TEST SITE HORROR

GUSTAVO BONDONI

SEVERED PRESS
HOBART TASMANIA

TEST SITE HORROR

PROLOGUE

Eighteen months earlier – South Ural Mountains

The speck in the grey sky grew larger and turned into a plane. The Antonov AN-26 was a familiar sight to Dr. Park Sun-Lee. Though it was a Soviet-era design, almost every country east of Germany or south of Italy still used them. They were rugged, simple and, most importantly, they could land on pretty much any strip in the world.

The one coming in, buffeted by the swirling wind of the mountain plateau, was not painted in Russian colors, but black. The daytime landing was an anomaly: this plane did most of its flying at night.

But it was a long flight from Antarctica, especially for a slow short-hauler.

It bounced a couple of times on landing, throwing up ice crystals and stones from improved surface of the strip and came to a halt forty meters away from the delegation that had arrived to meet the returning soldiers.

There were five of them in the reception committee. General Orlov, of course. He would never let a top-secret mission take place without being personally there to oversee it. If the Americans or the Chinese ever wanted to know what the GRU was up to, all they needed to do was follow Orlov around. His shock of unruly white hair would probably be easy enough to spot from orbit with the right lens.

Selene Grosjean, on the other hand, was a wild card. All Park knew about the woman was that everyone was afraid of her and that she sounded French when she spoke, looked about forty-five, had auburn hair and curves that he thought more appropriate to the set of a pornographic film than a secret project. Even packed in her winter furs, she resembled a walking hourglass.

Park hoped she would just help them receive the soldiers and then disappear. But, knowing his luck, she would be in his hair for the duration.

Fortunately, the final two members of the group were just a couple of gorillas with AK-47s. In uniform, even. Uncomplicated and comforting.

The plane's rear cargo ramp opened, and the flight crew began unloading something large covered with a blue tarp. Park's pulse began to race.

A large soldier approached. This guy was the perfect Russian: close-cropped blond hair, ice-blue eyes taller even than the gorillas. He had a scar on his right cheek which didn't destroy his looks but rather brought them into sharp relief. Stubble covered his face. He was wearing a black jumpsuit and had a rifle—not an AK-47, one Park couldn't identify—slung on his back.

He came to a halt in front of the general and saluted.

"Major Yevgeny Alexeyev reporting as requested, sir." His teeth were clenched hard enough that Park, standing a couple of meters back, could see the bulge of the jaw muscles.

"I know who you are, Major," Orlov replied.

Alexeyev said nothing.

"What can you tell me about the mission?"

"The mission was successful. We retrieved the objective and also secured a mature sample."

"Then why do you look like you're in a mood to kick babies, Major?"

"I'm just tired, sir."

"You're just lying, Major."

"Yes, sir."

"You have permission to speak freely. Nothing you say here will be reported or affect your career in any way."

For a split second, Alexeyev's eyes flickered to the French woman. It was a tiny lapse, an instinctive fraction of a second, but Park was watching for it. Orlov was in the chain of command. A soldier would, to a certain degree, believe him.

No one seemed to trust the woman, though.

Unfortunately for him, Alexeyev had no choice. Remaining silent would have been an insult. The general hadn't reached his exalted position and survived several régime changes by being a man whose orders one could ignore.

"Yes, sir. I am angry because, as usual, some imbecile in the intelligence department fucked up and sent us out with incomplete information. Or maybe they were just too stupid to realize that the true threat was the big monster, not the small ones."

"They didn't see it."

"The thing is as big as a five-story building. If they saw the small ones, they couldn't have missed the big one. Someone is playing games." He paused to glare at the general. "I lost four men on this disaster."

"Yours is a high-risk profession, Major."

The glare intensified. This time he also directed it at Miss Grosjean. Evidently, he was more angry than afraid—probably a good trait for a Spetsnaz Blue Beret on covert missions in Africa or Central Asia, but unwise on Russian soil. There, the FSB and the SVR were much more dangerous than any soldier, no matter how good. And if Grosjean wasn't SVR, Park would eat his fur hat. "I had to leave two of them on the ice, General. They are the first two men I've ever had to leave behind. They probably got eaten by the dinosaurs, like carrion. That is unacceptable, and I will have answers."

"I will get them for you. What you will do is return to base and rest with what remains of your unit. We'll take the samples."

Alexeyev saluted and turned away without another word. By this time, a Tigr was waiting by the plane and four weary men dragging a lot of equipment climbed in.

The vehicle had gone about a hundred meters when it exploded.

"Regrettable," Orlov said. "Those were good men."

Selene Grosjean nodded. "Sometimes, one must do what must be done. My own men are dealing with the pilots."

Park said nothing. He knew about politics, and Russians killing Russians was nothing new. They'd been doing it for at least a hundred years… probably much longer. His concern was that, once his job was done, his life expectancy would be measured in minutes.

Something would have to be done about that.

The group walked up to the plane. The eggs had been laid in a row alongside the pallet with the tarp over it and, though Park knew he would be mostly concerned with the embryos, he walked up to the lump and pulled away the plastic sheeting.

A huge head lay on its side, one yellow eye looking up at him, matte-colored in death. Teeth the length of his hand protruded from both jaws.

Mottled, greyish, leathery skin covered the enormous creature, a relic from a past that would never have allowed anything as weak as a human to evolve.

"It's magnificent," he whispered.

Orlov turned to him. "I hope this was worth it. You have your dinosaur now."

"It's not a dinosaur," Park replied. "It's a prehistoric reptile."

Now the general's mask of composure began to crack. "You mean we did all this, lost some of our best men, to retrieve a reptile? I can find reptiles on the walls of my dacha."

Park smiled. "Not like these, you can't. Not like these." He paused and lay a hand on the cold, leathery skin. "With these eggs and a few bird genes, I can build you all the dinosaurs you could ever want. Actually, I could build you more than you want."

The general grunted and walked off, leaving Miss Grosjean there to study Park in silence.

He didn't care. If she wanted to watch a scientist caressing a prehistoric creature, then let her.

Things like this didn't happen every day.

CHAPTER 1

Marianne Caruso smiled. She smelled a story.

Not the superficial piece she'd been assigned to cover. The press trip might have been an all-expenses-paid extravaganza, but it was obvious from the moment she entered the building that the whole thing was designed to direct the attention of people to what the lab wanted.

Or maybe away from what really mattered.

The product manager, a young executive-style woman who stumbled over the technical terms, droned on, gushing over a white cylindrical product as if it were the greatest invention in the history of mankind as opposed to just another gimmick that would bring hope of eternal youth to aging housewives just begging to be relieved of their money.

"And, since every YekLab treatment is designed specifically to respond to the genes that control human aging, we can dispense with preliminary testing of its effectiveness and go straight to safety testing on humans. You see, *we already know it works*. This allows us to move to market much quicker." She smiled, a dazzling display of corporate lip-gloss which Marianne, as an expert in the field, grudgingly admired. "That's why our launches are always well-attended: the press knows it will be revolutionary, and without long development times, you never hear about our progress until we have a viable product."

The woman was lying, of course. The reason no one ever heard about their products until launch time was that YekLab's security was tighter than Fort Knox. And if they really did human safety testing, no one had been able to find out where it was taking place. She raised her hand, holding a pen, which was an affectation she used to call attention away from the fact that she also had an audio and video recorder going, plus her cell phone as backup.

"Yes, Miss Caruso?"

Marianne put on her best fashion-magazine-dumb-journo-bimbo face and asked, innocently: "So you use some kind of machine to predict how the injections in that tube will react to human cells?"

"To the genes inside the cells, yes."

"The genes, of course. And this will modify the genes?"

"It can't modify the existing genes. What it does is inhibit the activation of the processes that cause skin aging at a genetic level."

"I see." She pretended to look down at her notes, then looked up even more innocently. "I assume you're using CRISPR-edited T-Virus cells to selectively stop the mRNA sequences you don't want activating stuff. But doesn't selling it now violate both the EU and the FDA guidelines regarding permanent cell-function modification in human hosts? I'm specifically referring to the year-long stability testing mandated by both organisms."

Marianne aimed the question at the marketing woman, but she was watching the other impeccably-suited members of the YekLab executive team attending the launch. Corporations always did this: the marketing team was placed in the spotlight, but everyone else attended the press conferences for damage control reasons.

A short man with oriental features—Chinese or Korean, definitely not Japanese—whispered in the ear of a large blond man—she would bet her life that the man was Russian—who immediately stood and walked towards the still-smiling but now speechless product manager.

As the man spewed inanities about how the process itself was the lab's secret sauce, but that they should all rest assured that every regulatory hurdle had been passed, Marianne pretended to listen raptly. They wouldn't believe the dumb-girl routine anymore, but as the guy seemed to be addressing the whole group and not her specifically, she watched the Asian man.

The man didn't stay to listen to the big Russian. Instead, he walked to a door at the far end of the enormous conference room they were using for the launch and disappeared.

But she had a photo. She could find out who he was, if necessary.

Now, though, she had a job to do... a boring one, but the one she was being paid for, and the one which had gotten her invited on this particular all-expenses-paid press trip. She needed to do a glowing write-up of the new beauty product for *Update!* Magazine. Terrence Vaidal, the magazine's virtuoso editor-in-chief would print her story without question, caveat about regulatory issues and all, but readers would not worry about technicalities. The product worked, that much was clear from the presentation they'd been shown before the marketing team had made the mistake of opening the session up for questions.

That was all that her readers really cared about.

What Marianne investigated during her downtime was her own affair. She'd offer it to Vaidal first, of course, and he would probably buy it. But the reality was that if she found what she suspected, it was the kind of piece that would find its true audience when it got syndicated to other outlets—particularly places like the New York Times. Vaidal was really good about allowing syndication. He knew her investigative work gave *Update!* prestige, but he also knew that that prestige came from the fact that she was nationally famous after the *Timeless* investigation… and that if she ever hit another home run like that one, he could make bank on her byline for life.

She didn't begrudge him a cent of it. He was the one who'd given her the lead for the *Timeless* story, after all.

By the time the presentation rolled to a close and the food made its appearance, Marianne had five pages of notes and the rest of the journalists were beginning to look at her funny. Did she really need that much for a simple cosmetics launch that would, in the big glossies, maybe have a quarter page?

But *Update!* wasn't *Vogue.* As a web-first medium, they could deep-dive into the products they featured, and different parts of the story could also be used on separate social media platforms where the majority of the magazine's audience resided.

She needed all the info she could get.

Besides, she could cut it to length anytime. But she couldn't come back and see the launch again and ask new questions.

She had enough. Now it was time to enjoy the food.

A tray of canapés drifted past and she snagged something with salmon on it. Delicious, especially as the hotel breakfast had been a rushed affair… she had overslept and been playing catch-up from then on.

The correspondent from *Caipi*, a major Brazilian lifestyle site Vaidal sometimes collaborated with, appeared at her elbow. Tatiana was a tall woman with peculiar greyish skin, light brown hair and green eyes. Beautiful in an exotic way.

"Late night?" the Brazilian asked, knowing eyes twinkling.

"None of your business," Marianne replied. "And yes. But not what you think. I spent it studying for the launch."

"That's unlike you."

"What, to study?"

"No. To arrive unprepared and have to study the night before. Your little act of being the perfectly petite gorgeous brunette next door might fool a lot of people, but you can't fool me. I remember that time you came to Rio for the Fashion week. I think there are some guys down there still talking about you."

"Not for my brain."

"Not at first, but then they got to comparing notes and realized just how much information you'd gotten out of them, and why your tell-all articles actually had more juicy truth in them than even the local rags, they soon changed their tune. Now, I think they cross themselves whenever anyone mentions your name."

Marianne laughed. Tatiana was one of the few fashion journos she considered a serious rival. Not just because she was sharp and had a great nose for a story, but because whenever she walked into a room, every head turned to stare at her—the women in envy, the men in admiration. Marianne had the same effect, but she worked damned hard at it, while she suspected that Tatiana would manage it just out of bed with her hair in disarray and wearing sweat pants.

Besides, she was a head taller, which rankled Marianne.

But she was also a straight shooter, and had never stabbed Marianne in the back, so that was something. *Maybe she doesn't consider you a threat*, Marianne thought. But immediately caught herself. *Nah. She's smarter than that.*

"Well, I guess it's better to be remembered for something than for nothing at all..." Marianne lunged at a passing tray and snagged something with caviar on it. She sighed.

"What are you doing here?" Tatiana asked.

Marianne knew what she meant. She'd reached the pinnacle of their profession. She had made the rounds and won awards for a piece of serious reporting. And now she was covering cosmetic launches? Yeah YekLab was big... but it was still fluff reporting.

"A girl's gotta eat, Tatiana."

"But that wasn't the dream, was it?"

"No. It was all supposed to change."

It *had* changed, she supposed, but sometimes she just wanted to be on a press trip. The thing was, Tatiana wouldn't believe her. Marianne herself wouldn't have believed it either a year before.

Luckily, every alarm in the building went off right then, saving Marianne from having to lie to a woman who could spot it a mile away.

"What's that?" Tatiana asked.

"I don't know." People were milling around, confused, although no one looked terribly worried. If this was a drill, the fact that it happened in the middle of a press intro was definitely going to cost someone their job.

Tatiana strode over to the execs, to ask what was happening, but Marianne didn't bother. They'd know soon enough.

Her own focus was on the door through which the boss—she was certain the Asian man was the boss—had disappeared.

For that reason, she saw exactly what happened, and caught it on video.

The sliding door exploded inwards, showering those nearest to it with glass. One woman with the lab group clutched her face and fell to her knees, blood pouring between her fingers.

The door was the least of their problems. It was what came through the door that truly mattered.

As far as Marianne could tell, it was some kind of dragon. A brown feathered dragon with hanging arms that made it look simian as opposed to reptilian. It shook the glass off its head and looked around. On seeing the room full of people, it screeched, a combination of birdsong and the roar of an enraged carnivore.

Everyone except for Marianne ran for the exit. She stayed perfectly still, and later wondered whether she'd been paralyzed with fear or actually trying to maintain the ideal camera angle.

Whatever the reason, she got an excellent look as the thing lumbered into the room and gave another roar.

The stricken woman, still clutching her face, looked up as if in a daze. She screamed and tried to rise, ignoring the glass on the floor which had to have been digging itself into the palm of her hand.

Marianne took a step towards her.

Whatever she'd been planning to do, however, was moot. The woman was on the other side of the large room and the creature, taller than a man and much longer, took two quick steps and closed its jaws around her head.

The mouth closed with a snap that echoed off the walls. Then the creature pulled up and shook the head. The woman came with it, a grotesque parody of a dancing marionette. Blood flew everywhere as the monster tugged on the woman's head, trying to tear it clean off.

The woman was dead. She had to be; that thing's teeth had carved into her neck and every Hollywood movie ever said that that meant immediate death.

Nevertheless, Marianne couldn't tear her eyes away from the grisly spectacle. Only when the woman's head finally separated from the tortured carcass that had once been a young executive at a cosmetics company, probably thinking about what parties to attend when she got back to Moscow, did Marianne come back to herself with a start.

The monster—now it reminded her more of a dinosaur from some science fiction film than a dragon—crunched on the loose head, the skull snapping audibly. Then it turned to look around. Yellow eyes fixed on Marianne.

Suddenly, something pulled on her and she was moving. Her arm, firmly in someone else's grip, propelled her out of the room and into the hallway beyond. Two turns later, she entered another room and a thick door slammed closed behind her with a hydraulic whoosh.

Tatiana released her arm. "Girl, I respect you like no one else in this business, but hasn't anyone told you that, to get the story, you need to come back alive?"

"Oh God, thank you." She hugged the Brazilian woman tightly around the neck and sobbed into her shoulder. It took her some minutes to regain her composure and look around.

They were in a brightly lit enclosure about five meters square. The windowless room held nothing but a few chairs and a table. Five of the suited executives were seated around the table. They seemed tense but not particularly frightened.

"Where are we?" Marianne asked Tatiana.

The taller woman shrugged. "Panic room," she replied. "I've been assured that nothing short of a direct missile hit will breach these walls."

"Oh. I'm glad to hear it," Marianne replied. She sat for a few minutes, regaining her composure. Little by little, she came back to herself. Screams filtered in through the walls, but she paid them little attention. The door certainly looked like it could hold against pretty much anything and besides, no dumb reptile, plumed or not, was going to figure out opaque doors any time soon. Glass was one thing—you could see through it. But steel was something else. Finally, she got her breathing under control and felt like herself again, and her instincts returned. She turned to the YekLab execs behind her and, with a smile that would convince nobody, she asked: "Just out of curiosity, why does a cosmetics lab need a panic room?"

***

Lieutenant Max Alexeyev didn't even have time to dress properly when the call came in. One minute he was playing Durak with Ivan, Vasily and Yuri, and the next, all four of them were trying to put their armor on inside the closed confines of an armored Jeep. Their driver, at least, was fully prepped.

"Where are we going?" Max demanded.

"To the lab."

The lab. Max's stomach roiled. The Yekaterinburg lab was the city's eternal nightmare. In the Soviet Era, it had been a biological weapons center and, to hear the population speak of it, the mess it had made when they'd had a weaponized anthrax leak in the 1970s made the Chernobyl disaster look like a country picnic. Of course, as none of it had been visible from space, Soviet Leadership had managed to contain the knowledge. By the time the news leaked out, it was a footnote. After the fall of communism, the city's name changed back to Yekaterinburg from Sverdlovsk, and that confused things further.

Most people who visited YekLab would have been hard-pressed to link it to the old bioweapons facility.

Max knew better. He knew exactly who ran the facility… and it wasn't the Boy Scouts. What he didn't know was what they were doing there, which is why an emergency call from that source turned on every one of his alarms.

"What's going on?"

"All they said was that we have a containment issue, and that we should bring heavy guns."

"Heavy guns? What about respirators and hazmat suits? Did they have another anthrax leak?"

"They specifically said we won't need any of that."

"What the hell?"

The only scenario he could think of was an attack on the facility. Maybe an American or Chinese special forces strike that went wrong. But at noon? In broad daylight? It made very little sense.

Of course, they'd learn what was happening only after they got into a firefight, usually losing any kind of strategic advantage they might have had from deploying without panic.

"Damn," he said.

"Lighten up. Maybe it's just zombies," Vasily said. "They probably let one of their superbugs get away from them and turned the staff into the walking dead. All we need to do is to aim for the head." He made a shooting motion with his rifle.

"Just stop."

"Sorry." Vasily wasn't a bad guy, but he could be an asshole. The man knew that Max hated the lab because his brother had been sent out on a mission to Antarctica by the lab people and had never come back. All that remained were the medals the government had sent the only surviving family member—Max himself. But the lab was the only reason to have a Spetsnaz unit in Yekaterinburg, and he suspected he was about to find out exactly what it was they were defending against.

The driver spoke over the radio and then turned back to the troops. "Okay, the mission is biological containment."

"Viruses? Bacteria? What?"

"None of that. Large animals, apparently. It sounded like headquarters is completely confused."

"The fog of war," Max mumbled to himself. "Nice day for it."

The cars they passed along the highway seemed unconcerned. Traffic flowed the same way as it always did. No one seemed to be escaping from the city in a panicked rush. In front of them, a second Tigr sped towards the event... whatever it was.

The lab was a five-story concrete structure that occupied an entire city block. A typical Soviet-era building with rounded corners and a courtyard in the middle. Smoke poured out of a second-story window and the police had cordoned-off the area. Their driver ignored the cars and tore through the yellow tape, coming to a halt at the open front door.

"Alexeyev, do you hear me?"

Colonel Petrov's voice was unmistakable. "Yes, sir."

"Good. Stay at the door. No one goes in, and nothing comes out until the next squad arrives. They should be there in two minutes."

So Max and his men stood in the doorway, waiting and listening to the sounds coming from within. Human screams mingled with strange roars and thumps. At one point, a man ran towards the door from inside. Max and his men screamed at him to stop.

"But the monsters."

"Stay where you are! Get down on the ground. If anything comes this way, we'll deal with it."

"You won't be able to!" The man seemed at the edge of panic. But if he tried to reach the door, Max would have to cut him in half. Orders were orders and he didn't know what was happening inside. For all he knew, this guy was carrying some lethal bug.

"Don't worry. We can deal with anything in there. Now get down or we'll have to fire through you to deal with it."

The man lay down, covered his head with his hands and whimpered.

Ten meters to Max's right, a fourth-story window shattered and something fell to the ground with a hard thump. Max looked to see a woman in a red dress crumpled on the concrete. She had probably been around fifty and quite overweight, and now she was lying motionless. "Ivan, check on her."

Ivan rushed over and felt for a pulse. Then he ran back to Max's position. "She's still alive."

"Get one of the cops to deal with it and come back."

"Yes, sir."

Petrov's reinforcements arrived at the same time Ivan returned.

"Sir, our backup is here," Max told the colonel.

"Perfect. Put them on perimeter and get inside. Shoot anything that looks like a monster."

"A monster?"

"I'm watching the video. Trust me, you'll know it when you see it."

"Size?"

"Like small cars."

"Oh, good. So they won't be hiding in cabinets?"

"Not very likely."

"What about people?"

"Get as many out of there as you can."

"All right. We're going in."

"Wait," Petrov said. "Whatever you do, don't blow anything up in the cellar. Just seal it off if you have to. It has blast doors. If any of the creatures are down there, we'll deal with them later."

"You," Max shouted to the guy on the floor. "You can get up now. Run past us and don't stop until you get to the cops. Tell them you were inside and the soldiers sent you."

The man didn't need to be told twice. He ran past, blubbering. "Thank you. Thank you," he sobbed.

Ivan grinned. "Either that guy is a major pussy or we're headed for a meat grinder."

"I know where my money is."

"No bet. You always get us the choice assignments."

"For that, you get point. Lead the way and let me know if you run into Godzilla."

They entered the building.

The floor was polished concrete, slippery as hell, but about as sinister as the sunlight outside. It looked like exactly what it was: an old Soviet-era building turned into an office block. Open doors led into offices.

"Where are we going?" Max asked Petrov over the radio.

"Clear the central courtyard first. That will let the people trapped on the ground floor out."

"I suspect the ones on the upper floors are also in danger."

"Yes, but there are only four of you inside right now. There are a lot more people on the ground floor. Apparently, the only way out is through the courtyard, so we need to clear that first."

"Yes, sir." Like most modern Russians, Max had a very low opinion of the Soviets. It was just like them to design a building with only one way out. Well, only one way out if you didn't choose to jump through a window. It was probably so everyone would have to file past the security desk manned by the KGB.

"Max," Ivan called back from the door that led to the courtyard. "I think you might want to see this."

Seeing that the man was not particularly alarmed, Max closed the gap and looked through the shattered glass of the door.

"What is it?"

"How the hell should I know? Why don't you ask the Colonel?"

"Colonel, what am I looking at?"

"A target. No more questions now. You have a mission. Carry it out."

Feeding on what appeared to be a dead human body on the manicured grass in the middle of the rectangle formed by the four sides of the laboratory building was a grey lizard. With feathers. At least the colonel had been right about size; it was pretty much exactly like a small car.

After every third bite the creature stood on its hind legs and sniffed the air. It was much taller than Max and its head was short and stubby with powerful jaws. The front legs were long, not like the pictures of Tyrannosaurus, but actually useful forelimbs. This creature was using those legs to manipulate its food.

Max raised his rifle to his shoulder. "Shoot one burst on my mark," he said, as the other two soldiers from his group crept forward. "Now."

Four AK-47s opened up at once, the sound echoing in the enclosed space. Each soldier fired three rounds.

Then they waited to see what the thing would do.

The creature turned to look at its tormentors and Max tensed. In creature features, this was the part where the monster charged, impervious to light weaponry, and tore them apart.

For a second, it seemed like the Hollywood scenario would come true. The creature's eyes locked on them and it took a step forward, then another and a third, each quicker than the last.

Then it faltered and stumbled as blood flowed copiously from twelve well-grouped bullet holes. About halfway to the troops, it fell on its face.

"One down," he told the colonel. "How many of those things are loose?"

"About twenty."

"About?"

"None of the people inside when they got loose stopped to count. Just shoot the ones you see, will you?"

"Yes, sir."

**

Marianne strained to listen. The door was thick, and apparently the acoustics of the material meant that only high-pitched sounds made it into the room. There had been some screaming at first. Some time later she heard what sounded like gunfire, but it was hard to tell.

It probably was gunfire, she concluded. If the monster she'd seen in the conference room was any indication of what was outside their door, a certain amount of gunfire was inevitable.

She sighed. She'd thought she was done with gunfire for the rest of her life.

"How do we get out of here?" she asked the execs. After the initial excitement, they'd taken the whole thing extremely well, sitting in the back and raiding the tiny fridge. It was probably the only corporate snack fridge on the planet that had vodka in it. Only Marianne and Tatiana seemed impatient to get out.

"We wait. Activating this room lights up an alarm in the police station and they send someone out here to make sure we're okay. When the coast is clear they enter the code that unlocks the door and out we go."

"Are the cops going to be able to deal with those dinosaurs?"

The man speaking to her smiled. "This is Russia. The cops can deal with anything. Just relax and have some vodka."

The man's sleazy smile made Marianne wish she was out in the hall with the dinosaurs. Balding office workers with incipient potbellies never knew when they were out of their league, but in this guy's case she suspected that all bipedal vertebrates were out of his league.

As if on cue, the door behind her whooshed open and she turned with a gasp to find a big blond guy staring back. Close-cropped blond hair, high cheekbones and ice-blue eyes distracted her from the fact that he was pointing an assault rifle at her chest and wearing black commando gear.

But only for a second. She had worked in the fashion industry long enough that she could put gorgeous guys in a mental parking lot to think about later. "Are you the cavalry?"

The man ignored the question and barked something in Russian. The guy who'd offered her the drink stood and replied, suddenly all corporate and serious again. The glass of vodka, Marianne noted, was nowhere to be seen.

The soldier said something else and everyone stood and picked up their belongings. They filed out of the hall into the second-story corridor they'd walked through earlier. Now, it was soiled with blood and one of the windows was shattered. Strangely, there was no glass on the floor, which made Marianne suspect that the window had exploded outward.

There was a human body at the end of the stairs, and one of the dinosaur-things, covered in blood, a little further on. It wasn't moving.

The soldier caught Marianne looking at it. She was trying to get a good picture on the video, but the leader of the soldiers must have misinterpreted. "Don't worry, miss," he said in English with a thick accent, "we have killed them all."

"It's a pity, isn't it?"

"I don't know. I'd rather be talking to you than being eaten."

She looked at him sharply. Was it a joke? A pickup line? A simple observation of truth? The man's face betrayed nothing, of course. He was probably some crazy commando type who thought women were an unimportant part of life. To be sought out when necessary but otherwise nonessential.

The thought made her angry, so she turned her highest wattage smile at the man. This one had been known to make Hollywood actors forget their groupies. "Well, I'm glad you didn't get eaten, and thanks for letting us out."

"You are very welcome. It is my pleasure."

They crossed a couple more open spaces and descended two flights of stairs before crossing the courtyard—featuring another shot-up lizard—and exiting via the main entrance.

"The ambulances will check you. Then you go home. The police have called taxis, yes?"

"Yes. Thank you," Marianne replied.

The guy only lingered a second before he turned away and rejoined his men.

"Damn," she said to herself. "I must be getting old."

And then she turned herself over to the nearest doctor. Between the fact that everyone seemed to be in shock and the language barrier, it took her several minutes to convince the woman that she was perfectly all right.

By then, the soldiers were gone.

CHAPTER 2

"This is the craziest thing I've ever seen."

The internet connection was crappy as hell, but Terrence Vaidal's expression, even on Skype, was always eloquent. He couldn't believe what Marianne had just sent him.

"It's absolutely on the level. I shot the footage myself, and the story describes exactly what I saw. None of it is hearsay, and none of it is third-party testimony. It's real and it's mine."

On the other end of the video call, she could see her editor typing. "I can't find news of this anywhere."

"Do you think the Russians are advertising it? There were just a few of us in there. I don't know who else survived, and I'm sure the only reason they didn't take my footage away from me is that I never told them I was filming and everyone was too confused to do anything anyway. I usually only film for my own records and use whatever imagery their press department sends us. But this is a special case." She grinned. "Either way, I'm just glad you got the footage safe and sound. I have a feeling this whole area is going to go into firewall lockdown as soon as someone recovers from the shock enough to remember to do it. Keep that safe for me."

"You don't want me to run it?"

"Of course I want you to run it, but I'm not losing any sleep over it. If you don't run it, Tatiana will, and *Caipi* will scoop you again. I'll just sell my take to *The New Yorker*. Either way, I get paid and I have an exclusive for an important world event. But I have a feeling that in a few minutes I'm not going to be able to speak to you at all, so I'll do that when I get back."

"Look, I really don't think—"

As if on cue, the connection cut off. Marianne tried to reconnect, but there was no internet to connect to. Not on the hotel wifi and not through her phone.

Inwardly, however, she exulted. Her story was safely filed. Nothing that they did now would change that. They could take her camera and her notes with no consequences whatsoever. And if they decided to silence her completely... well, Vaidal would take that as a sign that she was on to something and run the story. No one was going to stop it.

Now, it was time to speak to Veronika.

***

Terrence Vaidal sat back and cursed Marianne. When she was on staff, she acted out in every way possible up to and including having an affair with the husband of one of the owners of the media conglomerate that owned *Update!*

Fortunately for her, the old bat had never found out what her much younger husband was up to, because that was one transgression Vaidal would have been powerless to shield Marianne from. It would have been the end of her career in media. In fact, the next one the guy dallied with was still blacklisted.

He thought that after she resigned to go freelance, his Marianne-Caruso-related ulcers would subside, but every so often, she did something like this.

Granted, it was never quite like this... but the sensation was familiar.

Real journalism was about triple-checking every fact, vetting every source, making sure you were printing something as close to the truth as you could. Opinion pieces were all very well, but news had to be based on fact, not speculation or personal preference.

He watched the video again, trying to decide if it was real or if it was something Marianne had somehow faked. That, in its turn, led him down the path of trying to remember if Marianne had seemed out of sorts. Had he done anything to make her mad? Might she have picked up some addiction? PTSD from the *Timeless* affair?

He didn't think so.

While he pondered, a clock ticked in his head, counting down the minutes until Firminha Barbosa at *Caipi* published Tatiana Close's story. She would, of course, no questions asked, and it would soon syndicate around the world.

If Marianne was telling the truth and not suffering some kind of psychotic episode.

"Damn the woman," he said to himself. But that was unhelpful. The clock kept ticking. "Damn, damn, damn, damn." Vaidal pressed on the button that summoned his assistant. It was an affectation, a remnant from an earlier time, but since it was a time he considered more elegant than the current age—an era in which some poor misguided souls actively looked down upon elegance as a tool of the oppressor—he welcomed it.

Sarah popped her head in. "Get me Lola. Tell her she's going to hate what I'm about to ask."

Lola was as blond and bubbly and uninteresting as Marianne was bewitching, but she was just as good a journalist, which was all that mattered. Well, all that mattered with Lola... Marianne had already made it very clear that nothing more would happen between them.

She sat down, knowing that Vaidal liked to speak first. She generally let him get the gushers off his chest before contributing sound ideas.

"I need you to edit and frame something Marianne sent us."

"Marianne *Caruso*? You're going to lay hands on Marianne's copy? Like more than just a copy-edit?"

"Yes."

"She'll murder you. Worse, once she's murdered you and I get your job, she will never sell us anything else again."

Vaidal shrugged. "Oh, come off it. Marianne isn't that difficult to work with." He let Lola fume a little. Her hatred of her predecessor as *Update!*'s star journo was natural. All she ever heard since she'd crossed the street from *WSJ* was *Marianne this, and Marianne tha*t. "That's a risk I have to take. This is a time-sensitive piece and Marianne had to do a rush job on it. Plus we need to make it extremely clear that we didn't generate this content but purchased it as is from il Gran Caruso."

"Okay. Now you're making me curious. What did she come up with this time?"

"You won't believe me if I tell you."

"Bit of a waste of time calling me up here, then, wasn't it?"

"I have to show you a video first."

* * *

Veronica Bee raised her head as Marianne crashed into her room.

"You should really lock your door, Ronnie," she admonished.

"In a hotel? Why? The likelihood of an occupied room being attacked in a hotel is..."

"Spare me the lecture," Marianne said. "There's something you need to see."

Ronnie watched the video Marianne had shot in silence. Then she looked up.

"So you want to know how they faked it, and who did it? I won't really be able to tell you much until the internet comes back."

"It's not coming back."

Ronnie frowned. "Why not?"

"Because that video isn't faked. I filmed it myself."

Veronica leaned back on her chair. "Are you going to start on me, too? Just because I'm not cut out to be a fashion journalist, you guys don't all need to treat me like dirt."

Marianne gaped at her. "I'm actually not kidding. Look, I was nearly killed by one of those things. The person filming is me." Then she glared back at the research assistant, a woman who'd been allowed on this trip partly because YekLab was paying for it but mostly because Marianne had vouched for her. "But if you think I'm messing with you, fine. I'll do the rest of this alone."

Veronica gaped. "You're telling me I should believe this?"

"I'm telling you it's real. I was there and I need to know what we're looking at here."

"You promise me this isn't a setup?"

"I swear. I'm not messing with you."

The researcher took a few moments to gather her thoughts. Marianne knew just how easily someone like her would get bullied in an office like *Update!*'s. She wasn't physically unattractive, but she was... bland. That wasn't the problem, however. The problem was that she insisted on making a statement with her clothes and hairstyle, and that statement was: 'I demand to be evaluated only on my mind, so I dress in what appear to be burlap sacks and cut my hair short despite not having the best face for it in the hope that you will look beyond it.' The effect was awful, especially if one lived in New York and worked in media. The worst part about it was that it was the result of special effort to look like crap. Had she worn jeans and t-shirts, not only would she have been more comfortable, but also looked about a million times better. And shoulder-length hair would have been a titanic improvement.

Finally, the researcher nodded. "I guess I should trust you."

"Yes, you should. Now what do you think of that?"

"Wow. A dinosaur, no doubt about it."

Marianne shook her head. "But what about the feathers? Isn't it like some kind of flying dragon thing? Look, the dead one we saw when we got out of the room has feathers, too."

"Those feathers aren't to fly with. Don't be silly."

Marianne bit back the grin that was trying to get out. For a woman who wanted to be loved for her personality, there were a few things that needed ironing out.

If Veronica noticed her words might have been offensive, she didn't show it. She just went on. "A lot of dinosaurs had feathers. In fact, dinosaurs still exist, except we call them birds. Now I think I saw a decent angle on that one a few minutes ago, let me rewind. There, I think I could probably identify it from that shot."

"No, you can't. Network's down, remember?" Besides, at least now she knew it was a dinosaur. That made her story even more significant... especially if Vaidal ran it before *Caipi* did.

"Pfft. Who needs the internet? I'll check the database."

"You have a database about dinosaurs?"

"I have gigs and gigs of Wikepedia copied onto a hard drive, even managed to keep the hyperlinks by reprogramming a browser with the address lookup instructions. You never know when you'll need to research without a connection. In fact, I'm pretty sure the most important things you'll ever need to know will happen when you have no internet." As she spoke, Veronica rifled through her bag, discarding thumb drives and discs until she came to the one she wanted. "Here we go. Now that thing looks like one of the later dinosaurs, doesn't it? So... Cretaceous, most likely."

The researcher began flipping through drawings at high speed, not spending more than a few seconds on each.

"This one... no."

Marianne let her work and paced around the room, wondering if she was making a huge mistake, but desperate to know what she'd stumbled on. Ten minutes later, Ronnie exclaimed, "Ah. This is you, isn't it, dearie... Marianne, we found him. Deinonychus." She read the description. "Ooh. You were a bit of an asshole, weren't you?"

"I hope you're talking to the dinosaur. No, scratch that, I hope you're not talking to the dinosaur."

"Lay off," Ronnie said. "Have a look." She turned the laptop towards Marianne and smiled. The thing on the screen looked very similar to the one that had terrorized the product launch.

"The colors are wrong. The one I saw was brighter."

"These things lived a hundred million years ago, Marianne. The only reason we know about them is because of calcified impressions in rock. So scientists pretty much had to guess at coloration."

"But there's a real one. A living one, I mean. I saw it myself."

"Then someone built it in a lab. Probably using the creatures from Antarctica as a basis."

"I have no idea what you're talking about."

"Just a conspiracy theory based on some leaked footage from an Argentine Antarctic base that failed a couple of years ago. There's people who say it was attacked by a huge dinosaur and a bunch of little ones."

"Sounds like a Godzilla movie."

"That's what they claim, yeah," Ronnie replied. "I didn't believe it... especially the parts of Russians being present and stealing some eggs. But now..."

"You think they're engineering this stuff?"

"Remember that question I told you to ask about CRISPR?"

"Yeah, worked like a charm, by the way. I'll show you the woman's face sometime. It's on the video. Priceless."

"Well, once you know what DNA you want to build, CRISPR is part of the toolbox that allows you to build it. It's the scissors, if you like, clipping strands." She studied the picture of the dinosaur and then looked at the video. "They don't have an original genome, of course, so they probably looked at the characteristics they wanted and built up those things. But why anyone would create a Deinonychus is beyond me. It's just a bigger, meaner version of velociraptor... you know, the one in *Jurassic Park*..."

"I know what a velociraptor is," Marianne replied, trying not to let her impatience show. She'd been this close to winning a Pulitzer, but the geek squad still treated her like a dumb ornament. In fairness, though, Ronnie was right about Marianne knowing velociraptors because of *Jurassic Park*.

"Well, this one is worse. One of the killing machines of its age. With a claw specially designed to disembowel things. Why would they want this?"

"Terror weapon? Super soldier? Because someone went nuts in the lab and decided he wanted to watch the world burn? It's our job to find out."

Ronnie's eyes widened. "You mean..."

"Of course I do. That's what a real journalist does. You go after the story, and you don't stop until your readers get answers." Marianne held Ronnie's gaze. "Now, you told me you were going to get information about YekLab, the background and the corporate structure."

"You told me you didn't need it, and to research competitive beauty products instead. That no one was interested in the corporate stuff, so we didn't need to spend time on it."

"Turns out I was wrong. So you didn't do that research?"

"Actually, I did. I just didn't show it to you, even though I really wanted to."

"Really wanted to? Why?"

"Because the lab facility you visited used to belong to the Soviet military. It's the site of the most famous biological warfare accident in history, the Sverdlovsk Anthrax Leak."

"You should have told me that."

"You told me not to," Ronnie retorted.

"I know. But sometimes you have to disobey orders in order to be effective at your job. Ask Vaidal sometime... he's the one who taught me that and he's been regretting it ever since."

Ronnie shrugged. "It's too late for that, but I also found out that there's no real records about who owns YekLab. This isn't just the usual Russian obfuscation of ownership to protect oligarchs. This is deeper-level stuff; none of the holding companies involved seems to really exist—if you follow the trail deep enough it goes up in smoke. So I'd say yes, it's a covert operation, but I'm not sure whose it might be."

"And they grow the dinosaurs in the basement, or wherever they used to grow the Anthrax."

"I doubt it. If they're growing dinosaurs, they're doing it at their complex in Gora Yezhovaya." She held up a hand. "It's the only other asset listed to this company, and it's perfect. Here's a picture of it from above, a bunch of enormous buildings on a huge complex in the mountains. Other than skiers in winter and an occasional hiker, it's out of sight. Look at this place here. I don't know of too many other buildings with that kind of footprint."

Marianne's heart sank. "We can't get there. They'll never let me out of the city on a plane, not until the fuss over the lab dies down, and Russia's too big to drive across."

"No need to take a plane. This place is just about sixty miles away. It's the skiing spot for Yekaterinburg people. We can rent a car and be there in an hour."

Marianne thought about it. It was four in the afternoon already, but daylight lasted a long time in Russia in July. They had time to drive out there, have a look and get back to the hotel before nightfall. If they could get a car in time.

"How do you rent a car in this place?" she said.

Ronnie smiled. "Leave that to me."

***

"And did you see how I took out the one on the second floor?" Ivan said. "Boom, boom, two shots to the head and it came down the stairs. One dead ugly dinosaur."

"Yeah, you almost dropped it on top of us," Yuri replied dourly. "But you're right about the shooting. Did you see the one that charged at me from behind the filing cabinets?"

"I've never seen anyone run so fast," Ivan replied. They all laughed.

Max smiled as he drove. The adrenalin had long since worn off, and they'd spent the rest of the day in debriefing. Yuri had been in combat—if you could really call that glorified hunting expedition combat—for the first time, while Ivan and Vasily had only limited live-fire experience. Max, of course, had been in Chechnya quite often, both in open conflict and in very unofficial incursions. His incursions tended to happen at night, though, so it was a nice change to be able to see what he was doing and to be allowed to discuss it with his men.

After they'd been debriefed, they'd each been taken back to barracks individually. As the officer, Max had been the last to be liberated from the officials, and was delighted to find that his troops had waited for him before going to lunch. They were good guys.

So they'd liberated a Tigr from the motor pool and headed back towards the city. There was a service station on Route 352 near Tatavuy that served food that was both affordable enough for the enlisted men and almost edible.

An orange Lada Niva approached along the other lane, and Max looked to see who'd be driving something that loud.

He almost steered them into the trees as he realized that the driver was none other than the dark-haired journalist from the lab. What was she doing?

His heart sank as he realized that the only thing along this highway was Gora Yezhovaya... and he didn't think she would be attempting to ski there. July wasn't the best skiing month. She must have been on her way to the facility, and would probably get herself into big trouble.

That was too bad, but he shrugged. She would probably get deported and never be allowed back into Russia, but she was no longer his problem. He'd already done what he could for her when his men secured the main lab building in Yekaterinburg.

The next car that passed caught his eye because it was a black sedan with dark-tinted windows. The kind that the FSB drove.

He couldn't see the driver as the car passed, but he just managed to catch a glimpse of the passenger.

Selene Grosjean. The witch woman.

Following Marianne.

That was bad. It was one thing for a journalist to run afoul of the guards outside the complex, get themselves arrested and be deported through official channels with a note of complaint to their government, and quite another for the charming Miss Caruso to fall into the clutches of the FSB or whatever dark agency Miss Grosjean worked for. When those people grabbed you, you just disappeared from the face of the earth, never to be heard from again.

He hit the brakes and, when the speed was low enough, pulled the handbrake and executed a neat U-turn on the two-lane blacktop.

"What the hell?" one of his men yelled.

"Sorry guys," Max replied, "lunch is going to have to wait."

They groaned. "What? Why?" came from every seat but his.

"Remember the pretty reporter from the lab?"

"Which one, the tall one or the short one?" Max had no doubt that the men had already discussed in graphic detail what they'd do to each of them if they weren't completely unobtainable.

"The short one. The American."

"Nah, we don't remember her. You kept her close by so no one could talk to her."

"Well, she's headed down the road towards the facility."

"So what? Let the guards deal with it."

"Selene Grosjean is following her."

Silence followed the pronouncement. Grosjean was the one beautiful woman they never, ever, made lewd jokes about. In an earlier era, the men would have crossed themselves.

"Maybe we shouldn't get involved," Ivan said.

"You know how that would end."

"But the FSB…"

"I know. But I just can't let her do it. Not to this girl. I'm sorry guys. How about this… anyone who prefers to stay out of this can get off now, no hard feelings. If the shit hits the fan, you can claim that you tried to stop me and I ordered you out of the car. You'll be free and clear of any responsibility. Just let me know and I'll let you off."

Silence greeted his proposal. Max knew that none of the men would speak unless the others did first, so he forced the issue. "Ivan, you know what we're getting into. I meant what I said about no hard feelings. This is my folly, not something you need to tag along in. Do you want off?"

"I'm with you to the end. Which is going to be bitter, but I'm with you."

He got the same answer from each of the men. Loyalty ruled the day, albeit with a strong undercurrent of fatalism. They were convinced that they were going to die for this, of course.

Max smiled. "Spoken like true Russians, my friends." He pulled a flask from his pocket, unscrewed the cap and took a pull. Then he passed it to Ivan in the passenger seat. "Here, taste some real vodka, made with water from Lake Lagoda. Not the crap you people drink in Moscow."

Ivan took a long drink. "Tastes like dog piss," he said, before passing it back.

"You would know," Vasily said as he drank.

Round finished, the flask made its way back to Max who took a last pull before replacing it in his pocket.

The black car was just barely in sight up ahead. He didn't want to get any closer because the witch woman—or her driver—would spot them.

***

Half an hour later, they pulled into the dirt lot for official vehicles located next to the main vehicle entrance and got out of the Tigr.

Max pointed a hundred meters further down the road to the service access, where Marianne had parked, and where Grosjean's car was just pulling up. "She's probably trying to see if the guard will let her in. I don't think our friends in the black car will let them."

"Speaking of which," Vasily said, emerging from the guard post next to them where he'd gone to report their presence, "the guard isn't here."

"He probably crossed the road to take a piss," Max replied, nodding towards the forest that began right beside the tarmac. "Might be better if we don't waste time explaining ourselves. Let's get moving."

They hadn't brought their rifles. None of them was in the habit of dressing for battle when they went to lunch on a sleepy summer afternoon, not even after a midmorning dinosaur hunt. But each of them had their handguns—newly assigned Lebedev PL-15s—and unless the witch woman had packed her car full of goons, that, plus the element of surprise should be enough to decide any unpleasantness in their favor.

They advanced slowly through the trees on the far side of the road, Ivan on point, trying to spot any lookouts. When he reached the place where the cars were parked, he turned back and signaled that the coast was clear.

"Do you see them?" Max asked.

Ivan pointed. Visible over the hood of the Lada Niva, a man, presumably the driver of the car, was looking at someone on the floor beneath him. Selene Grosjean, beside the man, had her attention on the same point. "They made the women kneel down," Ivan whispered.

"Okay. We'll go across behind them. Vasily, check the car for more men. I'll lead."

They ran silently across the road, weapons raised. If they were spotted, they could quickly take over the situation.

But their quarry wasn't expecting company. As he crouched behind the car, Max heard Grosjean asking questions.

"Who sent you?"

And Marianne's voice, full of fear, but also defiant. "My magazine sent me. I'm a journalist. After seeing a dinosaur attack in a lab, looking at the lab's other properties in the area is a logical next step."

"For your sake, I hope you're lying, because if not, you have nothing of value to offer." The woman paused. "And you really, really want to have something of value to offer me. Otherwise, I'll just shoot you."

"You wouldn't dare. We're international journalists."

Selene's laughter tinkled through the air. "Yes. International journalists who, not knowing that some parts of Russia can be dangerous, unwisely drove out into the countryside where they were accosted by drunken men, raped and murdered. You'd be surprised how little attention people will pay, especially since the government won't have anything to deny because I won't tell them. Now talk."

"I told you the truth already," Marianne replied. He could hear the desperation in the young woman's voice.

"Yevgeny, kill the ugly one, please."

Max jumped up from his concealment, raised his pistol and put a round into the back of Yevgeny's head. He didn't even think about it, just fired.

The man hadn't even hit the ground when Max turned his pistol towards Selene. The woman turned, held his gaze for a second, then glared at the rest of his men. She calmly raised the cigarette she was holding to her mouth and took a long drag. Then she smiled. "Well, you boys have just fucked your lives up completely, haven't you?"

"This is illegal," Max said, feeling foolish even as the words left his mouth.

"Illegal is what I do. When I have your families pulled out of their beds in the middle of the night and tortured to death, that won't be legal, either. But it will happen."

"I don't have a family."

"Ah. But what about your men? Are they prepared to sacrifice their wives and children?"

The men behind him shuffled uncomfortably, but Max was certain they'd hold. Hopefully.

"You're just giving me reasons to put a bullet between your eyes. What you just said to them applies equally to you."

Grosjean laughed. "Angry like that... you remind me of someone. I wonder who it is." She shrugged. "No matter. No one will believe I died accidentally. A lot of people would love for that to happen, but no one would be dumb enough to believe it. And Yevgeny here isn't the kind of guy common criminals just ambush and murder. Not even to get to me." She wriggled suggestively, an obscene image. "So they'll investigate everything, starting with the bullets. I see you're using the new fancy pistols... you should have thought it over a little more if you were planning on killing people. No one but you Spetsnaz boys are using those yet. And I assume you didn't walk here, which means you've got a vehicle that can be traced. You're dead if you kill me and dead if you don't. In fact, the only chance you have of living through this is to convince me that I don't want to have you disemboweled. That won't be easy."

She threw the cigarette butt over the chain-link fence that separated them from the complex and put her hands on her hips. "So go ahead. Shoot me if you dare."

"I would do it just to make the world a better place," Max replied. "But I won't. Yuri, please check her for weapons. Vasily, there are restraints in the Tigr, please bring me a set. We're taking her back with us."

"Yes, sir." The two men leapt into action.

Yuri soon produced a Makarov pistol and a stiletto and ordered Selene to sit down. She winked at him and said: "I haven't been touched like that in ages. Do you mind if I smoke another?"

Vasily returned with a set of cable ties and they secured the woman's wrists. "Aren't you going to do my legs, too? I'm a martial arts expert."

"No. If it looks like you'll try to kick us to death, we'll just take a few steps back and kneecap you."

That earned him a hard look. "I'm going to enjoy having you killed."

"I strive to bring pleasure."

He stepped out from behind the car and into Marianne's line of sight. Her eyes registered surprise when she saw him. "You're the guy from the lab."

"Yes," he replied, switching to English. "Are you all right? You can stand up now, you're not in any more danger." He helped the women to their feet.

Marianne's companion was shaking. "I need to change my underwear," she said.

"Maybe they'll let you use a bathroom inside."

"No. I'll do it in the car." Without ceremony, she disappeared into the Lada.

Max turned to Ivan. "The thing about the bathroom raises an interesting question. Why isn't the guard here? We just shot a man ten meters from the gate and no one called the police or came out to see what's going on."

"The guard is probably hiding under his desk waiting for the coast to clear."

"Go look. You too, Yuri."

The little cabin door was unlocked. "Empty."

"This one and the other one too. No guards? Damn, there's something strange going on. This is a military installation, there should be people guarding the door."

"Actually," Selene chimed in, "it's ours. But you're right, there should be people here. Lots of people."

"I'm going in," he said. "Keep an eye on Grosjean. Don't listen to anything she says." Max paused. "No. We'd better all go in. Damn."

Grosjean smiled. "Don't trust your men not to cave?"

"No. I don't trust you not to have some kind of seeking device on you, and I don't want to leave them out in the open waiting for me. Hard to kill people inside a building from the air without also killing the person you're trying to rescue."

"Yeah, right," Grosjean said.

"What about them?" Ivan asked, pointing to the reporter and her companion.

"I'm coming with you," Marianne replied. Though she didn't speak Russian, the meaning must have been perfectly clear.

"Out of the question," Max retorted.

"Definitely in the question. I'm not going anywhere until someone explains to me why that bitch over there decided to try and kill us. And I feel a lot more comfortable when the guys with the guns are on our side."

"I'm not sure whose side we're on anymore. We might get you into more trouble, especially since Miss Grosjean over there…"

"You're actually telling a reporter my name? Are you a complete idiot, soldier?"

"…has a reputation for disobeying orders and freelancing. So it's possible that, while we have her in our custody, you would be able to get on a plane out of Russia."

Marianne shook her head. "What if she isn't working alone? What if they're waiting for us at the hotel? No thanks."

Max shrugged. "Fine. Come with us."

"Soldier, what's your name?" Selene said.

"I'll tell you later," Max replied.

"You'll tell me now."

"Fine, my name is Max. And that's all you'll get."

"Max." She rolled it around her tongue, thinking. "Are you sure we haven't met before? Well, no matter. I want to say just one thing: if you allow an American reporter into that building over there, you will be shot for treason even if you get away with whatever you're planning to do with me."

Max smiled at her. "They can only shoot me once."

***

Park Sun-Lee's phone rang. "Yes, Mr. Buddha." It was ridiculous to have to call the hacker that, but the guy was good, really good. Good enough that none of Park's connections had managed to unearth his real identity. For all Park knew, it might be a woman.

All he knew for certain was that whoever the hacker was, the Electric Buddha wasn't Russian.

"We've picked up the news item you asked me about."

"Who ran it?" Park asked, hiding his delight. The Russians had clamped down fast, and he thought that the reporters might not have had time to get the piece out. Of course he had his own news article ready to go, but having it come from a major media outlet was much better.

"*Update!*"

"Perfect. Please amplify it. I want the full treatment—memes, social posts, the works. I want people to *see* this."

"Yes. For the price I sent you?"

"Yes." The Buddha was expensive, but Park had plenty of money. The important part was that it could never be traced back to him. "Let me know if we go over budget, though."

"I never go over budget… Wait a second, I'm getting another alert. *Caipi* just published, too."

"Good. Amplify that one as well."

"Yes. I will call you if I need further instructions." The Buddha hung up.

Park quickly called up his browser—internet lockdowns didn't affect his satellite phone—and navigated to the *Update!* website.

He smiled. He was expecting a lurid story, maybe even a quick snapshot. But video? Who was this Marianne Caruso woman? He owed her a huge debt of gratitude.

Park's advertising campaign was now well and truly underway. Soon, the entire world would know what was happening, and he could organize the press tour.

After that, it would be time to disappear for a while. The Russians were not going to be happy.

CHAPTER 3

The lobby was quite small. Just inside, a reception desk faced the glass. Like the guard post, it, too, was unmanned.

Max started to push the door closed and hesitated when he felt the heft. The normal-looking metal-and-glass door weighed a ton, like the concrete door to the bomb shelter at the base. He almost dismissed it as a faulty hinge or something, but some instinct stopped him. Upon further study, he realized the glass was a few centimeters thick and the lock consisted of big bolts more suitable for a vault.

"Armored," he told Ivan, who was nearest. "I wonder who they think will attack this place."

"If you knew what you were getting into, you wouldn't ask such stupid questions," Selene Grosjean said. "And you definitely wouldn't bring an American in here to see it."

"From what I know about you and Park Sun-Lee, nationality has little to do with anything."

"We work for Moscow."

"Ah, but *who* in Moscow? A lot of the soldiers at the base are beginning to wonder. Either way, one foreigner more or less will make little difference to this." He looked around. "Besides, maybe this is for the best. That armor makes me think there should be guards here. Armed guards. The fact that they're missing makes me think there's something wrong that goes well beyond internal politics. I'm going to go in, and I won't stop until we run into someone who can tell us what's happening."

"You should call your superiors. You're making an enormous mistake."

"We tried. Cell coverage is down. In fact, I can't get my phone to respond at all."

"That's just because they run a scrambler here. Go five hundred meters in any direction and call for instructions. Trust me on this."

"*Trust* you? I thought all you wanted was my head on a platter."

"At least with me you'd know who was coming for you."

"We're going down that corridor. It would be helpful if you'd tell me what we'll find."

"I don't actually know. Never been here before."

"Why don't I believe you?" Max said.

"Probably childhood trauma. Maybe a mother who didn't love you or an older brother who abused you."

Max turned away suddenly, but he couldn't close his ears to her mocking tones. "Was it something I said?"

A long corridor, windowless but well-lit, stretched out before them, ending at a door. Offices opened up from the main corridor, some obviously in use, others completely sterile, and all empty of human presence.

"What kind of work do they do here?" he asked Grosjean.

"Telling you would be treason. I don't want to be standing beside you when they shoot you."

"You're beginning to irritate me," Max said. "I think something really serious is going on. Knowing what it is might help us deal with it."

They reached the door. This one consisted of riveted metal armor, painted grey and much more aligned with his ideal of what a secure location should have. The door had a large dent in it... bulging it out from the inside.

To Max's surprise, it opened as soon as he turned the handle.

They stepped through the door into a tropical wonderland.

Everyone ooh'd as they looked down over a sea of green illuminated from above by a glass roof larger than anything ever built over a sporting arena. Thick columns disguised as trees supported the vaulted transparencies. The vastness was more inferred than visible, as mist obscured everything more than fifty meters away. The humid air pasted clothes to skin.

"Are you sure we're still in Russia?" Marianne asked, awed.

"Unless my government has some kind of science fiction portal, yes, I'm sure." He turned to the witch woman and said, in English in deference to the reporter, "What is this place?"

"They call it the feeding ground," Selene replied with a smirk.

"Why?"

"Oh, you'll find out. You shouldn't have let the door close."

Max turned back and saw that the door had no handle on the inside, but only a keypad. "Tell me the code."

Now the woman laughed. "I never come in here so I don't need to know the code, and if there's one thing you should know, it's that 'need to know' is pretty much a religious concept in this place."

"But it makes no sense. Why build this place so that just anyone can get in and no one can get out?"

"Because no one is worried about people getting in. That is a problem that takes care of itself. And as for no one getting out, there's your mistake. It's built that way so no*thing* can get out."

Ivan, who'd been looking into the mist, spoke. "There are things in there."

"How can you see under the tree canopies?" Max asked.

"I can't. There are things in the mist. Flying things." He pointed to where a slightly darker grey shadow could barely be seen moving in the clouds of vapor. As Max watched, the image grew more distinct and the shadow became some kind of large bird.

No. The distance was deceiving, not a large bird, but some colossus that should never have been able to remain aloft.

And it was coming straight towards them.

"Run!" Max shouted as the thing came into focus. Leathery wings and huge talons appeared. The group sprinted along the balcony towards a set of stairs leading down, the only cover in sight. Completely exposed, their footsteps clanging on the metal gridwork, they were the perfect targets for an aerial strike.

Ivan decided he wasn't going to run anymore and turned to face the oncoming bird. He raised his gun and fired several times.

He might as well have spit on the thing for all the damage it did. A talon raked the front of his t-shirt and blood welled. Ivan staggered and clutched at the railing, his face turning pale.

"No!" Max cried. He rushed back to where his soldier stood looking down, the blood creeping over the green shirt. He grabbed the man's arm and pulled.

While the flying creature circled for another strike, they reached the stairs and descended into a mezzanine formed by the landing between flights. A man lay on his back. His head was gone.

"Well, that explains where at least one of the guards went," Max said. Then he turned to Ivan. "You okay?"

Ivan was studying a couple of deep gashes on his chest. "Hurts like hell, but it didn't get past the ribs. It's going to leave a mark, though."

"Well, you deserve it for trying to shoot at it with a pistol. What the hell were you thinking?"

Ivan shrugged. "The ones at the lab fell pretty easily."

"Yeah, we unloaded rifle clips into them."

"That's what the dead guy should've done," Ivan said, nodding towards the corpse. "At least I managed to hit the thing."

Lying beside the headless guard lay the most beautiful sight Max had ever seen—a well-used Kalashnikov AK-47. He bent to pick it up.

"Won't be much good against any of the big ones," Selene said.

"I thought you didn't know what was in here," Max replied.

The woman shrugged, a beautiful sight. "For someone who claims not to trust me, it seems like you believe everything I say. Could you untie me, at least? I don't particularly want to stumble and break my nose."

"If you fall, a broken nose will be the least of your problems."

Max dropped to one knee and inspected the body. There was nothing remarkable about the guard except that his head was missing and his clothes were drenched in gore. He hadn't been dead too long—the body was still warm.

The group huddled close, the soldiers trying to get a better look at the dead man, the journalist and her companion not wanting to leave the dubious cover of the landing which, though not armored, at least had a grating between it and the outer world.

Max straightened and turned to them. "We need to look for…"

A crash against the grating interrupted him. Their friend the flying lizard had returned, and was grabbing onto the grid. Bat-like, it clung to the metal with its claws while two hooks on the wings stabilized it. The creature tried to push its beak through holes in the grating several sizes too small for that operation.

"Not the smartest thing on the planet," Marianne said. "It could come in by the walkway. I wonder how it survived in the wild."

Marianne's friend, the short-haired stocky one who'd been almost silent since being rescued, spoke. "It probably didn't. If they're recreating dinosaurs using CRISPR editing, they can only select for things like appearance and size. They can't program in instinct or experience. That's probably what this simulated jungle is for. To see what they do in the wild, which designs work and which need to be tweaked."

Selene snorted. "So you're the smart one? And you work with the pretty one? How cute."

"Screw you," the other woman replied, causing Selene even more laughter.

The creature didn't look like it would be able to reach them, and it didn't look like it would ever figure out that there was a big hole along the side that led straight to the tasty morsels it desired.

Unfortunately, all of that would be of no importance extremely soon. The metal holding up the grating began to creak and groan, as the enormous weight of the flying lizard told. The grate began buckling out and the monster flapped its wings a couple of times to steady itself. The movement tore even more metal away, and their already dubious cover became worthless.

Max raised the rifle to his shoulder and fired, trying to hit the thing's tiny head through the openings. He smiled in satisfaction as three bullets smashed into the tiny skull.

It fell backwards, sprawled into the trees below. The grating went with it.

"Okay," Max said. "We need to move. Any ideas where to go?"

"How about back to the door? Sure, it's out in the open, but we can hold anything off now that we have a decent gun."

Max pulled the clip off and grimaced. "We have maybe ten shots. I'd rather try to find an emergency exit or something."

"Do you have a map?" Selene said.

"Shut up," Max snapped. "I vote we go down and check the perimeter of the space. There has to be a door in here somewhere, an emergency exit of some kind. What happens if the keypads malfunction? No one would design a building which locks people inside if a glitch happens."

"Well," Selene said. "Unless the designers aren't really concerned about the value of their researchers."

Max nearly hit her with the butt of the rifle, but held up just in time. It was what she wanted. To prove what, exactly, he didn't know. But he was absolutely certain she wanted to make him react. Maybe to drive a wedge between him and his troops? Hell, that was easy to counter: he'd let his men take turns hitting her.

A dull thud shook the building, a sound he'd heard infinite times in his military career: an explosion. He placed it at the other side of the enclosure straight across from where they stood.

Ivan grinned. "I vote we go that way," he said. Then grimaced with the effort of speech.

So they did.

**

At the foot of the stairs, Marianne felt the ground under her feet. Soft, loamy grass. Completely different from the surface they'd been kneeling on, awaiting death just fifteen minutes before. That had been hard dirt, dry and rocky, the grass hardy stuff that had actually survived countless Russian winters. This felt like a moss bed in a rainforest.

They crept slowly behind two of the soldiers, but ahead of the woman who'd captured them. Max brought up the rear. Marianne made space for Ronnie to come up beside her. "Look, I'm sorry I got you into this."

"It's not your fault. I was the one who insisted on coming."

"Yeah, but I should have told you it would be dangerous."

"You didn't know," Ronnie replied.

Marianne took another couple of steps before the guilt grew too strong. "Actually, I did know. I knew we were walking into a hornet's nest, and I was pretty sure the people who run YekLab work for the Russian military. I let you come along anyway."

"I pretty much guessed all of that myself," Ronnie replied. "Except I don't think this is fully a Russian thing."

"Because of Grosjean?"

"That and the man in the video who left the meeting through the same door the dinosaur entered. He didn't look Russian."

"Poor guy. He was probably one of the first to die."

Ronnie took a while to answer. "He didn't look like a guy about to die, either. He looked to me like a guy about to watch other people die."

"You got all that from my crappy video?"

"I watch a lot of videos."

"So what do you think?"

"I think if you ran his picture through a police database, you'll find some interesting stuff. I'd start with the terrorist organizations."

"Why?"

"Because they're the ones with the major bioweapons programs. No one else admits to having them, so when you need to recruit new talent, there aren't many recruiting options. LinkedIn's terrorist section is quite small."

Marianne laughed. "You have a vivid imagination, Ronnie."

"Five buck says I'm right."

"Hell, if we get out, I'll give you the five bucks even if we're wrong."

"Why are you so calm?"

"Because this isn't the first time I've gotten involved in something like this. I once had a bunch of Eastern European smugglers chase me all over Greece for the privilege of shooting me."

"How did you get out of that?"

"I had a really good friend. A bunch of people who turned out to be really good friends, in fact. I'm hoping our soldier boy back there is also a good friend. If not, we might make it out of this and find ourselves in a Russian maximum-security prison."

Ronnie swallowed. "You're a famous reporter."

"Yeah. So someone will send a strongly worded note of protest. Do you think the Russians give a damn about that? Nobody is going to start a war over one journalist, no matter how much we like to pretend otherwise."

"I think you underestimate how important public opinion and social media is," Ronnie said.

Marianne bit back her reply. People who gave their opinion on Twitter liked to think that it mattered, liked to believe they were changing the world. What harm was there in letting Ronnie keep her illusions? For her part, Marianne would keep working to make it a non-issue. They needed to get themselves out of this mess and not rely on outside help.

How they would do that, she had no idea. For now, she was following a bunch of Russian commandos towards the site of an explosion. Had anyone asked her if she could think of any situation in which that could be the safest course of action, she would have just laughed.

Shows what she knew.

A concrete walkway followed the contour of the outer wall, and then the dirt started. In some places, it was covered with grass, in others with some kind of bright green lichen. It was soggy everywhere, and squelched underfoot. The vegetation reminded her of the Amazon tours she'd taken while she was down in Brazil. As did the humidity and heat.

Strangely, though, mosquitoes appeared to be absent.

Small blessings were better than none at all.

They walked between the trees and she marveled at the soldiers. They were traversing the same jungle she was, but they did it soundlessly, advancing with a sort of tense readiness that made it look like they could jump through the canopies of the trees or bite the head off a dinosaur without warning.

By comparison, the three much smaller women were making all the noise. Marianne had even had to remove her heels, which she hated to do; the one thing she was always self-conscious about was her height. But sinking into the mud with every step was a good way to destroy an expensive pair.

Every few steps, the French woman would moan for them to untie her hands until Max told her that if she made another sound, he would gag her.

If looks could kill...

The injured soldier, Ivan, was just ahead of her. Blood dripped from his uniform, but when Max spoke to him in Russian, the man just responded something short and reassuring and kept walking.

But Marianne was used to watching people walk. Her first mentor at *Update!* had been a former runway model who'd taught her to spot which of the girls had a real future by ignoring the face—irrelevant for most models—and concentrating on the way they held themselves and how they walked.

This man walked like someone on his last ounce of energy. Only determination, sheer physical fitness and training were keeping him upright.

She left Ronnie's side and matched him. "Are you really all right?" she asked him.

The man smiled, a painful gesture, but genuinely grateful "Hurts, but I've had worse," Ivan replied in halting English.

She believed him. He wasn't looking to be a hero, wasn't looking to gain sympathy. He was just stating the facts of life. But the front of his shirt and pants were covered in gore. Even if the injury itself wasn't life-threatening, she wasn't certain anyone could lose that much blood and not feel it.

But there was little she could do.

The man in front halted suddenly. Ivan put his hand on her shoulder and indicated that she should crouch behind a bush.

A huge creature, much bigger than the one in the lab, stomped past, its head lost among the tree leaves.

But the soldier in the lead wasn't pointing at the big creature. He was pointing to the right.

Marianne heard it. Something was pushing its way through the underbrush at top speed. The big monster stopped and turned to face it, but the creature coming through burst through the leaves just in front of the soldiers.

Marianne had time to see that it looked like the one she'd run into in the lab before Max opened up on it with the machine gun.

It fell with a whimper and Max winked at her. "Good thing we had practice. Unfortunately, I've got maybe three bullets left now."

Marianne was horrified. The noise had blasted through the jungle. Everything in the area must have been converging on them. "Should we run?"

"No. Wait. Listen."

Thunder echoed. "What is it?"

"The big one. Running. It is making so much noise that nothing could miss it."

"This is all wrong," Ronnie said.

"What is?" Max said.

"The dinosaurs. They shouldn't be making that much noise. It's like they've never lived in a forest before."

"I thought that was what they were supposed to be testing in here," Marianne said.

"I guess it might be, but these things are worse than I expected. I mean even the base genetic material…" She paused. "Oh."

"What?"

"Well, I just remembered about the Antarctic incident. The monster they took from there was aquatic. If they used that as a base…"

"Antarctica?" Max said, suddenly intense. "What about it?"

"They say a Russian team took some nothosaur eggs from the creatures that attacked the Argentine base in Antarctica. Don't you guys watch the news?"

Marianne smiled. "Not the kind of news you watch, dear. Deep internet conspiracy stuff isn't everyone's cup of tea."

Ronnie snorted. "Which is why you don't know what's going on. Look around you. All of this could have been built easily using the right kind of DNA. And where could a Russian facility have gotten that?"

"From my brother," Max said. "He was the one they sent. He brought it all back." He turned to look at the French woman. "And then he conveniently disappeared." He pulled a pistol out of his holster and aimed it between Selene's eyes. "Tell me you had nothing to do with it."

The woman didn't flinch. "Maybe I did and maybe I didn't. You should really ask the Director about that kind of thing, though. The real question is whether you could live with yourself shooting an unarmed woman without even knowing if she's guilty or not."

"You're not some innocent child caught in a crossfire, Selene. I suspect I could live with myself quite easily."

But he put the gun away. "Come on."

They started out again, but it was immediately apparent that Ivan needed help. He staggered to his feet and would have gone straight back down had Ronnie not rushed in and caught his arm on her shoulder, covering herself in blood in the process.

Max and Ivan spoke in Russian, and it was easy to understand what was being said: Max insisting that the soldier needed help, the other man waving it off. Finally, one of the other men took Ronnie's place, supporting the wounded soldier, and they set off.

The jungle was quiet, the men tense. Marianne's uneasiness had a specific source, and it had little to do with dinosaurs. The place was quiet because there was no wind, no birds in the trees, no insects. It was a lab, sure as if the walls had been painted white and it had been full of glass tubes or the apparatus from Dr. Frankenstein's workshop. It had been built just detailed enough to test out dinosaur designs, but it didn't work as a forest.

She wondered if the dinosaurs were fooled.

***

Max burned with anger. The witch-woman wasn't telling them all she knew and that infuriated him. It was almost as if her twisted sense of revenge for the humiliation of being questioned had overcome everything else and she no longer cared if he splattered her brains all over the mossy floor, just as long as she could watch the rest of them perish as well.

The right thing to do would be to shoot her and leave the body to whatever carrion eaters existed among the thunder lizards. But he couldn't bring himself to do it even though he knew she deserved it. Even his men would applaud the decision, and the Americans... well, they might pretend squeamishness but when someone makes you kneel on the ground to accept your execution, you don't really mind if someone shoots them.

But she could tell him about his brother. He was sure of it. That woman had been there.

The real problem was how to make her talk. She would probably enjoy any kind of torture he could dream up. She was sick. Everyone knew that.

They'd reached the halfway point of the enclosure. The explosion had happened just on the other side of a deep valley ahead, and he wondered where everything was. In the first hundred meters they'd run into two creatures and then... nothing. It was almost as if the place was emptying out.

If that were so, they needed to find how they were leaving. Ivan wouldn't be able to walk much longer... Yuri was already grunting with the effort of keeping them both vertical.

They crested the valley rim and Max's heart sank.

Some asshole had decided that putting a swamp in the middle of the complex would be a good idea. He wished he could grab that guy's neck and squeeze.

"Don't even think about going through that," he told Vasily, who was about to test the depth of the water. "They're probably testing water nasties in there. We go around."

Ivan groaned and Max turned to see how the man was holding up.

That saved him. Something about the size of a large dog jumped at him and he barely managed to twist around to make it miss. It landed in the water with a splash, all tail and scales.

He pulled out his handgun and took a bead on it. It looked like a miniature version of one of the velociraptors from those American movies, and its head exploded in satisfying chunks when he shot it.

Ten more took its place.

Max, Yuri and Vasily began to fire at the pack that struck them, shooting each creature as it approached.

Their assailants didn't growl or screech, but instead made barely audible squeaking sounds. Were they coordinating their strikes? If so, Max couldn't see the pattern unless one counted that whenever he blew one away, another took its place.

They weren't too smart, though. Instead of hiding in the underbrush, the dinosaurs stayed out in the open where his men could shoot them.

On the other hand, they were fast and agile and were hard to hit when they came straight towards you. Max had his hands full just keeping them off himself and Marianne.

He saw Ivan fall to the ground to his left, but remained focused on the attacking creatures. Blinking at the wrong time could mean missing one, and missing one could get them all killed. They weren't big, but those jaws looked strong and full of teeth.

Four of the creatures together jumped on Ivan's prone figure just as three others struck at the men with guns. Ivan screamed and Max saw that Marianne's companion rushed over to help, waving her arms and yelling at the top of her lungs.

Two of the dinosaurs bolted, the third kept worrying at the fallen soldier, and the final one held its ground and lunged at the approaching woman.

She fell to the ground and started beating at it with her fists.

But that was all he saw. The distraction of watching the woman's actions was enough for him to miss a shot and one of the creatures jumped onto his chest. The impact knocked him backwards and he landed with a gasp on his back, losing his pistol in the process. The scaly monster was heavier than it looked, and he drove his forearm into its neck to keep it away.

The defense would have been effective against a human assailant, but the reptile's neck was more flexible and it managed to grab hold of the cloth of his uniform jacket and begin to pull. Then it adjusted its grip and took hold of his shoulder through the jacket. Max felt the pressure mount and gritted his teeth in pain; the only thing between the monster's teeth and his skin were a couple of layers of cloth.

He reached down with his left hand and unbuttoned the sheath on his leg. He pulled on the knife within and felt it stick. The serrated back of the blade had caught in the cloth. The dinosaur felt the motion and released his arm. The thing's head snapped towards his face.

Just before it reached him, the blade broke free and he buried it in the creature's skull and tossed the dead weight to one side.

In the same movement, Max rolled, grabbed the pistol with his right hand and stood, ready to shoot anything that came towards him.

The pack was gone, and they'd taken Ivan's body with them.

Vasily, Yuri and Max exchanged a look. "Which way did they go?" Max barked.

"That way," Vasily replied, indicating a direction with his head. "But look there."

Marianne was kneeling over her friend, holding a limp hand in her own and sobbing. Max approached and put his hand on her shoulder.

Marianne looked up. "She's hurt. Can you help her?"

Knowing his men would warn him if danger approached, Max knelt beside the fallen woman. The blank, open eyes told him everything he needed to know, but he still went through the motions of checking for a pulse. Even as he felt for it, he realized that the blood covering the body was hers.

"She's gone," he said.

"Oh God. Marianne buried her head in her friend's chest. "Ronnie, I'm so sorry. This is all my fault. I'm sorry."

Max stood. He'd never been good at comforting grieving women. Or men for that matter. When the colonel had told him about his brother, he'd just nodded and left, not wanting to subject anyone to the embarrassment of having to console a grown man.

His men apparently felt the same, none of them daring to interrupt Marianne's mourning, even though all three knew they needed to get moving, to get out of that killing field before something bigger with just as many teeth stumbled on them.

But to force her to stand, to force her to walk... they just couldn't bring themselves to do it.

Finally, Vasily spoke.

"Has anyone seen Grosjean?"

The French woman was nowhere to be seen.

***

Selene Grosjean watched the soldiers disappear into the distance, the leader supporting the Caruso woman on his arm. She glared at them.

"Don't you dare get yourselves killed before I can catch you," she whispered. "I want you to suffer much more than what you'll get if our little beasties kill you first."

Then she looked around. Seeing the coast was clear, she removed herself from the canopy and shimmied down the tree she'd climbed—a branchless pole only accessible to her because she trained rigorously every day—and strode towards the wall. The tree's rough bark had also made short work of the cable tie holding her wrists together.

The soldiers weren't dumb. They'd tried to use their cell phones to call for help. Unfortunately for them, those phones wouldn't work inside this complex. But hers would.

She called up Park Sun-Lee's number, but hesitated before pressing 'call' and decided to put her phone away. The North Korean was up to something, and she wasn't certain that whatever plans the man had included her.

And if they didn't include her, they didn't include Russia.

That meant that, before calling him, she had to find out what was going on. There weren't many people who could have coordinated the disaster at the press launch. She was one of them. Park was another. Maybe, with insane amounts of luck, someone else could have pulled it off.

But everything seemed to point to Park.

Then there was the question of the explosion in this enclosure. Again, the ability to get inside in order to cause something to happen pointed directly at the project leader. Very few others could have made it past security.

Which meant that this war might have to be fought on a couple of fronts. She might have to put off the satisfaction of gutting that soldier like a fish for some time.

She punched the security code into the balcony lock and took a last look out at the enclosure. The place should have been crawling with dinosaurs but, instead, it felt completely empty.

The explosion had opened an exit somewhere.

Someone was about to have a few thousand prehistoric visitors.

CHAPTER 4

Park Sun-Lee knocked on the hotel room door.

"Who is it?" a woman's voice asked from inside.

"I'm with the YekLab team."

The door opened and the Brazilian reporter, Tatiana Close, looked out at him. It always amazed Park that people would just open doors and talk to strangers. They clearly lived in a very different world than he did. "I remember you from the lab. You were with the executives."

"Yes. Could you come with me?"

Suspicion crossed the woman's features. "Where?"

"Not very far. Just out into the hotel gardens. We won't leave the grounds, but what I'd like to say to you is private."

"We can talk right here."

"I sincerely doubt your room is private."

"Oh." The woman looked more annoyed than appalled by the thought that her room might be bugged or that someone might have planted a camera inside. "All right."

They made their way down the elevator, through the lobby and out into the garden. A couple of guests were still in the pool despite night having fallen half an hour before.

"We should be able to talk here," Park said.

"I'm listening."

"How would you like the story of the year?"

"I think I already have it. From the lab, although I got a call a couple of hours ago that informed me that Marianne scooped me by one hour."

"That was just a little incident," Park said, waving his hand dismissively. "I'm talking about something serious, a major violation of human rights on the part of the Russian government, not a minor industrial accident with a handful of dead and injured."

"What do I think? I think I'm suspicious. Why aren't you taking this proposition to Miss Caruso? After all, she's the biggest name on this press junket. You could help her win that Pulitzer this year."

Park felt the color rising in his cheeks. "I admit that I tried, but she is unavailable."

"Did she tell you to jump under a bus?" Tatiana paused and then laughed. "Or more likely she already has a handle on the story herself, and decided to cut you out."

"As a matter of fact, I don't know. She was seen leaving her hotel this afternoon and no one has heard of her since. I'm on a bit of a schedule, so I can't wait for her to come back. For all I know, she's spending the night in the mountains with a boyfriend."

"You don't know Marianne. If there's a story out there, she will be chasing it."

"I was told she is very... er... sexually active."

"She knows how to prioritize. Trust me, she's hunting your story."

Park shrugged. "No matter. The situation I will be revealing to you is well beyond her capacity to ferret out. If you're interested, be at the heliport near the airport at 7 AM tomorrow morning."

"Will I be alone?"

"Perhaps. You're the first of the journalists I've located so far. I will be speaking to three more of your colleagues tonight. Depending on their answer there will be between one and four of you on the flight. If none of you show up," he shrugged, "I guess I'll just have to locate Miss Caruso. I think she is the kind to jump at the chance. Thank you for your time."

As the tall Brazilian woman walked back towards the hotel, Park smiled. By the expression on her face when he mentioned that he'd find Caruso, he knew that the woman would be punctual, and she would get into the helicopter even if she had to go alone.

One outlet was enough. What he planned to show the press tomorrow should be truly spectacular.

Of course, once he was done, he needed to get the hell out of Russia. Africa, he'd heard, was wonderfully anarchic this time of year.

He would remain there until such time as the Russians took the price off his head.

***

Marianne stared up a long, ill-lit tunnel big enough to drive a truck through as two of the soldiers whittled saplings into spears. Their walk around the swamp had taken-in the soggy and uneven terrain-nearly half an hour.

One annoyance they didn't encounter, however, was anything resembling a dinosaur. The prehistoric monsters had seemingly disappeared.

And now, as she stared up a concrete hallway that was too long for the end to be visible, she knew where.

The doors that had kept the corridor separate from the animal enclosure were thick, reinforced with steel. But they'd been blown inward by the force of the explosion that they'd heard earlier.

Max handed her a long, straight stick, one end sharpened to a point. "What am I supposed to do with this?" she asked.

"Whatever you can. We're nearly out of rifle bullets and we have to escape through that tunnel, which is where the monsters seem to have gone."

"Why don't we just stay here?" Marianne asked. "If the monsters are out there, wouldn't it make more sense to wait for someone to come let us out?"

Max chuckled. "You seem to be a sophisticated woman, but it's clear you don't understand Russia. The first people in here will not be a rescue team. They will be people who work for a very secret part of the government."

"The FSB or the SVK?"

"I'm impressed by your knowledge, but those will only come if we're lucky. Those are official agencies… and this place seems to me to be extremely unofficial. We'll probably be picked up by an agency even I've never heard of, taken to a place that doesn't appear on any maps and tortured in ways that were specially invented for us. Then we'll be buried in unmarked graves in a wilderness no one ever visits."

Now it was Marianne's turn to laugh. "That doesn't leave too many options. How many places could possibly meet all those descriptions?"

"Russia is a big country. Trust me, it is much better to go through that tunnel and hope the people sent to look for us come in through the office. Because if that tunnel leads out, it's our only chance of living through this."

"And if it doesn't?"

"If it doesn't, it probably leads to someplace even more secret than the enclosure, so you'll be able to see things that are so confidential they'd kill you for seeing them. Luckily, that won't make any difference because they'll already kill you for what you've seen. So there's no risk in going that way. Besides, as a reporter, you're supposed to be nosy, so this should make you happy. Come on."

They set off down the tunnel, which was peppered with droppings, some quite large. As they passed a pile of excrement as tall as her knees, one of the soldiers said something in Russian, and the others laughed. She didn't ask for a translation.

The tunnel looked as if it had been built a long time ago and then never used. Apart from the animal waste and tracks, the concrete appeared crisp and unscuffed, but there were signs of age. Water seeping through seams had created calcium deposits in places, even miniature stalagmites.

"This is longer than I expected. It must go completely under the hill," Max said. His voice echoed in the huge space.

"What do you think it is?"

Max looked around. "Something Soviet, and that means a military installation. Maybe a tunnel connecting to a nuclear missile storage bunker. See? It's big enough that MAZ missile trucks could wheel through here. Then, you could set them up on any stretch of open concrete outside and boom! No more New York."

On that cheerful note, they trudged on. Every once in a while, they encountered a small dinosaur, but nothing that wanted to stand up to the pack of primates invading their space. Most scurried away, a few backed into the wall and watched them warily as they passed.

"What do you think made them go this way?" Marianne asked.

The soldier shrugged. "Everything I know about these creatures was told to me by your friend. I'm sorry about her, by the way. She seemed like a good person. Smart."

"It wasn't your fault," Marianne replied.

"We should have been able to protect her against a bunch of animals. I'll never forgive myself."

Marianne put her hand on his arm. "Let's just concentrate on getting out of here alive. I don't blame you."

Finally, when it seemed they must be reaching the Earth's core, the lights in the corridor suddenly cut off about three hundred meters ahead.

***

Max gestured to Vasily. "Go have a look," he said.

They stopped and waited for the soldier to return. Marianne took the time in the concrete tunnel to put her shoes back on. He couldn't believe she hadn't complained even once. Most of the women he'd ever gone out with—at least the ones who looked like this one did—would have screamed bloody murder all the way. Those that didn't dissolve into hysterics at the first sight of one of the creatures.

He suspected there was steel under the soft exterior of this American journalist. The clothes, the makeup… apparently they were a front, camouflage to hide a resilient, competent individual.

But she probably wouldn't be much good in a fight, resilient or not. She barely seemed to know which end of the spear they'd made should go into the dinosaur, and which she was supposed to hold, and she looked much too wispy to fight them, as if the slightest wind would blow her away... not to mention a dinosaur.

Then he caught himself. For that matter, neither he nor his men had trained with spears. It wasn't the kind of thing you expected to have to use on a modern battlefield.

Vasily returned. "It opens onto a hillside with a road leading to a parking lot or something."

"A ballistic missile staging ground," Max clarified.

"Whatever. I didn't see any missiles, anyway. I could see a few of the animals grazing nearby, but most of them seem to have wandered off. It's too dark to see where they might have gone."

"Good work."

They walked to the exit and stopped just inside.

"Don't you think it would be better to stay in the tunnel until it gets light?" Marianne asked.

"Not really," Max replied. "What I said back there still applies. Someone's going to be around here soon to secure this installation. We don't want to be here when that happens." He stepped resolutely out into the crisp night air and breathed deeply. After the hothouse humidity of the big chamber and the stench of the polluted tunnel, the fresh scent of mountain breeze felt wonderful.

Yuri spoke. "We should try to get back to the road."

"If anyone comes, they might be watching the car," Vasily pointed out.

"We can always stop another car and get them to drive us to the city. Civilians shouldn't be much of a problem."

"Yeah," Max said. "You're right." They turned to look at the tunnel behind them, trying to gauge the direction they needed to hike over the mountain at their back to arrive at the road. "My phone is working now, but we must be out of reach of any cell towers. I have zero bars."

"Same here," Yuri replied. Vasily shook his head and even Marianne tried to find reception and failed. How she'd managed to keep her purse on her shoulder through everything they'd encountered was beyond him, but there it was.

They would have to climb up the mountain, so Max did something he'd been postponing. "Here," he told Marianne. "Take this." He pulled a pair of shoes out of a bag he'd tied to his belt. They were black lace-down boots, ankle-high, rubber-soled and ugly as sin.

In the dim light from the tunnel, she looked down on them. "What's this?"

"Those are your friend's shoes. You need to put them on."

Marianne dropped them and looked into his eyes. "You took her shoes?"

"She didn't need them anymore. You do. See if they fit."

"No... I can't."

"You have to. We can't carry you, and you certainly can't climb rocks in those heels. You need to help us help you."

"Oh God."

For a second, he thought she would break down and cry, refuse to wear the shoes. But after a moment's hesitation, she sat on the slope and pulled them on.

"How are they?" Max asked.

"A little big, but otherwise all right. I'll survive."

Then she stood and, with a scream of pure rage, threw her own shoes down the slope.

They set out in silence, climbing the gentle hill and taking turns using their phones for illumination.

Suddenly, they came to a rock cliffside, too steep to climb easily. They walked along it, trying to find a way up, but ten minutes later, had made no progress. "We're getting pushed way off track," Yuri said.

Max stopped. "This makes no sense. These hills shouldn't be this rocky, and they definitely shouldn't be this steep. I've hiked here for years and never found anything like this."

Vasily laughed. "Yeah, we know all about your hikes. You used to call them training exercises, remember? As I recall, you liked to set off in the morning and return the following day... and not stop for anyone who collapsed."

Yuri laughed. "Yeah, remember the time—"

A shift in the shadows, a sudden darkness, a rush of air and Yuri was simply gone. "What the fuck!" Vasily said.

Max shone his light into the darkness and saw an enormous silhouette in the night. "Run!" he shouted and, grabbing Marianne's arm, rushed back towards the tunnel, Vasily hot on their heels.

Gunfire tore through the night as the soldier tried to fend off the monster crashing behind them.

The terrain was treacherous. He had to pull Marianne bodily to her feet several times as they ran. Rocks rolled down the hill below them.

Finally, the light of the tunnel mouth became visible ahead. They ran towards it, but Max knew they would never make it in time. Vasily was ahead of him now. He knew his only chance was to drop the woman. She was slowing him down.

Somehow, however, he just couldn't bring himself to let go.

He pulled her over a rock, barely clearing it when the big thing arrived. He couldn't see the monster's shape, just a shadow of enormity in the blackness as it put a huge foot onto the stone they'd just laboriously scaled.

The enormous stone shifted, then dislodged, then rolled. Behind it, a good chunk of mountain dirt slid onto the creature pursuing them. Not enough to really hurt it, but maybe enough to slow it down, Max thought.

Then the shadow lost its footing and began to tumble down the slope, gaining speed as it disappeared from sight.

"Wow," Vasily said. "That had to hurt."

Max shook his head. "Come on. We need to find a place to wait for dawn. We can't fight if we can't see them coming. I'd prefer not to stay in the tunnel if we can avoid it."

They trudged on, occasionally shining their lights into the darkness in a vain attempt to spot anything approaching before they, in turn, were seen.

In the end, they stayed in the tunnel.

***

Two identical helicopters waited on the pads beside the hangars. Whoever this guy Park was, he had some pull. The guards at the gate had straightened when she mentioned his name and ushered her inside without asking a single question—even though Tatiana had arrived an hour early.

Dawn had just finished breaking and the air was cool and crisp, with the moisture of evaporating dew giving that inimitable early-summer-morning sense to the air. She laughed at herself. Normally, she would only have experienced this kind of early morning on the way home, dressed to the nines and returning from a party. Preferably with some good-looking guy on her arm.

But Yekaterinburg wasn't Rio. Hell, it wasn't even Sao Paulo. She doubted everyone danced till dawn the way they did as a matter of course back home.

Since there was nobody around, she sat on a bench under the glass roof of something that looked like a bus stop and studied the helicopters.

They were green, and that was as far as her expertise went. They looked a bit bigger than the ones she sometimes traveled on in Brazil, but other than that, they were just helicopters. She'd never been particularly interested in machinery.

She took a couple of pictures of the aircraft. Someone back home would be able to tell her what they were and to spin some speculation about which of Russia's myriad of intelligence, military and paramilitary organizations used them. But that wasn't the real reason she'd been early.

Simply put, she'd come an hour beforehand to make certain she wasn't late. For the first time since she graduated from being *Caipi*'s cub reporter, she was nervous about a story.

This piece could take many forms, but one thing was definite: it wasn't a fluff piece. It also wasn't a piece about a cosmetics company or a profile of a fashion designer. This was serious journalism. People were dead and injured, and she, Tatiana Close, could help the world come to a better understanding of why it had happened.

It might not win her awards. It might not make her famous.

That didn't matter. What mattered was that she would finally be doing something that made a difference, minor though it might be.

Most of all, however, she would be able to look Marianne in the eye again. She remembered the last time they'd met, in Río, for the fashion week two years earlier. Marianne had already been a formidable force in their little microcosm, but outside the fashion world, very few people knew her name.

Tatiana, on the other hand was inextricably tied to Brazilian high society. You couldn't have a party unless she was there, and the popular magazines that women pored through while getting their hair done would never pass up an opportunity to speculate about whether the guy on her arm on any given evening was something serious or not.

Marianne had been a moth orbiting her flame during fashion week—a bright moth, but a moth nonetheless. Now, Marianne was a hugely respected journalist. First, she'd managed to track down the author of *Timeless*, a bestseller whose mystique—and sales—had been increased a millionfold by the fact that no one knew who had written it. Then her piece on the criminal organizations of the Aegean Sea, complete with details and locations, had stunned the world—no one expected that from her, and it threw dark shadows on the sunniest of Aegean islands. But it was her piece about the monastic community on Mount Athos in *The New Yorker* which had catapulted her to fame.

Not only had Marianne apparently been on the peninsula—which was famously off limits not only to human women, but also to cows, mares and anything else of the female persuasion that stood still long enough for the monks to expel it—but she'd been *inside* the monasteries and spoken with a select few of the monks. No woman had ever managed that before, much less a journalist.

The fact that the monks, in their misogynistic medieval cluelessness, had been useful idiots in the game the smugglers played was just the cherry on top. It was what made the story a masterpiece. And every single word, despite the best attempts of people to knock holes in it, had held up to cross examination.

So when Marianne had walked into YekLab the morning of the dinosaur escape, fashionably late, but still there before the presentation started, Tatiana had felt something she hardly imagined possible: she'd felt intimidated by a woman she had once considered a peer and still considered a friend.

Now, she would even things up. This was the first step.

But that wasn't the only reason she was there. She had a hard time believing that Marianne would miss a story as big as this one promised to be. So she wanted to be there early, because if Marianne showed up, she wanted to have been there before her. She wanted the other woman to respect her work ethic, to realize Tatiana, unlike the pieces she often wrote, was not inconsequential.

The morning chill burned away and people started arriving. One of the European correspondents—from an English paper, if she wasn't mistaken—arrived first.

Then Park walked into the heliport flanked by four men in helmets—probably the flight crews.

Three more journalists she recognized from the press event and four other men she didn't recognize, but who walked like they owned the world, completed the group.

"All aboard," Park said with a smile, waving them into the helicopters. In the end, the journalists and Park piled into one aircraft and the big men into the other. She wondered if that was intentional.

The seats were uncomfortable, just a row of canvas supports and padded backs on each side of the aircraft. The helicopter was noisy.

But, as the vehicle she was seated in left the ground, Tatiana couldn't help but smile broadly in relief.

There was no sign of Marianne.

***

Marianne watched the sun rise. The two men had decided that they were safer in the tunnel after all, and they'd taken turns keeping watch while she slept.

Unfortunately, she'd found it nearly impossible to get any rest as the hard ground and the knowledge that they were surrounded by prehistoric monstrosities conspired to keep her from falling asleep for more than a few minutes at a time. Every sound, real or imagined, woke her with a gasp.

The soldier whose turn it was to sleep didn't seem to have the same issues. First Vasily, then Max were sound asleep every time she checked on them. For a second, she almost envied the soldiers' life. Simple, dangerous, possibly brutal at times, but it must have been nice to trust your coworkers so completely. The thought of throwing a press room into a life-threatening situation almost made her laugh out loud. The hardest part would be trying to stay out of the way as journalists stabbed each other in the back and threw the dead—and the slower living members of the group—to whatever was endangering them.

"It's beautiful," she said as the sky brightened to reveal a grassy valley surrounded by cliffs.

Vasily smiled, indicating that, though he didn't speak any English, the sentiment had come through.

Max, who'd been outside, probably answering a call of nature, returned. "It's unnatural," he said.

"What is?"

"This place. The Urals are old mountains. Eroded over hundreds of millions of years. So normally, they're just rounded hills that you can't even tell are supposed to be mountains. Those cliffs shouldn't be there. In fact, I'd be willing to bet that this whole place was built on purpose."

Marianne looked again. "Impossible. It's huge."

Max sighed. "I suppose you're right. There might be some other explanation. An impact crater or something. But the cliffs have definitely been worked on. Over there, you can see where they poured concrete over the rock. And the cliff we tried to climb last night has been hacked at to make it sheer."

"But why?"

"My guess is that the Soviets built it to keep people out of this area. It's the perfect place to launch missiles from trucks. You have to be almost directly overhead to hit them. Cruise missiles wouldn't work, you need to use conventional bombs. Pretty smart."

"Do you think people still use it for nuclear missiles?"

"No. I'm certain that they don't."

Marianne wasn't going to press him on that. The man was clearly military, and she suspected he wasn't just a regular grunt. The fact that he'd been the one sent to clear YekLab of dinosaurs made that a good bet. He probably knew what he was talking about. "Well, someone seems to be using it."

"Yeah. I'd guess it's the lab people."

"What for?"

"Can you think of a better way to keep a bunch of dinosaurs contained than to have them in a huge outdoor space they can't climb out of?"

Marianne looked out over the space. "Can *we* climb it?"

"We can have a look, but I'm not optimistic." He studied the cliff above the tunnel mouth. "The very top looks sheer all around. But there's some good news. I thought I saw a light just before dawn. Down there."

***

Hiram smiled as he unrolled his prayer mat. These summer days were his favorite. Perhaps not the perfect dry weather of the Afghan mountains he dimly remembered from his childhood, but beautiful all the same.

Water, in particular, was much easier to come by. There was no need to walk down the mountain to get it. He missed the conversations with his older brother, a boy so full of wisdom that his death still made him cry forty years later, but certainly didn't miss the blisters and the dust.

A rivulet ran through his field, a field that the Soviet government had given him when he was old enough to express the opinion that he wanted to be a farmer, and which the post-communist government had signed over to him.

As more and more people chose to farm this area, a village had grown up around his farm. It was isolated, and no one made enough to own a vehicle and traverse the single tunnel through the mountains, but that was not a problem for Hiram. He'd seen war first-hand. So closely, in fact, that he'd been rescued, bleeding and bloody, by an enemy soldier, treated by an enemy surgeon, and given land in an enemy country.

He had no desire to leave his little valley, no use for the outside world. This was a peaceful place and the world could look after itself. Or blow itself up. It made no difference to him.

Hiram was happier here in Russia than he'd ever been before. He'd even met Irina, and fathered Dmitri. This was home, now, even if his neighbors still looked at him funny when he prayed facing Mecca.

He finished his morning prayer and rolled the mat back up, reveling in the sense of the air upon his skin, a sense of being one with creation. Peace was important to him, and this morning was particularly peaceful.

He filled two buckets and began the short walk through the trees that gave shade to his wooden house.

Insects buzzed, a bird chirped. Someone screamed.

Hiram dropped the buckets to the ground and looked around, waiting for the sound to repeat itself. It didn't, but it sounded like it had come from the Galshibii farm, his closest neighbors. Holding up his hand to keep branches from hurting his eyes, he sprinted in that direction.

The house came into view, clapboard construction almost identical to his own, and he slowed. There didn't seem to be anything obviously wrong. No fire or smoke, at least.

The front door was on the opposite side so he crossed the neighbors' garden and went around the house.

And froze. A huge creature loomed in the front garden, firmly planted among the vegetables. Had it stood fully erect, the creature would have been taller than the house, but it was bent over something. Something wearing an undyed dress.

It resembled one of the lizards from the mountains of his childhood, greyish, with thin fur or down, and a blunt snout. Other than that, it was like nothing he had ever imagined in his life. There had certainly never been anything similar in their peaceful little corner.

He stumbled, snapping a branch underfoot, and the monster raised its bloody maw to look in his direction. It roared, the fury rooting him to the spot.

Then, forgetting the morsel at its feet, it straightened and charged.

Hiram found his footing and turned to run, crossing the back garden faster than he thought he could go. He knew that if he could reach the thicket of trees, the advantage would be his: the creature was too big to maneuver in there. Then, he needed to get home and warn Irina and Dmitri. The thought of them in danger gave his feet wings.

But the creature's size made it fast. Too fast for Hiram.

He was still ten meters from the nearest trees when the enormous mouth descended, wide open, to surround his head. The last thing he saw were teeth.

The jaws closed with a crunch that echoed inside the monster's mouth.

Hiram felt nothing more.

***

"Oh God," Marianne said. She disappeared around the corner of the house and Max could hear the sound of heaving.

"Go keep an eye on her," he told Vasily.

The soldier nodded and, gripping his spear like a talisman, disappeared after her.

Max studied the half-eaten woman on the ground. Both legs and one arm had been torn away, and there was a huge bite on the torso that resembled the photos he'd seen of shark victims. Whatever had attacked this woman had a huge jaw… much bigger than any of the monsters he'd seen over the past twenty-four hours.

Marianne and Vasily returned. The journalist looked pale.

"You okay?"

She nodded.

"Good. Let's hope this cottage has a phone, or a radio or something."

Vasily looked up. Max knew exactly what the other man was searching for, but he also knew no success would be forthcoming. He'd already searched and seen no phone lines, and no power lines. If any of those utilities were present, the wiring would be underground.

This seemed really far out in the boonies for underground cables, but he wouldn't give up hope.

He should have. The house, though clean and well-kept seemed more like the shack of a well-to-do peasant of the 19th century than anything else. Two rooms—one for eating and cooking, the other a small bedroom containing a narrow cot and an ancient armoire—were lit by open shutters. "Nothing," Max said.

"Maybe they have a shotgun or something."

"I doubt it. This is a woman's house," Max replied.

Vasily laughed. "You never met my Aunt Olga, I take it."

"From what you've told us about her, I'm the only man in the country who hasn't."

That brought another burst of laughter. "True. But they all knew that Olga was not someone you lied to or trifled with. She had expansive tastes, but no one messed with her. She had a farm out in the middle of nowhere, and didn't move away after her husband died. My brothers and I often wondered if she hadn't killed him, too."

"Too?"

Vasily waved it away. "All the others were self-defense. The police chief said so himself."

"All the others…"

But Vasily was too busy pulling open cupboards and overturning the mattress to hear him.

Max found a metal mug that smelled clean and filled it with water from a jug on the bedside table. Marianne smiled wanly but took a sip. Seeing that she managed to hold it down, she took a longer draught and sighed. "I bet you're sorry you ever saw me."

"Well, maybe a little. But if I had to land in the deepest of shit, I'm actually glad it happened this way. You seem worth saving."

"How would you know? You never saw me before today and all you've seen of me is a frightened girl who can't stay out of trouble or control her stomach when she sees a body. It's a good thing I haven't eaten since yesterday."

"I've seen soldiers break down completely after much less than what's happened to you. I've seen men soil themselves and beg when they knew they were about to be executed. You kept your head." He smirked. "And besides, I googled you after we left YekLab. I had a list of the journalists… it wasn't hard."

"Ah."

"You don't like that?"

"I hate it. Every time I meet someone, they do that. It gets boring after a while."

"I would think it was amazing," Max said. "Everyone wants to be famous."

"I know. I wanted to be famous, too. But now, sometimes, I just want to be me."

He chuckled. "You know… I don't think that's ever going to be a problem for you."

Vasily entered and began ransacking the cupboards in the kitchen area.

"You're not going to find a gun there."

"You never know. And besides, I'm not looking for a gun. Ah, good." He pulled a large round loaf of bread from a shelf and rummaged around some more until he found a yellow wedge of cheese. Finally, he took a knife from a drawer and cut the food into three equal portions. "I don't think she'll miss this," he said.

"Vasily, you're a pig," Max informed him.

"Don't you want it?" Vasily replied, reaching for the food.

"Get away from that or I'll shoot you."

Vasily laughed.

Max sat beside Marianne. She pulled a tiny piece of bread from the chunk she'd received and ate it cautiously. Then she took a bite. Moments later, all her food had disappeared.

"Seems like you're feeling better."

"I didn't realize how hungry I was. Of course, I missed dinner last night."

"What now?" Vasily said.

"We need to find some way to get out of here."

"Why not just hole up here?"

"Because either the army will come and hand us over to the witch-woman or the army won't come and the dinosaurs will eventually figure out that the houses have food in them. And then we'll be eaten."

Vasily grunted.

"I saw more houses to the north. Maybe one of them has a phone, or a radio, or even a gun and some ammo. At least in the daytime, those things won't be able to ambush us again."

They left the safety of the house, looking carefully before exiting. Once Max was sure the coast was clear, they ran towards a small wooded area which offered concealment. On the way there, they found another corpse, but didn't stop to study it. Even from ten meters away, Max could tell there wasn't much left.

The village looked like it had been hit by a tornado. Planks lay everywhere, beside bodies and clothing and two overturned carts. The remains of two horses, half-eaten, attracted flies on the ground.

But Max had no eyes for the carnage. Above one house stood a small metallic-looking ball. He directed Vasily's attention that way. "Webcam," Max said.

"That means there's a connection."

"Maybe it's just security."

"Do you really think these guys would use webcams?"

"How should I know?" Max asked.

"They wouldn't. Someone is doing surveillance on these people."

"But why?"

Marianne looked from one to the other. She didn't understand a word of Russian but understanding gleamed in her eyes. "They're watching these people. They were waiting for this. Someone wanted to show this to everyone, so they filmed it. It's a test ground. And they're testing on humans. That's why it's impossible to get out. This place is controlled by the lab."

Max knew she was right. "And we're in the middle of the proving ground." Then he paused and cocked his head. "Is that a helicopter?"

CHAPTER 5

Selene growled, fury rising as she reviewed the findings. There were fifteen pages of notes—someone must have spent the entire night typing—but there were only two lines that really mattered, and they appeared at the very end of the document:

We found no damage to the enclosures and no evidence of the doors being forced. Our attempts to verify if the open code came from an outside source reveals no firewall breaches.

Not broken and not hacked. That meant an inside job. Someone with the access codes had ordered the doors to open and let the deinonychus specimens out just when a group of journalists was present.

Only four people had those codes, and two of them had been in the conference room when the first dinosaur made its appearance—nowhere near the door mechanism. Moreover, those two were Russian citizens and career government researchers.

The third person who had the codes was Selene herself. She had no real use for them, wasn't involved in the science of what was going on in any way, but she had insisted. It was a matter of principle that she needed to be privy to every secret.

And she most certainly hadn't been the one to open the door.

Which left Park Sun-Lee.

The North Korean was the father of the project, the mad scientist without whom the research would never have gotten off the ground. Everyone had always considered his defection to Russia a godsend, too good to be true.

In her experience, things that seemed too good to be true usually were. Especially in Russia.

So Sun-Lee—who'd left the press event minutes before the disaster—was her man.

But what was his game? Why throw away a good thing, a sure thing?

Probably something better, but she didn't have any idea of what it might be.

She would find out, of course, but it would have to wait. Now that she knew all the data and research was safe, and that the incident had been limited to physically letting the dinosaurs out in both installations, and to planting the bomb that had let them into the tunnel, she had more pressing business to pursue.

Revenge.

She wanted that Spetsnaz asshole. She would personally break him, and when he was well and truly broken, she would tell him about his brother, how he didn't die a hero's death but was discarded like the worthless piece of rifle-toting meat he was. She'd been surprised to find out that this man was linked to that one... but it was fitting. She would kill them both.

But she wouldn't kill the journalist. She'd leave her to the experts. There were men on her payroll that knew how to make the suffering last for days on end. They'd humiliate her and abuse her first, of course, while offering hope that that was as far as it would go.

Only then would they start truly torturing her.

First, of course, she needed to capture them alive. That might prove challenging.

Surveillance video showed them exiting the tunnel two hours earlier, just after dawn, their initial party reduced to three members. It was a good thing she escaped when she had; Max's inability to protect his people bordered on incompetence... and with her hands tied, she would have been dead meat.

There was no way out of the test area, which meant that they would be trapped inside with the dinosaurs and prehistoric reptiles and God knew what else.

She sighed and ordered her bodyguards out of the office. At least there was a silver lining: the fact that Max had allowed a journalist to enter one of the most secret places in Russia was more than enough grounds for her to take them into custody. What happened afterwards was her own business; all she really had to do was to justify the initial capture. If that was approved—and there was no way this one wouldn't be—then the methods she used to extract information afterwards were no one's business but her own. Detainees, unfortunately sometimes died while incarcerated. It was a fact of life. Sad.

Selene opened the safe in her wall and pulled out two items. The first was a MAC 50 semiautomatic pistol which she placed in a specially-designed holster under her arm which would, when she wore a jacket, hide the gun's bulk from anyone not specifically looking for it. It was one of the few times in her new career where her silicone enhancements actually made her life easier.

The second item was a hard disk, a copy of a drive that Park Sun-Lee had in his possession. She'd had to order a team to crack the North Korean's own safety deposit box late one night to make this copy.

When she found out what it was, she'd been shocked but not surprised. It was exactly the kind of thing she expected from Park and it explained a lot of his research which otherwise seemed just a little too theoretical for the results that the government expected of him.

"Well, Mr. Pairetti," she said, addressing the hard drive. "We'll soon found out what you're made of... and whether Park's theories are actually practicable." She put the drive in a backpack and shouldered it. "This should be fun."

***

She'd been working in her office in YekLab in Yekaterinburg and now it was time to return to the other facility. The good thing is that she had a driver this time around. The better thing was that the hundred kilometers passed in utter silence. Her men were well attuned to her needs, and they were also aware that opening their mouth at an inopportune time would lead to unpleasantness. Being surrounded by competent people was a balm for her rage, but not enough to keep it from boiling under the surface.

It had always been that way. Her father had been the ambassador to France when she was growing up. It was a natural position for him, since he was a Frenchman who'd defected to the Soviet Union after being grievously injured in the Paris Student Riots in 1968.

Selene herself had been born twenty years later, and had been brought up in one of the most beautiful cities on the planet.

When her father had been relieved of his position as ambassador in the early 2000s, she was a teenager. The family attempted to stay in France, but the authorities had smiled and explained that once you were a defector, you were always a defector, and they'd been summarily deported back to Russia. That last day in Paris was also the last day she remembered not being angry.

Moscow was not, could never be, Paris, and the life they'd taken away from her poisoned every moment of Selene's waking hours, and her dreams after that. She had once read a line from Edgar Allan Poe— every teen in Russia read Poe, the man often captured the national temperament perfectly—that read: *Either the memory of past bliss is the anguish of today; or the agonies which are have their origins in ecstasies which might have been.* Both halves of that phrase tortured her.

Even when she became a well-known model, the anger still burned. She never enjoyed the fruits of her labor, the would-be lovers who bought her the finest gifts. The anger ruined every possible moment of enjoyment. The only true release she had was orgasm... but lovers who saw her as arm candy were never very concerned with her pleasure.

The rage boiled over on the day she was denied entry to France for the crime of being her father's daughter.

That was when *they* spotted her.

A college professor noticed her anger and intelligence and spoke to her about a possible outlet. A beautiful woman who spoke French perfectly and English with a French accent, combined with a mind that shone when she let it made her perfect material for... certain Russian agencies with international interests.

She became a spy, a honey-trap. In fact, the very best of her agency's femme fatales. At first, her assignments were simple: get so-and-so to give her information; make sure another man was at a certain place at a certain time, gain access to a building and get compromising pictures of a politician. Routine stuff that women much less talented could have managed just as well.

But those higher up had bigger plans, and one day the instructions changed. She'd been told to get acquainted—a euphemism which no longer needed clarification—with an apparently innocuous Russian émigré in London. Once she'd succeeded, the order came down the line: *inject him with this.*

The pinprick of the injection had woken the man and the poison had killed him painfully, while Selene watched every twisted moment of it. Her target, an indifferent lover, if that, writhed and contorted on the floor while she smiled and told him what she thought of his fumbling attempts at being a man.

Then she put him back on the bed, wiped the froth from his mouth and let herself out. A few hours and several train rides later, she walked off the ferry that linked Holyhead with Dublin and boarded a plane to Istanbul. Once in Turkey, a private plane flew her back to Russia.

She found out who she'd murdered only when the man, a prominent informant against the Russian Premier, made front page news all over the world.

It was the proudest moment of her life.

From then on, her career skyrocketed, and, being a little too hot to send back out into the field, she was given greater and greater oversight of domestic clandestine projects, and a small team to help her carry it out.

Anyone who failed to meet her expectations failed to survive the encounter. Many people who were simply inconvenient did likewise.

Killing people quelled the rage, just a little, just for a while.

Nevertheless, Selene never killed arbitrarily, but never risked information getting loose, which meant that she didn't have to kill arbitrarily. She just had to be thorough, and the chance to snuff out inconsequential people followed. Normally, her job gave her every satisfaction.

But not today. Today was shaping up to be the mother of all bad days.

They arrived at the complex and she had to wait while one of her men raised the barrier.

"Get someone to man the guard posts," she said.

"What should I tell them happened to the night shift?" her driver asked. It was the kind of question she liked. The man didn't want to know what had really happened to the men on duty. He just wanted information on how to deal with the question he was inevitably going to get.

"They were killed by a rogue Spetsnaz unit who also entered the compound and released the specimens within. Also, please bring the Tigr parked over there inside. I want to keep it as proof of their guilt. Also, I believe you will find one of your colleagues at the other guard post. Make sure the body is properly disposed of."

"Of course."

She smiled, satisfied. The dead man would never be seen or heard of again. The body would be gone forever, and the man's record deleted.

They drove into the parking lot and she gestured for one of the three men to accompany her inside while the other two dealt with her instructions. No one from the government or the military would come snooping around. Not even the FSB or the SVR would interfere. This complex, and the research that went on inside needed to be completely deniable, so any organization the public or the western world knew about was removed from the loop as a matter of course. Even some of the finances had to come from selling legitimate beauty-care products in order to keep the project's footprint as invisible as possible.

Now it appeared that the operation's cover had been blown sky-high by the very man who'd set it up.

The rage burned brighter for a second, but she calmed herself by thinking of how that bastard of a soldier would scream when she cut his balls off with a hot knife. Maybe she'd start with that. He would know from the outset that, even if he survived, he would never again be a man.

Or maybe crush them in a vice. That could work as well, even if it was a bit crude.

But to capture a Spetsnaz unit, even a decimated one, you needed an unfair advantage. That would require a bit of work, some of which was still in the experimental stage.

"Is the team here?" she asked the man.

"Yes. They arrived thirty minutes ago."

"Good. Let's get down there."

She walked the same corridors the soldiers had marched her down the previous evening but, instead of entering the containment area, this time she made a sharp turn to a stairwell that led down.

The vast sub-basement seemed deserted, but they followed a dim hall to a workroom where two men and a woman waited, dressed in white lab coats.

"All right. We have five Deinonychus specimens left because the traitor Sun-Lee had a fuse blow on him and couldn't get the door open. I need you to sedate them and hook them up to the transfer machine."

"The doors lock automatically when there's a system error," one of the men said.

"Then get them unlocked and do it. The next person who brings me a problem and not a solution will be shot in the head by my colleague here. That goes double for anyone who tells me I can't have you shot or complains about anything. Understood?" The man with her pulled a gun out from somewhere within his suit. "Good. Then this will make the next part go much smoother. Which of you worked with Park on the transfer protocols?"

One of the men raised his hand. "I did. And Anna." He hesitated, as if about to say more, but one glance at Selene's companion changed his mind.

Selene laughed. "You guys learn quickly. We normally have to make examples of someone before the rest realize I mean what I say. And yes, I know it's a highly experimental procedure that's never been tried before, but we're going to do it anyway and we're going to make it work."

"Actually, it has been tried. We transferred a diplodocus mind to a nothosaur. Unfortunately, the diplodocus drowned. We still have the nothosaur somewhere, but it isn't doing well. The stupid thing insists on trying to eat plants. So you can even say it's been successfully done."

"Good. Have you ever tried it with human minds?"

In his face, she saw the huge objections and the struggle to keep them contained. The woman also looked like she was about to jump in and earn a bullet to the temple. But they managed to stay quiet. "Not yet."

"Good. Then you'll be doing something new today. Exciting, huh?" She turned to the third man. "Now why should I keep you around?"

The other man said nothing.

"Can you open the doors?" Selene asked.

"I think so."

"Good. And once you do that, I need you to sedate the dinosaurs so your actually useful friends can work on them. I don't want to send them in there unless you get killed."

The guy swallowed and set about the task. Ten minutes later, after much sweating and cursing, a set of doors on the other side of the foot-thick plexiglass wall opened to reveal five dinosaurs that looked like a ridiculous mix between an ostrich and a tyrannosaur. She knew they were Deinonychus, and that they were one of the nastiest creatures ever to roam the cretaceous, but she still giggled every time she saw one. Of course, being behind a thick partition made it easier to laugh.

"Interesting technique," Selene mused. "I would have thought it would be smarter to sedate them one at a time to avoid the rest tearing you to pieces… but I guess you're the expert. Now do it before they start damaging one another."

He swallowed but didn't protest, and grabbed five separate dart guns. It seemed like a silly way to tranquilize dinosaurs, but she supposed these guys actually did know what they were about.

The man opened a steel door in the partition. Through the glass, Selene could see that the steel door opened onto a steel box, kind of like an airlock. The second door opened just a fraction and the muzzle of one of the dart guns poked through.

It was impossible to miss at that range, and the dinosaurs didn't even realize what was happening to them as the researcher got them plugged one at a time without being seen or being in any real danger. He returned, pale, and lay the spent dispensers on the table.

Selene gave him a smile. "I'm impressed. And don't worry. I don't shoot people for no reason. If this works, you will all be well rewarded."

They didn't look like they believed her, but she didn't care. For once she was telling the truth. These scientists already knew what was happening here, and news of Park's defection would be common knowledge in a few hours. There was no advantage to killing them and many advantages to keeping them alive. After all, they were now Russia's foremost experts in the field of creating dinosaurs from the genetic material of a nothosaur. Not a skillset that could be easily replaced, and not one whose loss she was eager to explain to her superiors.

"All right. I have the mind I want to transfer right here. How do we hook them up?"

"That's the device right there," the woman said, indicating a small wheeled table full of white and grey electronic equipment. "We have to do them one at a time because the output wires need to plug in here."

"I imagined the machine would be bigger. How long will this take?"

"It's normally nearly instantaneous, but a human brain is something like…" she turned to the man who'd tranquilized the dinosaurs. "What? Three petabytes?"

"A little less than that, but yeah, thereabouts."

She thought for a moment. "Each one will take fifteen minutes."

That wasn't too bad. But they didn't look comfortable. "What aren't you telling me?" she said.

"I…"

"I won't shoot you for answering questions."

"All right," the woman replied. "I'm not sure if we can put that much into a brain the size of a dinosaur's."

She shrugged. "Then put in as much as you can. I just need them to be able to follow basic instructions."

They exchanged glances. "Yes, ma'am."

"I'll be back in one hour and fifteen minutes. I expect you to be done by then."

***

Five deinonychus dinosaurs staggered to and fro like drunken sailors.

"Was the transfer successful?" Selene asked the scientists.

The woman stepped forward. "We… we think so."

"Why aren't you certain?"

"Because it's never been done before. We won't know for sure until we see how they react. We don't even know if what we did is viable. Sun-Lee wanted to run some tests in Central America, transferring human minds into animal hosts… but that program was scrapped."

Selene knew what the woman was talking about. The main thrust of the program had been something very different, including getting hold of samples of another researcher's labors… and Park had never mentioned his intention of testing the mind transfer. He'd gone on and on about wanting to capture some colossal monster that the other researcher had created combining DNA in ways that Russia was still years away from being able to attempt... and that no one else in the world even dreamed possible.

"Understood. How long until I can speak to them?"

"If it worked, a few more minutes for the first one."

After a while, the dinosaurs began to stand more firmly. One of them looked around and, realizing what kind of creatures it was locked in with, attempted to run. But the doorknob defeated its claws.

"Looks like at least one of them is alert. I'm going in."

"You can talk to them from here..."

"I'm going in. You've done the best I could ask. Go home."

"Really?"

"Of course. Come in again tomorrow, and we'll see about reorganizing YekLab now that Sun-Lee is out. Your help today will not be forgotten."

They filed out, looking behind them with the expression of death row prisoners who couldn't quite believe that they had been reprieved. Good. Working with people smart enough to be afraid of her was always easier.

She looked at the man who'd accompanied her and grinned. "I'm going in alone. If this didn't work, at least my death will be legendary."

The man said nothing. He knew better than to argue.

Selene opened the outer door of the airlock-like entrance, and then the inner one. These doors were quite thick, but they had no sophisticated locks. After all, they weren't meant to stop humans but beasts who couldn't work a doorknob.

Inside, the smell of the animals was nearly overpowering. Pools of excrement, wet like bird droppings, decorated the concrete floor. All five heads turned to track her as she entered, but none of them approached.

"Hello," she said in English.

Her audience flinched.

"Can you hear me?"

The dinosaurs—or at least whatever part of the human mind that the scientists had been able to transfer into the dinosaurs—tried to answer, and the results were pathetic. A series of squawks and hisses came back to her.

"Oh. Right. You don't have vocal cords. Just nod your heads if you can understand me."

The creatures, one by one, nodded.

"Good. Do you feel all right?"

She waited for them to nod.

"All right then. I'm going to explain what's happening here, and what I expect from you."

She looked around the room. Five monsters watched her in rapt attention.

"Good. My name is Selene, and you, I've been told, are called Luca Pairetti. Is that right?"

They all nodded. Then they all seemed to look around in confusion as if wondering why all the rest were nodding.

"Yes. You're all Luca Pairetti." She shrugged. "It was the only mind I had. Now listen up. You've been transferred to your current bodies—they're quite ugly dinosaur bodies, in fact—for two reasons. The first is to complete a mission. The second is to pay us back for your transgression. If you succeed, we both win. I will have captured a man and a woman that I need to control, and you will be transferred to healthy bodies. Human bodies."

She didn't know what Pairetti had done to earn his transformation into an involuntary research subject. That had been run by an entirely different organization, with closer ties to the *Mafiya* than to the government. All she knew was that, one day, Park had appeared with a hard drive and a smile.

"Can you see well, with those eyes? You," she pointed at one of the dinosaurs. "How many fingers am I holding up? Nod once for each finger you see."

She held up three fingers. The creature nodded three times.

"Good enough, I guess. Now, do you agree with the terms? If not, I'll just leave you here until you have no choice but to start eating each other." She gave them her best smile.

The creatures nodded.

"Good. Come on. Let's see if you can squeeze out through the door and save me the hassle of having to open the main entrance. I'll brief you on the way."

***

It took nearly thirty minutes to herd the dinosaurs around the simulated biosphere and into the tunnel.

The way the creatures moved didn't inspire confidence: they were clumsy and slow. Considering the fearsome reputation that preceded Deinonychus, she hoped the walk would help her monsters learn to control their bodies.

She was also happy that she'd brought three of her men along as backup. Armed with AK-15s, they should be able to deal with a lot of what the dinosaurs couldn't. The creatures were mainly there to scare off the smaller stuff and make the big stuff think twice so she could concentrate on the main objective, which was to bring back Max and Marianne. Max and Marianne. Corny names that sounded alike. It was fitting that they should die together, echoing each other's screams as they did.

Also, if all else failed, the dinosaurs should be able to absorb a lot of ammunition before dropping dead.

Sounded like something that should be in a bad American song. *Little ditty 'bout Max and Marianne…*

The tunnel stretched out ahead when her phone rang. It was the guy she'd left at the facility. She had him listed on her contacts as Number 3.

"Boss?"

"Yes, what's up?"

"Helicopters just landed in the test site."

That meant they were inside the valley with all the dinosaurs.

"What? Military?"

Had the military sent in its own strike force? She wouldn't put it past the GRU to interfere, of course. Internecine warfare among Russian security agencies was a long-standing and honored tradition.

But Orlov was supposed to be one of the good guys which, in her profession meant that he stayed bribed once you bought him. An open assault, visible from space, didn't seem like something he'd do.

"Not military. But not exactly civilian, either. They come up as helicopters with defensive ability owned by Tarsos."

Tarsos. Military contractors who worked for… well, they worked for anyone with hard currency and a problem that could be solved by the judicious application of ammunition. They were bottom-feeders, but generally effective as such organizations went.

"So who hired them?"

"Sending you a picture. You're not going to believe this."

The image downloaded quickly and she chuckled. Luck was not something she ever counted on but, when it happened to be on your side, one had to thank the universe.

Park Sun-Lee didn't know he was a bird, much less that he was one of two.

But Selene did, and she was coming with a stone.

***

Park addressed the grouped journalists. "I'm sure you're all wondering why I brought you here."

Heads nodded.

"I wanted to show you something, something so awful that it could bring down the Russian government itself. Failing that, I'm convinced that at least a few heads high up the food chain will roll."

"And how do you know about all of this?" one of the reporters asked, as if on cue.

"Because I'm going to reveal a project that I was once a part of."

"So you got fired and are out for revenge?"

"Quite the contrary. My departure will be a huge blow to this project, as I am the director and also the lead scientist. But I can't be a part of this any longer. My conscience just won't allow it."

"Why?"

"Look around. Do you see the mountains? This is an old impact crater, a few tens of thousands of years old. But the top of the crater has been molded to create a sheer cliff. It's impossible to climb without ropes and equipment. The only way in or out is through a tunnel in the cliffside, over there." He waved in the general direction of the YekLab complex. "Or, of course, by air."

"So, it's a fortress. What is it supposed to keep out? And what's so valuable that you need something this size to store it?"

"Well, back in the Soviet era, this spot was a launch site for missiles. You could drive them in here and fire them directly from the mouth of the tunnel, out of sight from observers. But now... now, no one is trying to keep people out. No. They're using this place to keep people in."

"You mean, like a prison?"

"No. I mean like farmers. This area has been split into farms. Each was given to a person who had no other way of contributing to society. Many were refugees, or political malcontents unsuited to the old Soviet way of life. They probably suspected they were being used as camouflage for the missile site, but they didn't care. There weren't many options for people like that back then."

"But that all ended thirty years ago."

"Yes, but the missiles only went away a few years ago... and after that, YekLab built a facility near here. Yes, the same YekLab you almost got eaten at. This place is much bigger and it holds many, many more lines of research."

"And the farmers?" the Brazilian, Tatiana asked. She obviously didn't want to lose sight of the humanitarian angle.

He gave her a smile. "Thanks for keeping me on track. There's so much to tell, you see. Yes, the farmers were allowed to stay. The powers that be considered their presence here valuable."

"As camouflage?"

"Oh, no. There's no more need for camouflage. No. They're being kept here for an entirely different purpose. They're test subjects."

"Wait. I heard there was a biological weapons factory here once. They're testing them on humans? On your own people?"

"Oh, they're testing biological weapons on humans, all right. But you're thinking of the wrong kind. The weapons they test here aren't germs or bacteria. They're much, much bigger than that. In fact, you already saw one on the day of the conference."

Stunned silence greeted him as the reporters processed what he'd just said.

"I brought you here today because there's a full-scale test in progress. Right now."

One of the reporters raised her hand. "Do you mean that they've released a monster into this place to see if it... if it kills someone?"

"No. I mean that they released dozens of dinosaurs into this place, with the objective of seeing how quickly they kill everyone."

"Oh God. How many people live in this zone?"

"About fifty."

"That's monstrous."

"Yes. Now you understand why my conscience wouldn't let me stay at work for these people, even though I have fifteen years of research tied up here."

Tatiana, since her one question, had remained silent. Now she spoke again. "But why us? We're just fashion magazine reporters for the most part. Why didn't you call in the international press, the heavy hitters? And people experienced in battlefield conditions?"

Park smiled. He could get to like this one. She knew all the tricks and had asked exactly what he wanted her to. "That's an excellent question," he replied. "The answer is that if I'd called on the international press, certain people in Moscow would have become extremely nervous, and I would have had to answer a lot of questions." He was proud of that answer. Every single word of it was true. "But don't worry about your inexperience on the battlefield. You won't be in any danger. My men are well-equipped to face anything that we might encounter. They're armed with both high-powered automatic rifles and with sonic weaponry. The creatures we're here to see are very sensitive to sound blasts because they have highly developed hearing. We left those characteristics in them so that we could control them during development. The plan is to remove them once they're fully deployed."

"Fully deployed? What are people going to use these things for?"

"As terror weapons. With suitable modifications, they can be given higher intelligence for missions where the terrain makes sending humans difficult, or for situations in which troop risk might be too great."

"You mean suicide missions?"

"Precisely." And now came the important part. He faced the journalists squarely and enunciated clearly. English was one of his six languages, and he knew that most of the reporters weren't native speakers. Clarity would be paramount. "Fortunately, I am the only one who knows how to make the next round of modifications... and I won't be making them for the Russians."

"And what will stop them from coming after you?"

"Nothing at all. But by the time they realize that I've left, I will be somewhere they can't reach me. We won't be here more than an hour. Now, would you like to see the true horror of what's happening here?"

"No," said one of the reporters.

But when he set off towards the village, they followed him.

CHAPTER 6

Tatiana followed Sun-Lee down a rocky path that led from the cracked, ancient concrete lot where the helicopters had set down towards a cluster of tall trees beyond which the roof of a house could be seen.

Up ahead, four men with guns and one with an unusual megaphone-like contraption—evidently the sound weapon—walked warily down the path. They were uniformly well-muscled and moved like big cats. Though Tatiana was the first to appreciate good-looking men, something about these left her cold. Brazilian guys were just as well-muscled and handsome, but they were warm and human as well. The men with Park looked like they'd kill you without even blinking. She wasn't the kind to chase violent thugs.

But in certain situations, it was extremely comforting to have them along.

Something rustled in the trees and six dinosaurs emerged. Tatiana's heart began to thump in her chest, and these weren't even big ones. To her eye, they looked to be about a quarter of the size of the creatures that had overrun YekLab, about waist-high on a person. They took one look at the group of humans advancing on them and disappeared back into the trees.

For a second, as the morning sun beat down and she watched the dinosaurs scuttle away, there was nothing in her line of sight to indicate that she didn't live a hundred million years in the past. Grass. Rock. Trees. Dinosaurs. Only when a bird, frightened by the movement in the trees, burst from the upper branches, did the spell break. She wasn't an expert on prehistoric creatures, but she knew birds didn't exist when the thunder lizards walked the earth.

As they advanced, the single building that had been visible from the landing site turned out to be a group of wooden houses which appeared to have been bombed. The front of the houses were torn out, windows gone, doors bashed in.

A group of minute scavengers clustered around something, growling at one another with tiny voices. Like the dinosaurs, they scattered at the humans' approach. Obviously, theirs was a world where hiding from anything larger than you was a key survival trait.

Tatiana turned away as the form on the ground was revealed. She'd seen plenty of bodies when she was just starting out. In her first job, the editor of *Folha* had assigned her to the police beat, a typical tactic to see if she had what it took to be a reporter. The effect hadn't been to scare her away, but it had taught her that bodies were not as interesting as their surroundings, which often gave a better clue as to why there was a body on the ground in the first place.

So she looked around. If the trees and the dinosaurs belonged in the past, so did the village, albeit a more recent past. The path in front of the houses, the de facto main street of the village, consisted of hard-packed dirt and there was no sign of motorized vehicles that might have justified anything else. None of the typical accoutrements associated with farms were present. No pickups, no tractors, not even an old clapped-out banger in a yard.

In addition, there were no electric wires or telephone poles in evidence. These people lived in the past. No. These people had been intentionally left in the past in order to ensure that they were completely helpless when the time to use them as human guinea pigs came.

It made sense. There was no need to give lab rats computers before you injected them.

Park Sun-Lee waited until his men gave him the all-clear before standing in front of the nearest house, another clapboard construction, painted pale yellow.

"As you can see, the dinosaurs have been here already. These houses are typical Russian rural homes, and sturdier than much of what you'll find in the countries around us. Some places might build with stone, but they don't even use wooden doors. Can you imagine how much protection a curtain would be against some of the creatures they've released into this valley?

"In case anyone is skeptical about what happened here, I'd like to point out a couple of pieces of evidence. First, look down that hill. Do you see those lumps in the distance beside the trees? Those are diplodocus. They really did release all kinds of dinosaurs here. Of course, diplodocus was a plant eater, but that makes little difference, because they're only here to support the predators that feed on them. The lab bred them expressly for that purpose."

Tatiana looked in the direction Sun-Lee pointed. She saw something that might have been a little hill... until it moved. The distance made it hard to judge size, but if those trees were the same height as the ones nearby, she did not want to tangle with anything that ate diplodocus. Sun-Lee appeared confident in his men, but she suspected that anything large enough to eat that wouldn't even notice their little weapons and sonic blaster or whatever it was. But maybe the thugs could buy the rest of them enough time to run back to the choppers while the dinosaurs ate the soldiers.

"The second piece of evidence is a little more concrete. See these farmhouses? They were built specifically for the people here. They have no amenities whatsoever. No electricity, no running water. They're heated by burning wood that the farmers themselves cut from the trees. There are more than enough natural resources to keep them alive. Every once in a while, the government releases deer into the forests, too, and the farmers hunt that. They think their life is hard, but bountiful and peaceful.

"One thing they would never, ever have had is a telephone connection, because giving your missile-launch decoy population the capacity to call NATO and tell them when a missile was being prepped is the very definition of stupid. Their only communication with the outside world happened once a month, when a person from the government would drive down here and ask them what they needed, take some of their surplus in trade so that no one suspected what was really going on."

He pointed at the roof. "But, as you can see, each house has clusters of security cameras on the roof. Those round pods over there. I'll ask one of my men to retrieve one so you can have a closer look. Those, as you can imagine, aren't for use by the inhabitants, but are connected wirelessly to YekLab's systems."

"How? I don't see any wireless networks here," a German woman who Tatiana hadn't met before coming there asked, glancing at her phone.

"There's a cell tower hidden in the woods over there on a military frequency. You won't get anything unless you have a specially designed phone."

Tatiana's peers walked around listlessly, the journalists not truly able to cope with the magnitude of the atrocity. These were fashion reporters and perfume critics. Their outrage was reserved for people who disagreed with whatever socially-conscious agendas on social media or insisted on combining black pants with brown shoes. Faced with any situation more serious than someone who failed to give adequate lip service to the current social or political hot-button topic, they fell apart.

And, she realized, she was doing exactly the same thing. That was unacceptable. She was from Brazil. She was tougher than these soft people full of first world problems.

"Can we take pictures?" she asked.

"Of course," Sun-Lee replied. "Not much use in showing you this if you can't share it with your readers."

After getting a few shots of the damaged buildings, Tatiana strode determinedly over to the one dead body she could see—well-gnawed by the scavengers—and took a few pictures of it. She knew *Caipi* would never run anything that graphic, but she needed to document this, perhaps for a publication that dared to show the unvarnished truth.

She turned back to Sun-Lee. "What else is there? All we've seen is one dead person who could have had an accident, and a couple of broken houses. Other than that, we have to take your word for everything."

"You've also seen some dinosaurs."

"Herbivores and little things that run as soon as we come close. Nothing that comes close to confirming your story."

Their host smiled as the other reporters watched, slack-jawed. "Then we'll have to get a little closer, won't we?"

Tatiana returned his smile. "If you want us to be able to report truth, yes."

He barked something in Russian and the men strode forward, eyes scanning the plain. Ahead, mere dots in the distance, another cluster of buildings came into view. At that distance, it was impossible to make out whether any larger dinosaurs were close to the houses, but they'd soon find out.

Tatiana wasn't afraid. All she could really think of was to wonder if Marianne, had she been present, would have acted the way she had. Then she caught herself. Trying to live up to the approval of an impossibly idealized version of another reporter was a good way to go nuts. She should be proud of herself when she got back, if she got her story.

Besides, this place was starting to get on her nerves. How could a meadow on a summer morning feel creepy? She didn't know, but this one certainly managed.

Besides, she felt an itch between her shoulder blades, as if someone was watching them.

***

Marianne watched from the trees, mouth agape. Was that Tatiana? What the hell was she doing here? She wanted to jump out of concealment and scream that she should get the hell out of there, but she was pretty sure the soldiers with her would shoot her if she tried. They were on her side... but only as long as their side and hers happened to be aligned.

Exposing their position was not something they would appreciate.

Max turned her way. "That's your reporter friend, isn't it?"

"Yes."

"Why is she with Park Sun-Lee?"

"How should I know? Reporters don't share their scoops with each other."

"Well, those are the men I was afraid of. It's extremely clear they're here to hunt us down. Sun-Lee works with Selene Grosjean, the woman who was going to shoot you. No one is really sure who works for who, so they're probably working for different agencies within the government, and are only temporarily collaborating. He's bad news, too. North Korean. He's the one who cooked up all the dinosaurs we've seen, or at least he must have been a part of it. He's the head of YekLab."

She studied the scene below. Tatiana didn't look like she was under any duress. She appeared perfectly at ease, studying the broken buildings and asking questions. Vintage Tatiana even if this wasn't the kind of place one would normally have expected to find her: not one runway model or beautiful male hanger-on in sight. For a second, Marianne envied her colleague for getting information that was forbidden to Marianne herself.

"I suppose going down there to ask for a ride on the helicopters is out of the question?"

"Completely. But we may be able to borrow one, if they left the pilots behind."

Marianne smiled. "Well, I'm already a fugitive from the KGB, so I guess adding aerial piracy to my list of crimes won't hurt too much."

"The KGB no longer exists," Max replied, suddenly icy. "We don't talk about them anymore."

"Look, I'm sorry."

"No matter. Let's see about the helicopters. I want to get back to base and tear someone's head off."

"Can you drop me off at the hotel?"

As soon as she said it, Marianne felt a wave of anguish. The only thing waiting for her at the hotel were some clothes she could do perfectly well without and a room next to hers that would remain empty because its occupant lay dead in a dinosaur pen ten thousand miles from home, all because Marianne couldn't leave a dangerous story well enough alone.

"You'll be safer at the base," Max replied.

She said nothing. She couldn't. But Max didn't seem to be expecting a reply, so she followed, choking down her anguish, as he cut across the woods. They soon reached the other side of the small clump of trees and the helicopters came into view.

Standing directly between the troops and the aircraft was a dinosaur that could very easily have been the same one that had nearly eaten her in YekLab.

"Well, now we know what we're going to waste our last AK bullets on," Max said. "Too bad about the noise, but it can't be helped. With any luck we'll be in the air before Sun-Lee catches up to us."

He put his spear on the ground, put the rifle on his shoulder and fired a burst into the dinosaur and waited for it to collapse as the empty rifle clicked. He discarded it, and then pulled his handgun out of its holster, picked up the spear and strode out into the open towards the fallen monster.

Only then did they see the other deinonychus.

It saw them at the same moment.

***

Happy Bunagu watched the video time and again. The email had come from the Electric Buddha, and therefore was absolutely trustworthy. Could someone really be thinking of putting these things on the market?

When his watch ended, he stood and walked towards the captain's rooms. The warlord had taken over the mission building, a single-story brick rectangle with a corrugated roof—the only house for fifty miles around that was wired for light. The jungle night in central Africa was pitch dark, but he could find his way with his eyes closed. The light from his cell phone was mainly to keep the animals out of his way.

The door, like the windows, had been bashed in when the captain had taken the village. The white priest and his treasonous acolytes had thought they would be safe inside, but the door had fallen almost immediately. He still remembered the resignation of the white man and the huge, terrified eyes of his black collaborators as the captain read the charges and sentenced them to death. The fact that Happy had pulled one of the triggers was the reason he was still pulling headquarters duty; the warlord liked to keep his friends close.

He knocked on the shattered remains of the door.

"What is it?"

"You have to see this, Captain."

"Happy? Is that you?"

"Yeah."

"Come in, then."

Happy entered. The long room was illuminated by candles—the generator had packed up and no one was willing to deliver the parts they needed to fix it into the lawless lands on the border between Nigeria and Cameroon. Especially not since the captain had established his fiefdom.

The working generator in the village proper was used for important things: keeping cell phones charged and powering the satellite dish which gave the rebels their internet access. The boss could get drunk and get laid by candlelight, but his men couldn't stay in contact with the outside world without communications. And if they didn't know what was going on, they wouldn't be able to hold their territory, inconsequential though it might be.

Cigarette smoke hung in the dim light. One of the captain's women was smoking, another lay fully nude on the bed, the remaining two must have had the evening off. Or maybe he'd loaned them out to his lieutenants. Happy was a trusted soldier, but he was too far down the food chain for that kind of reward to come his way.

Jacques, the only white man tolerated in the captain's presence—he was the captain's blood brother, whatever that meant—snored on a chair in his underwear, a bottle in one hand.

The captain slapped at a bug. "Well, what is it?" he said.

"Sorry. Look at this. It came from the Buddha." Happy handed over his phone.

Three minutes later, the captain handed it back. "You're a fool. This is fake."

"It came from the Buddha."

"But it's ridiculous. Those are dinosaurs."

"Yes. And they're for sale."

"Probably more than we can afford."

"Buddha's email says there is a special price for Africa. Look."

"Interesting. Ask him how much. One of those in the forest..." The captain smiled. "You did well to bring this to me."

"He says they aren't ready yet."

"Then I want to be first in line. Boko Haram will hate us. We'll show them how to really sow terror."

"Yes, boss."

Happy left without saying that he thought Boko Haram's outrage would be more focused on the fact that they were playing with God's creation than with envy that another insurgency would deploy dinosaurs first. Boko Haram would denounce them for being heathen infidels.

He would let the captain think of those things. Anyway, Boko Haram was far away, up in the north, and besides, Happy didn't think even those fanatics would want to tangle with a dinosaur.

***

The monster paused a second, as if unsure what to make of this group of people and their loud banging. Then, it shrugged and charged straight toward him.

Max, hand still vibrating from shooting the AK-47, clutched his spear and tried to slam it into the creature's belly. He didn't quite get the point planted in the center of his target and it slid across the dinosaur's skin, tearing feathers away, twisting the spear to one side, and wrenching his arms in the process.

Max dove out of the way as a fearsomely-clawed back leg sliced the air above his head. He kept rolling until he managed to regain his footing a reasonable distance from the creature.

"Vasily, look out. It's too strong. I don't think you'll be able to stab it."

"You've obviously never hunted boar in the forest. Try to bring it this way."

Max sprinted across the grass as fast as he could move. The initial rush had taken him in the opposite direction from his soldier, and he'd also dropped the spear. He debated whether to shoot the dinosaur or do what Vasily suggested. In the end, he decided to trust the other man and circled around.

The arc he chose wasn't wide enough. One of the dinosaur's forelegs, which served it as arms, shot out and clipped a foot as he passed. He tripped and flew through the air at full tilt.

Max got lucky. He rolled with the impact and popped back to his feet in a single instinctive motion. He was running in the right direction as soon as he got back. In fact, he might have gained a fraction of a second in the spill.

He made straight for Vasily. Twenty meters, ten. He felt the floor shaking with pursuit. He knew he was losing ground, but didn't dare turn around to look. If he turned, he was a dead man.

So he ran. The final ten meters should have taken him less than two seconds. Instead, time seemed to stretch out until he was certain that every instant would be his last.

He passed a hair's breadth from Vasily, as close as he dared.

Behind him, he heard a thump and an enormous outgassing of air. He got himself stopped and turned around.

The dinosaur reared up, and stepped towards Vasily, who backed away slowly.

Max looked for any sign of a wound, but failed to see anything. He was about to turn and keep running when he noticed a greenish-white stub protruding from among the creature's feathers.

The butt of Vasily's spear. It had gone almost all the way through the dinosaur. It was as good as dead.

It seemed to take a long time for that realization to reach the thing's tiny brain, however.

The monster was still moving towards Vasily, mouth open, when it stumbled once and collapsed to the ground.

Marianne reached Max a moment later. She hugged him and said. "I thought you were dead for sure. When you fell…"

Max didn't even hesitate. He kissed her full on the lips.

To his delight, she kissed him back.

"Typical," Vasily said in Russian. "I was the one who killed the thing and saved your ass, and you get the girl."

Marianne pulled away and cocked her head. "Hold that thought," she told Max. Then she walked over to Vasily and planted a kiss on his cheek, right next to the man's lips. Then she said, slowly and clearly: "thank you," before pulling away.

"Yeah, whatever," Vasily said. But he looked pleased.

Marianne turned back to Max. "I can't believe this is the kind of thing you do for a living. I mean you've already lost two men and it's like nothing. And you could have died, too. Both of you. How can you deal with the violence?" She looked from one to the other. "I nearly fainted when that thing came for us. Why aren't you afraid?"

"To be honest, the training takes over. Look at me now." He held up a hand so Marianne could see how badly it was shaking. "And no, this isn't what we do for a living. We mostly keep our barracks clean and our skills sharp so when this kind of thing happens, we can react the way we did. We're Spetsnaz. When we go into battle, we go with the express intention of killing many, many people. Often, we hit people who never even know we're there. We do not expect losses unless someone fucks up or intelligence is faulty. The whole point to special forces is to kill a lot of people and get out without anyone being able to respond effectively."

"That sounds unfair."

"War does not exist to be fair. It exists to be won." He held her gaze. "And I'd much rather face a dozen of those things than do the duty that is waiting for me if we survive this."

"What's that?" Marianne asked, no longer questioning, but small and vulnerable.

"I have to tell Ivan and Yuri's families that they're not coming back. And I can't even tell them what they died for. The government will never admit this happened at all, except maybe to admit that a rogue civilian laboratory acted in illegal ways and are being dealt with. And that is the way it should be." He walked to where Vasily was inspecting the dead creature. "How did you manage to plant the spear? It threw me off like a fly."

"You should spend more time in the gym," Vasily replied, flexing a bicep.

"Come on. I'd like to be of some use next time."

"All right. Look here." They walked a few paces past the place where the dinosaur had fallen. "You see this gouge in the dirt? That's where I planted the butt of the spear. Now this spear wasn't very long, so I had to crouch behind it to hold it in place, but the point is that, in trying to get at me, the monster impaled itself. I didn't have to hold the spear. The ground did it for me."

Max shook his head admiringly. "That was smart. Good work. Now let's go get those choppers."

***

Selene watched the Korean and his troops and wondered what the hell they were doing. Was he giving a fucking guided tour? Had he gone completely insane?

She didn't know, and hoped never to find out. Her main priority— even more than locating and gutting Max—was to turn Sun-Lee into a corpse and to eliminate the witnesses to his malfeasance. Moscow didn't really need to know about any of this, and they could be told that the accident at YekLab—which had indeed been reported in the international press—was just that, an unfortunate loss of containment, and that Sun-Lee had died in the effort to put things right. It wasn't even a lie.

But if Sun-Lee got out... or, even worse, if one of the foreigners did, the project would be completely compromised, and every aspect of operational security would be torn apart until Moscow was satisfied.

That included her, and when her superiors tore apart a failed operative, they didn't mess around... and the tearing apart was not metaphoric. She would never be seen again, and the only thing anyone would hear from her would be the screams of pain and the supplications that they let her die.

She was tough. She was angry. But she was also a realist. No one held out under the kind of torture she would be subjected to. If it came to that, she would put a bullet in her head when they came to arrest her. Of course, before that, she'd try to run. But the kind of people she'd be running from tended to get their man in the end.

There would be time to consider such matters later, however. Now, she needed to do everything in her power to contain the situation. Her assets numbered five dinosaurs and three men with guns. The dinosaurs wouldn't be much use while Sun-Lee's soldiers were loaded for elephants and also had the sonic weapon. Selene had seen what those amplified blasts could do to the creatures developed by the lab. She would need to neutralize that one before bringing her dinosaurs into play.

She began to give her men their instructions.

***

Park led them towards the larger village on the banks of the river that crossed the enclosure. He checked his watch repeatedly. Time was of the essence. Selene would have arrived at the facility in the morning to find the security disabled and the guards dead. She'd probably send a team out to discover where the dinosaurs had gone. That team would have found the hole in the wall and assumed that the dinosaurs would have escaped that way.

If everything went to schedule, Selene would be finding out about what he did just about now.

Then, she'd need some time to put two and two together and come find him. He estimated that she couldn't reach the valley for another three hours—not unless she was willing to sacrifice manpower and use the facility personnel. That would be a mistake, because Sun-Lee's people were much, much better than those glorified street cops.

So he still had at least three hours by his calculations. To be on the safe side, he wanted to be out of here in one. Two on the outside. One chopper would take the reporters back to Yekaterinburg. The other would take him and his men to Kazakhstan. From there, he'd make his way to Gabon. There was a man he wanted to speak to, and the trail started in Libreville.

So he didn't want to get too far from the aircraft. Already, he needed to budget at least twenty-five minutes to get back. That would only increase the further they walked.

"Look!" one of the reporters yelled.

In the middle of a rough square formed by the houses, a villager attempted to enter one of the buildings, chased by a trio of small dinosaurs. "Those are velociraptors," he told the journalists.

"They look a bit small for that," the German woman said.

"The ones in the film were much bigger than real ones. These are much closer to reality," Park replied.

The man never made it. One of his pursuers hamstrung him, and the rest were on him in an instant.

"Can't we do anything?" Tatiana, the Brazilian, asked.

"We're too far away. The rifles would kill the man, and the sonic blaster works best at close range. Besides," he gestured at the journalists around her, "shouldn't you be filming instead of talking?"

"Filming? No! We need to help that man. They're killing him."

"That's what you wanted to see, isn't it? The truth about what was done here? Well, there you go. That's it. And you're missing it."

Tatiana took half a step towards the carnage, but one of the raptors happened to look that way and she stopped. Park smiled. She might have had a sudden case of conscience, but she wasn't stupid.

"Viktor," he said to the man with the sonic blaster. "Go clear the square, please."

The man nodded and stepped forward, apparently unafraid of facing the herd alone. He'd been part of that particular weapon's test phase and he knew precisely how effective it was. The other men fanned out behind, to cover his back, the only way a dinosaur could reach him.

The group followed the gunmen down the hill until Park gave everyone but Viktor the signal to stop.

He was maybe fifty yards from the nearest house when three loud reports echoed in the still air.

Gunshots. From the direction of the choppers. There was something going on back there.

"Come on!" he shouted. "We need to get back to the helicopters."

"But what about the village?" Tatiana asked.

"You should have enough to go on, now." He turned and shouted down the hillside. "Victor! Get back up here. We're leaving."

The man with the sonic blaster began to run in their direction.

He never made it. A shot rang out—much closer than the previous burst, somewhere in the vicinity of the village—and the man fell to the ground, blaster useless under him.

Sun-Lee's remaining men turned to face the village again and dropped to the ground. Sun-Lee spotted muzzle flashes—three separate sources of fire—from the village, pinning his men to the ground.

Then, from the side, five deinonychus-unmistakable with their wing-sized arms—ran in from a small clump of trees on his men's left flank.

He stared. He'd spent the past eighteen months building, discarding and rebuilding different dinosaurs. He knew each and every one of them by sight. Those five deinonychus were easily identified by the coloring on their wings—dark bands unique to that particular batch.

Those five had been locked in a jammed containment cage. He hadn't been able to release them into the feeding habitat and, as a consequence, they should never have been able to reach the tunnel and arrive here.

He swallowed. Someone had let them out and brought them here.

Worse, deinonychus, like all the other dinosaurs, shouldn't have been able to participate in a coordinated strike except on a limited basis. Which meant that, in most cases, their sudden appearance at the worst possible moment would have been a coincidence.

Unfortunately, there was another possible explanation. It would mean that Selene had been spying on him all that time, but that was something he'd expected. Worse, though, it would mean that Selene had found out about what he was doing much earlier than he expected. Worst of all, it would mean that Selene was here.

When the first dinosaur reached one of his men and, instead of trying to charge straight towards the armed man, zigzagged across the grass and then stood on the arm holding the gun, his fears were confirmed and an icy feeling ran up his spine.

Those dinosaurs were thinking strategically, and they knew what guns were. They should never, ever have been able to do that. At best, they should have been startled by the noise. They were operating way beyond their natural capacity.

Sun-Lee didn't even bother to tell the journalists to save themselves. He ran like the devil himself was after him.

In a way, it was true. For evil, the devil had little on Selene.

CHAPTER 7

Park Sun-Lee huddled beside a tree and ignored the questions the remaining journalists were screaming at him—he only vaguely registered that there were only one or two of them remaining. The rest had run off in panic, but he wasn't about to look for them; he had more pressing matters on his mind. His two remaining men were giving quite a good account of themselves.

One of them had dived into a small dip in the grassy terrain that allowed him enough protection to fire on the men in the village and to keep them pinned. The second man, too far to the right to be in the line of fire of the shooters using the buildings for cover, had shot down two of the deinonychus.

The three remaining dinosaurs had run off behind the houses. That behavior confirmed Park's suspicions that Selene had managed to apply some of his more theoretical research on a macro scale. All the equipment was there, and the only thing that had stopped Park from doing it himself was that shoehorning a human mind into a brain that small would drive the man insane.

Selene, of course, wouldn't care about that. She'd created dinosaurs that could strike when called, that feared guns and that, most tellingly, ignored no less than four fresh, dead bodies—two human, two dinosaur—in the vicinity.

That was utterly unnatural, and showed that the human overprinting had completely pushed the animal portions of the dinosaurs aside. Selene was unwittingly doing his own work for him.

As if to prove him right, a small pack of velociraptors, no more than five or six individuals that had probably been separated from a larger group, approached the deinonychus carcass furthest from Park. Ignoring the firefight going on around them, they set to work on the grisly business of getting food. Feathers flew as the sharp, tiny teeth tore at the fallen colossus. They knew they had to work fast: bigger creatures were never far away.

Meanwhile, the stalemate on the meadow—two sets of fire teams shooting at each other to little effect—continued until, with a roar, one of Sun-Lee's more vicious creations entered the fray.

A Cacharodontosaurus—the name meant shark-toothed lizard, which was why Park had decided to create two of the things in the first place, because it was so cool—lumbered into view. It resembled a thicker, more robust version of the hopelessly cliché T-Rex, with bigger front legs and a more solid head. The man closest to it, one of Park's troops, made the mistake of shooting at it. A long, panicked burst made it angry.

A single swoop of the enormous head pulled up half a man and a shower of blood. The other half remained on the floor, testament to the effectiveness of the dinosaur's huge teeth.

"We need to get back to the helicopters," he told the reporters. "Come this way."

Abandoning the remaining security man to his fate, they set off through the trees. Their cover was a mixed blessing: on one hand, the stand concealed them from view, but on the other, the dead leaves, piled knee-high in places, slowed them down. And if they ever needed to hurry, this was the time.

A woman behind him screamed, and Park turned to see shadows approaching between the trees, knee-high. A pack of saltopus; in fact, the only one he'd built. The little dinosaurs, twenty strong, had been the first animals Park had created from the captured nothosaur eggs.

Alone, a saltopus was little match for a human. But they worked in packs—they collaborated even more effectively than the more notorious raptors—and YekLab had already lost two assistants to the little bastards.

And now, Park had lost a German journalist. The woman fell into the underbrush with a crash and disappeared under a living carpet of housecat-sized monsters.

The woman took a really long time to die. When they reached the edge of the woods, she was still crying out for help.

Park stopped. Up ahead were two dear dinosaurs—one impaled on a spear of all things—and two soldiers, accompanied by a lean woman with dark hair.

His heart fell. Grosjean must have sent these men out to the helicopters, and Park had abandoned the single armed man remaining to him on the meadow behind them. The two soldiers, bloody and ragged—they must have had a really tough time with the dinosaurs—were walking towards the aircraft, and Park knew the pilot contractors would be extremely unlikely to risk their lives to avoid capture. Their company worked with every branch of the Russian armed forces and secret community; the CEO would get on the phone with the right people and the choppers—complete with unharmed pilots—would be released with no need for unpleasantness.

That meant Selene had him beat. She had at least two teams in the area, and Park had nothing. There was no way for him to fight back against her in military terms.

But there was one thing he could do. Scorched earth was always an option when faced with insurmountable odds.

He faced his companions. Another woman must have run off, because he was left with exactly two of the reporters. Of course, they didn't really matter, but he did want someone to survive to tell the story. The dinosaurs had proven that they could be deployed very effectively in war zones, and it would be nice that some news outlet could confirm his claims.

"We need to get into a tree."

"What about the helicopters?" the Brazilian woman asked. "Shouldn't we get out of here?"

"I'm afraid that's no longer an option. We need to take cover."

He started climbing, not waiting or caring whether the reporters followed suit. Even if they weren't there to corroborate his claims, the pteranodons would have flown out of the crater, visible to everyone. That should be proof enough that what he was saying was true.

Tatiana climbed a tree beside him, but the final reporter, a French woman, ran out of the woods at a ninety-degree angle to the direction they'd been traveling, shouting as she went. Park didn't bother calling after her.

Ensconced in a branch high enough to avoid casual detection but not so high that it wouldn't bear his weight, Park pulled his phone out of his pocket and opened an app represented by a big red circle on the screen. When the app opened, it prompted him for a password, then asked him a question about the lyrics of a song he learned in North Korea when he was five years old.

The app opened to display a user interface which he'd designed himself. It consisted of a single big red button in the middle of the screen.

Park took a deep breath and pushed the red button.

***

Krista watched the video again and again. She couldn't believe what she was seeing. A thing like that, one that couldn't be brought down with small-caliber bullets would be the perfect weapon to unleash the next time someone organized a demonstration that went contrary to her ideals.

She smiled to think of how easily an abortion-clinic protest could be dispersed if she just let a dinosaur out among the religious nuts.

It might solve one of her largest problems. The fact that political discourse was getting more and more polarized in the US as protests flared and people refused to compromise worked to her favor. In fact, she financed an important meme farm to heighten the childish behavior of random Americans on both sides of the divide.

Unfortunately, she had a problem. To really bring things to a flashpoint, one needed victims. Gun victims, for political reasons, were used differently from what she wanted. They were used to call attention to Second Amendment rights, and that wasn't what she wanted. She needed chaos and confusion, not prepared sound bites. You couldn't shoot protesters with automatic rifles or your intentions would immediately be lost in the subsequent shitshow.

But if these people were for real, then she would definitely have confusion. The Buddha had given her an email address.

Krista typed: *Send me a quote for a T-Rex. My one condition is that they have to deliver it, in a van, to Portland, Oregon. I will need to keep the van, so include it in the price.*

She imagined it wouldn't be cheap. Getting something like that into the country would likely be a nightmare, unless they could find a way to grow the thing here.

Money was no object, however. She could afford whatever they wanted for something that perfect.

Krista looked out over her manicured lawn and sighed. There would be upheaval, of course. Good people would suffer. But it was the only way to tear down the corrupt capitalist society they lived in and create something better.

In the long run, people would understand. They'd thank her.

***

As he died, Luca shook his head. It was hard to concentrate in this body. The only reason he hadn't gone completely insane already was that he had plenty of experience in transferring from one mind to another.

Of course, that bastard agent of his had promised to delete all the copies of his mind immediately when the transfer was finished. The man had obviously lied through his teeth.

Unsurprising. The business of transferring minds was illegal in every country that suspected it could be done, and would be made illegal everywhere else when governments decided it wasn't just science fiction. It wasn't a line of work that attracted honest people.

Except for Luca himself. His entire reputation was based on being the foremost straight shooter in the industry. Discreet and effective, he got client after client.

Of course, his actual service was a little less than exotic. He transferred into a client's mind for a few months and got their bodies in shape. It was incredible how much people would pay to look like an Olympic athlete without any of the suffering and hard work normally involved in that kind of transformation.

It allowed Luca to live like a king.

Correction, it allowed the *real* Luca to live like a king. A copy that no one knew existed could apparently be used for whatever anyone wanted to do with it, including dumping it into the weirdly wired brain of a huge chickensaurus.

He wondered what the real Luca was doing. Probably spending his millions on a beach in the South of France.

He roared. In a human body, it would have been a scream of frustration. He couldn't think right. Sometimes, such as when the woman spoke, he could barely make out her words, and while he was listening, everything else disappeared: he couldn't think of anything else, certainly couldn't remember who he'd been.

Worse, even when things were relaxed, he wasn't quite himself. For example, he couldn't recall, no matter how hard he tried, what job he'd been on when this copy had been made.

He remembered only snatches of faces. A woman. The name Romina floated around her. A vague sense of New York. That was it. Other stuff seemed to be missing, too, but he really couldn't put his finger on it.

And when the woman ordered him—several copies of him, it seemed, but he couldn't manage to count them, numbers were impossible in this head—to attack, he just blanked out and went. The body took over, and all he could remember from the charge were vague sensations. Grass. Sunlight. Food in the shape of a mammal.

Then he heard a sharp crack and felt pain, a pain that overwhelmed everything else. The pain of impending death.

Now he couldn't move the body at all. One of his eyes still saw the grass as he lay on his side. The other was under his head.

Perhaps it was for the best. This mind they'd transferred him to was stifling. It took all his discipline just to keep from losing his grip completely.

It felt… it felt almost like being trapped inside a box just slightly larger than he was. The box allowed movement, but you could only move one thing at a time. So you could scratch your nose, but only if you wedged yourself into a position that allowed nothing else to move.

That was the way this brain felt.

At least now there were few calls to use it. He was too weak to move, so balancing the unusual shape of his body was no longer a problem. No one was yelling orders at him, and he didn't have to charge at armed enemies. Hell, the sounds outside his immediate sphere were irrelevant to him; he was dying. The shooting went on while he ignored it.

That let him think more clearly than at any time since he'd been downloaded into this body.

As his blood drained onto the ground and the limited consciousness of this form allowed him a bit of thought, he realized that he was relieved.

The brain he was locked inside didn't allow him to feel surprise at that, and even acceptance was a difficult concept.

Death was less complicated for him: one moment he was, the next he wasn't.

* * *

Marianne stopped. "Did you hear that?"

"Gunfire," Max replied. "From the village."

"Why would they be shooting?"

"Because the whole place is infested with enormous monsters that enjoy eating human flesh? That's always a good bet. But that means they'll be retreating back this way. We should move."

Max jogged in the direction of the helicopter, and Vasily ran up beside him. "Those aren't all AK-47s," he said.

"I know," Max replied in Russian to keep Marianne from understanding. "There's something else going on, and I want no part of it. We should just grab a chopper and get the hell out of here."

"Where are you going to take it?"

"Back to base. I'll take my chances with the CO. He hates the witch woman more than most."

"But not more than you."

"I think she killed my brother."

"What if the colonel won't help?"

"Then we shoot our way out and run for it. The Kazakh border is a couple of hours away."

"Why not take the chopper directly?"

"Because I want to at least try to get some justice for Yevgeny."

Vasily said nothing more.

They went slower than Max would have liked; Marianne wasn't particularly fast. They might have actually made better time if they'd carried her, but any net gain in speed would have been nullified by the inevitable argument.

It would be fine, though. He checked behind him near-obsessively, but there was no sign of Sun-Lee or of whoever was shooting at him. The helicopters, safely nested on the tarmac of the launch area, were less than half a click away. Even at Marianne's speed, they'd be there in three minutes.

The earth shook beneath him and knocked Max to the ground while Vasily spilled beside him and Marianne behind.

He looked up to see the helicopters disappear as the cement collapsed into the earth below. The grinding shriek of torn metal reached them an instant later, audible over the rumbling of... could it possibly be an earthquake? Was his luck actually that bad?

The shaking stopped as suddenly as it had started.

They got up and ran to the tarmac. Max could see a huge hole in the center and, since they had no better ideas, they kept running to the edge. Only a second before they reached the hole did Max's sixth sense trigger his danger instinct.

"Wait! Move back," he said in Russian. "The hole. It's a square. There's no way that was caused by an earthquake. Get the girl and move away. I'm going to have a look."

"Why not run?"

"If it's a way out of here, I want to know about it."

"And if it's not?"

"We're probably dead anyway. Now move."

The fact that Vasily did as he was told was testament to how well his men had been trained. No one could possibly pretend that the regulations of the Russian Army still held sway. The action they were undertaking was strictly against other Russians, and yet none of his men had wavered at any point.

He just wished he could have seen them in action against Russia's true enemies.

But that was the life of a soldier, particularly a special forces soldier. You played the hand you were dealt, and this time, someone had decided to pull monsters from the bottom of the deck.

He'd act accordingly.

The hole was twenty meters square, and the interior was brightly lit by the late morning sun.

What he saw resembled a collapse in a parking garage. The tarmac had fallen to reveal a structure built up in several levels. He counted six stories to the rubble-strewn floor. There was an entire complex down there, dust-covered desks visible in the darkness of the floors. Two mangled helicopters lay in the rubble, small tongues of flame licking one of them.

But there was also something else down there, something spider-like and black, with the tail of a scorpion and way too many legs. It was climbing, skittering up the side, pulling itself up floor by floor.

Only when it reached a level three floors below his feet did Max stop to take a measure of scale.

It was enormous. Easily six or seven meters across the central body, the tail was even longer than that. Each leg was as thick as his torso... and there were eight of them. Pincers that looked like those of a lobster blown up a hundred times snapped around columns to gain a climbing grip. No, not like those of a lobster. Like those of a scorpion. They shone chitinously.

Max stepped back, and then again. He stared down at the approaching angel of death and couldn't move.

"Max!" Vasily shouted to him. "Is everything all right?"

That woke him from his trance. He turned and called back. "No! Get the hell out of here."

"What about you?"

"I'm right behind you."

And he was. He sprinted in the direction of his two companions. "Which way?" Vasily asked.

"Cover! Any kind of cover!"

They ran downhill toward the trees. When Max reached them, he didn't even ask, and simply picked up Marianne in his stride and threw her over his shoulder. She weighed next to nothing.

He felt her take a breath, and almost grinned. He knew he was about to get an earful for treating her with less than complete dignity, but she screamed instead.

"What the hell is that?"

"You tell me," he panted in reply. "I'm looking this way, remember."

"It's like a seriously fucked up spider."

"Oh, that. Yeah. That's what we're running from."

"It's coming this way."

He didn't reply. He already knew that.

"Oh God, it's too fast. We're never going to make it!"

Max looked back. They'd had a hundred-meter head start, but that was already down to fifty. They would never get anywhere near the trees in time. The thing moved like a train, thundering on eight chitinous legs.

They were most definitely dead.

But he still kept running. What else could he do? Maybe it would grab one of them and ignore the others long enough for them to reach safety. Ideally they should split up... but that wouldn't help. There was only one clump of trees anywhere nearby, and that was the one they were making for.

The creature halved the distance again, in seconds. Max could almost feel it at his back, pincers ready to slice through him.

The ground shook now with its proximity. Every instinct screamed that he should turn to see, but he knew that would slow him down.

"Run, Vasily," he shouted. Unburdened by Marianne, Vasily could run much faster than he'd been going. The man had actually been matching Max's pace. It was the bravest thing Max had ever seen, but now it was just foolhardy. He needed to sprint so at least one of them would survive.

The thing was so close now, he could actually see its shadow, and his burning legs were strained to breaking point.

Suddenly, the monster disappeared. Max didn't see it, he felt it. The wind no longer fluttering at his back, the sun no longer blocked. For some reason, it had fallen back. He was almost too scared to ask Marianne what was going on.

"It turned to the left. It's running that way," the woman reported.

"Why?" Max gasped. His lungs felt like they wanted to jump through his chest.

"I think it saw one of the dinosaurs, a big one. Over there." He felt her pointing but didn't turn to look. The trees were just a couple of hundred meters ahead. He'd look around once he reached them.

When he arrived, he fell to his knees, spilling Marianne into the dead leaves on the floor. He gasped for a minute before he could move again, all the while listening to Vasily and Marianne's running commentary.

"It's going for that little one," Vasily reported in Russian.

"I think it's trying to reach the big one. What did Ronnie call it? Oh yeah. The diplodocus," Marianne said in English.

"Oh, it went for the big one in the end. The big one sees it. It's turning to face it."

Max staggered to his feet and leaned on a tree beside them. They should probably concentrate on moving further into the woods, but the scene presented by the two monsters was too compelling to look away from.

The shiny black thing, insect-like and menacing, had stepped up to the diplodocus, dwarfed by the enormous herbivorous dinosaur. Even at this distance, Max thought one strike of a reptilian leg would tear the black monster a new asshole, or at least severely dent the armor.

The diplodocus advanced with a roar that reached them several seconds later.

The black monster held its ground and, as soon as the dinosaur was in range, reached out with a pincer.

Blood spurted from the diplodocus' chest, a great fountain.

Now wounded, the dinosaur went berserk. Rearing like a horse, it tried to come down on the spider-scorpion thing with both feet at once, but the insect monster was much too quick. It danced out of the way and snipped when it could.

The diplodocus kicked out with one leg. It missed again. It paid the price again.

The battle continued for several minutes, the prehistoric monster on the offensive, the one that looked like it had sprung from the screen during a 1950s science fiction film defending... but so effectively that it was the one dishing out the pain. A blundering attack from the dinosaur would be met with a surgical strike from the huge claw.

Soon, the blood loss, gallons and gallons of it, told on the diplodocus and it became sluggish. During one attempt to crush the other creature with its front legs, it stumbled and its long neck hit the ground.

That was all the smaller monster needed. It struck the center of the dinosaur's neck with a pincer and squeezed.

The neck was too big to sever, but the pincers cut through enough of it that Max knew the fight was over. The dinosaur tried to get up, but the energy just wasn't there.

The spider-monster seemed to know as well. It moved back a couple of steps and waited for the dinosaur to collapse completely.

Then it began to feed.

***

Tatiana's vantage point, a little higher up than Sun-Lee's, gave her a clear view of the hill leading up to the helicopters. She saw the aircraft disappear and witnessed the chase, the soldiers'—and Marianne's—narrow escape from a monster that could have come from an insane person's worst nightmare.

She had no idea how Marianne could have suddenly popped up again, but it was a measure of her respect for the other reporter's resourcefulness that Tatiana was unsurprised.

She wanted to call out to Marianne, to tell her to climb up with them, but just didn't dare. That thing might hear them, and if it did, they would die. She had no doubt about it. There could be no escape. The monster was death, immediate, painful death. No human power could save them once it knew they were there.

So she remained silent as the other group entered the woods, only whispering to Sun-Lee. "Did you see it?"

"No, what was it?"

"A monster."

"One of the dinosaurs?"

"No, something else. Something awful, too awful to describe, like a huge bug."

To her astonishment, Sun-Lee smiled. "Well, that was quick. It must have been truly itching to get out. I suppose one can't blame it. It's been locked up for five months."

"You knew about that thing?"

He suddenly started as if realizing for the first time that he was talking to someone else. He stared into her eyes for a moment and then nodded. "Yes. I knew about it. It's the culmination of the atrocities they are storing here."

"They can build those things?"

"No. Not really. Not here, anyway. The monster you saw was produced by a Frenchman called Philippe. No one really knows his last name because he never uses it. He doesn't use Philippe, either, but he'll admit to it if someone knows who he is."

"Is he working for the Russians, too?"

"Philippe? No... Philippe works for his own amusement. Or maybe he does it out of a belief that science should move forward unchecked by the morality of its day, that science is above ethics in the same way the weather is. He is an idealist, and the people he has most contempt for are those who try to stop him from researching anything he likes." He paused for a moment. "And what he likes to research is the extreme bleeding edge of what we can create with today's gene-editing tools. Moreover, he works with human genes, something that even the Russians would never attempt. He created the monster you saw."

"So where is he now?"

"No one knows. We captured that monster in Panama, and we've been working since to try to understand how the hell he put it together. As for the man himself, he's everywhere, but more often than not, he pops up in Africa. The French really want to arrest him, so he keeps well under cover. I've only met him once. We tried to get him to do some work for us... but things suddenly went very bad for him and he disappeared. All we got from him was the monster you saw and a couple of smaller samples."

"And the Russians let them out to kill those people we saw?"

"The Russians. Yes, the Russians let them out. Let it out. Yes." Sun-Lee shook his head. "You need to report this. Can you compose an article, and send photos?"

"I haven't got a network connection."

"I can fix that. My phone is a satellite phone and I can hotspot you."

"All right, let me transfer the pics from the camera to my phone. I still have plenty of battery life. Give me a minute."

She composed a quick email to her editor. She didn't tell him she was up a tree, probably doomed to become a monster's lunch. Instead, she tried to keep it professional, to make the story about the story, and not about her. If she died, they could give her any awards posthumously, but she wanted them to think about the immense story she'd discovered. No one, not even Marianne down in the underbrush, could scoop her this time.

"Sending it over," she said. Even the images went quickly, making her wonder why the man had such impressive bandwidth out in the middle of nowhere. But she wasn't in the habit of questioning good luck. You used it until it was used up, and then you waited for a little more to hit.

"You didn't ask for help," Sun-Lee said.

"No. The story was more important."

Sun-Lee nodded silently and kept looking down towards the floor of their little patch of forest.

"Any sign of them?"

"No dinosaurs. A lot of them are probably following after the monster. Others are probably hiding from it."

"Why would they follow something like that?"

"Many of the dinosaurs are carrion-eaters by preference. The movie might make you think velociraptors are hunters, but they'd much rather strip a dead carcass than make their own. Dead bodies don't fight back. So they follow bigger, badder dinosaurs and wait for them to kill something. Then they feed on the remains."

"Ugh. What if the big one sees them?"

"They run. But normally, the big hunters ignore them and concentrate on things with more meat on them."

A scream, distant but full of pain, reached them.

"I would guess," Sun-Lee said, "that the monster has found something worth hunting. Can you see what it is?"

"No, it went out of sight behind a tree."

Sounds on the forest floor beneath them echoed and they shut up.

Two men and a woman walked under the tree she was hanging from. Tatiana was so relieved to see a friendly face that she whispered, "Marianne. Marianne, up here."

Marianne looked around, confused.

"Up here," Tatiana repeated.

Finally, Marianne spotted her. "Tatiana? What are you doing up there?"

"I'm hiding from velociraptors and stuff."

"If you'd seen what we just saw, you'd welcome velociraptors."

Tatiana couldn't believe it. She'd just watched her colleague come within a hair's breadth of being torn to pieces, but she seemed unflustered by the experience. Ragged around the edges, looking like she'd been dragged through a hedge backwards, but not the nervous wreck she should have been. Certainly not the nervous wreck Tatiana would have been.

"I saw it. This is just awful."

"We need to tell the world about this."

"I already have. We got a message out just now."

"We?" Marianne said. "Who's we?"

Tatiana pointed towards the branches below her where Park Sun-Lee was perched, but the space was empty. A rustle below them announced the two men who'd been with Marianne before. Tatiana recognized two of the soldiers that had helped them escape from the YekLab panic room.

One of them had Sun-lee by the arm, the other was holding a gun to her host.

"Wait," Tatiana said. "He's one of the good guys. He's trying to tell the world what's happening here. Don't hurt him."

The big, blond soldier peered up at her and then turned to Marianne. "This guy is a snake second only to the witch-woman in sliminess. He is anything but one of the good guys. We should shoot him now." He waited, making it clear that he wanted her opinion, maybe because she knew Tatiana, maybe simply because he didn't want to look like an arbitrary monster.

Marianne hesitated. "Tatiana is the best journalist I know. She is also honest. If she thinks this is a good guy, we should at least listen to what she says."

"I think she doesn't know what she's talking about." The gun pointed at Sun-Lee's head didn't waver.

Sun-Lee looked him in the eye, unflinching. Tatiana couldn't believe these people. Was she the only one who would have fainted if someone pointed a gun at her?

"If you shoot me, you'll never get out of here alive," Sun-Lee said.

"I don't think you'll be much good in a fight," the soldier replied.

"Perhaps. But I know the way out."

"So do I. The tunnel. But we can't use it because Selene controls the complex at the far end."

"Not the tunnel. Another way. Only I know where it is and I won't tell you unless you take me with you and promise not to kill me after I tell you where it is."

The gun lowered and the soldier said something in Russian that sounded very unhappy.

"Dammit," he said. "But put a single foot wrong, and I'll shoot you myself." He looked up. "I hope you're right about him," he said to Tatiana. "Because if not, I'll shoot you, too. Now get down here so we can start moving."

Tatiana had barely reached the ground when something hit her in the chest. Marianne held her tight and sobbed. "I'm so glad you're all right."

Tatiana returned the hug. She had nothing to add.

CHAPTER 8

Selene looked down at the man on the floor, the man who'd been one of Sun-Lee's henchmen—surprisingly good at keeping them pinned and wasting her time. He'd taken a bullet to the right side of his chest, close to the liver, but he was still alive.

"Where did he come from?" she asked in Russian.

"There's no identification on him," one of the men with her replied after a quick search.

"Of course not," Selene replied, kneeling next to him. "You're a professional, aren't you? Never take identification with you on a job, not even a fake driver's license that could be traced back to someone. So tell me. Who are you, and who do you work for? You're not one of mine, and you certainly aren't one of Sun-Lee's security guys from the lab... so tell me."

The man said nothing. He stared at her, but she didn't know if it was a look of defiance or one of hopelessness.

His face certainly told her nothing else. Dark hair with just a hint of grey in it, and slightly swarthy features meant that he could be from anywhere in the south of Russia or any of the Stans. His features weren't distinctive enough for her to be able to hazard a guess.

That meant he'd chosen the right line of work: being unexceptional was an asset for certain jobs. They would need to take his fingerprints to gain any information on him.

Unless she got him to speak. Then, he would give himself away to her trained ear.

"How about this. If you talk, I'll get you a doctor and maybe you'll survive. After all, it's not a hired goon we want, it's Sun-Lee, so we can let you walk."

It was a lie, of course. Even if there was any hope of saving the guy, they would have stabilized him only in order to torture him to death. But there was no hope. A shot to the liver was pretty much a painful death sentence. Even if he'd been in a city, his life would likely have been forfeit. Out here? The chances of surviving were exactly zero.

She was banking on the fact that he wouldn't know that, and clutch at any straw.

"On the other hand, if you don't talk right now, I'll put a bullet in your brain. You have ten seconds."

He held her gaze, no spark of hope visible. She pointed the gun at him. "Three... two..."

He tried to speak, but spluttered, tried again, but pointed at his throat, his movements weak and sluggish.

"Pity," Selene said, and pressed the trigger.

At that range, Selene was incapable of missing, and she turned away to avoid splatter. There was no real need to check if he was dead... and exit wounds from head shots were always unpleasant.

She holstered her pistol and turned back to her remaining men—one had caught a bullet, leaving her with two—and the three dinosaurs with human brains. She briefly thought of shooting the dinosaurs just to remove distractions but, on further thought, decided to let them come along. They could be useful as cannon fodder if they ran into a lot of other creatures at once.

"Get the sonic weapon," she told her men. "That one really works."

They set off across grass. About halfway to the nearest trees, she stopped.

"What the hell is that?"

"I don't know," the man nearest her answered. "Sounds like an earthquake or something."

"The ground isn't moving," Selene shot back.

"Yeah, that's true."

"Move. I think this is trouble."

They sprinted across the grass and, about halfway to the trees, they stopped again, mouth agape.

"Please tell me you're seeing what I'm seeing," she said.

"I hope not. I'm seeing a spider as big as a house. With pincers. And a scorpion's tail."

"Good. Then I'm not hallucinating."

"What do we do?"

"Stay still. I don't think it saw us."

They remained where they were-even the uplifted deinonychus was rooted in place-until the monster disappeared around the hill.

Then they ran like hell for the trees.

Selene cursed as they went. That North Korean bastard had managed to hide this thing from her, and from everyone she worked with. How? She didn't know, but when she returned, everyone whose job it had been to report on Sun-Lee's activities would have one hell of a lot of explaining to do.

As she thought about it, she realized there was only one possible explanation that fit the facts: Panama. He'd captured the thing when in Panama.

The problem was that an operation of the size and equipment needed to grab a monster like that would have needed near-military resources... and she was certain they hadn't come from Russia.

That meant contractors... and that, in turn, meant money. Where he'd gotten it was another mystery that she would have to look into.

Damn. This was supposed to be a quick and easy jaunt to kill a few loose ends. It was suddenly getting complicated.

The plan had now changed. She could kill the soldier and the reporter bitch but she would need Sun-Lee alive. Unfortunately, that brought in additional complications: no one could know that the director was being put to the question... that way lay unwanted attention.

Well, she'd cross that bridge when she got to it.

They reached the trees and kept running. At least now, they were out of sight of anything they couldn't deal with. Stuff in the woods would be small enough to shoot... and they'd be unlikely to mess with her pet raptors.

"Move it! We need to catch up to Sun-Lee," Selene called back to the men running with her. She jumped around a particularly thick clump of trees and into a group of small dinosaurs. "Watch out!"

But the warning came too late. One of her men bowled straight into the little carnivores and was immediately swarmed. She brought up her gun to clear him and shot one off, but he was writhing so much that she didn't want to keep shooting for fear of hitting him.

The man's screams echoed in the trees, and the other guy went in and kicked at the creatures hanging all over him. Bones crunched as the boots fell.

Then, one of Selene's pet deinonychus joined the fray and the small raptors gave up any semblance of a fight. They disappeared into the trees, leaving only one dead dinosaur—shot by Selene—and the one her single remaining foot soldier had kicked. That one lay brokenly on the floor, trying to get up and mewling pitifully.

The other man was very dead. The little bastards had torn away a good chunk of his throat. It wasn't just a killing blow: they'd actually been feeding.

Selene picked up the dead man's rifle. Her gun was proving worse than useless. Then, she turned to one of the dinosaurs with them. "We're going that way. You take the lead."

They followed the beast through the trees and didn't see any other dinosaurs. The only indication that they were in a place where hundreds of prehistoric creatures had been released was the noise fleeing animals made as they moved out of the way of the advancing deinonychus.

When they emerged, she cursed. "They got away," she said.

"Were the two groups working together?"

"Of course not, they probably took a helicopter each." She stared at the empty space on the hill where the two helicopters should have been. "Wait a second. The whole place looks weird. I want to have a look."

They stepped past two of the dead dinosaurs and she stopped at the one furthest from the trees. Someone had stabbed it with a spear.

"Someone out here is a badass," the single man with her said. She was surprised. Her troops generally knew when to keep their mouths shut. This man must have been truly impressed by what he was seeing.

"Yeah. Too bad we're going to catch him and skin him alive."

She wasn't certain of that now. After all, if the soldiers were back at the Spetsnaz base, getting them out was going to be a real bitch. Orlov might have played ball so far, but if this Max guy had any intelligence at all, everyone would already know what had happened here even before she went after him. They'd know why he was being hunted, who was doing the hunting and what would happen to him.

Most of the soldiers would be dead set against letting her have her prize and, though she was powerful, there was no way she would be powerful enough to take on an entire Spetsnaz base.

Worse, they'd have leverage on her, leverage that Orlov could use with his superiors to get her recalled. And 'recall', in this case was a euphemism for 'disappeared'.

She decided to change the subject. "Did you hear a helicopter?"

Her man scratched his head. "No. Not at all. But there was a lot of shooting, so I'm not surprised I missed it."

"I didn't either. Let's get up there and see. That big chunk of concrete wasn't there when they landed. The blacktop was empty. Something isn't right."

They climbed the remaining portion of the hill. When they crested it, she gasped. An entire sector of the concrete lot had collapsed into the hill. The wreckage of two helicopters lay at the bottom. Across from them, a group of small dinosaurs were investigating a staircase that led down into the guts of the underground complex revealed by the collapse. She pointed. "That's where they went in. Let's go." Then, turning to the dinosaurs with her, Selene said: "Run up ahead and clear out the little things. Wait for me at the first landing."

"What do you think happened here?" the man asked.

He was more talkative than the rest, but she'd have to tolerate it for now as he was the last bit of muscle remaining to her. "I think this is where the Korean had his secret lab, and where he kept his ugly spider pet. He probably blew the roof when he realized that he wasn't going to make it to the helicopters... and released that... thing into the Russian countryside. It's just another thing he'll have to answer for once we grab him."

She started down the steps.

***

Vaseekar sat in his study, a carpeted, beautiful room in his mansion overlooking Palk Bay and studied the pictures on the article. Was it real? The Buddha never screwed around, of course, but his follow-ups to get the name of the seller and the pertinent contact details met with a swift 'not yet, all shall be revealed in due course' response.

Which meant that, if the Buddha wasn't screwing around, there was something else going on. If that was the case, he didn't want any part of it. The Sri Lankan police, forged by decades of guerrilla war, were a sophisticated, deadly enemy. Any misstep on his part would see his Reborn Tigers destroyed before they could fire a weapon in anger.

So he studied the article that the Buddha had sent. As far as he could tell, the original piece had been published in a Brazilian fluff magazine who happened to have a reporter in the area.

That certainly wasn't an auspicious start, and his Portuguese was nowhere near good enough to judge the quality of the writing. Google translate was absolutely no help. Now, he had to try to piece together the veracity of the journalism by seeing who picked it up after it originally ran. That was an interesting trail.

The usual bottom-feeders republished first. Online newspapers who specialized in gore and sensationalism without asking too many questions. Then some local outlets who might have been having a slow news day.

The heavy-hitters got in on the act a little later, with *USA Today* and *The New York Times* running pieces about the Russian Dinosaur Atrocity. The BBC stated that they were flying a team into the area, as did CNN.

It certainly sounded like people who knew what they were doing believed that this new technology to create genetic monsters existed. No one mentioned that it might be for sale, which was a good thing.

He wanted to catch the authorities by surprise... and this would do nicely.

Vaseekar began to compose an email to the Electric Buddha.

***

"There's food in that refrigerator," Sun-Lee said. "It's quite fresh. A man comes in once a week to clear out anything old and replace it. Since I never know when I'll be here, it's important to keep supplies up."

They were in an office, a perfectly normal one, with computers and a meeting table. It had tasteful grey carpeting and a wooden desk. Marianne found herself lounging on a leather recliner, enjoying the sensation of being able to rest. There was only one thing... "Do you have a bathroom?" she said.

"Behind the door."

She went in and stripped down to her underwear. Then she wet some paper towels and gave herself a lightning sponge bath, minus the sponge. Feeling human again, she dressed and emerged. Her clothes, she reflected, would need to go straight in the bin after she got back.

Max was arguing with Sun-Lee, gesticulating at the computers. He turned to Marianne in disgust. "This bastard claims there's no internet connection here."

"It's true," the North Korean said in English. "I didn't want anything on these computers to fall into Selene's hands. She'll be after us, you know. She already killed my men and the other journalists."

"I didn't see her killing the others," Tatiana said.

Sun-Lee held her gaze. "Trust me. As soon as she finds them, they're dead. If they're lucky, she'll be in too much of a hurry to bring them with her and she'll shoot them straight away. But unless you and your friend over there get out of here, no one will ever know what became of them."

"What about the rest of you?" Tatiana asked.

"Neither I or the soldiers will ever tell an outside agency what happened here... and the Russians won't broadcast this."

"My story got out," Tatiana said. "Less than an hour ago."

"Yes. But since my phone is now out of battery power and I didn't bring the charger with me, we can't use it to find out if it was published."

"Oh, it was definitely published," Tatiana said.

Marianne wished she was that confident. Had her own story gotten out? Even if it had, now it was old news. Tatiana's would have a ton of new information about the release of the dinosaurs into the midst of an unsuspecting rural population. But only Marianne knew why they'd been released, and where they came from.

In fact, she was starting to suspect that Sun-Lee might have been the one to blast open the tunnel in the first place. His little press trip here was a little too convenient to have simply been a coincidence. Even if he'd known that today was a planned release day, he could never have guessed that every dinosaur would have escaped without knowing of the breach.

But she said nothing. It would be much better to let the man think she had no clue. Maybe he'd let something slip.

Tatiana had the scoop this time around, and Marianne was happy for her. She'd been in the right place at the right time, true, but it appeared that she was also the only one of the journalists on the trip who'd managed to keep her head and survive long enough to get her story out. Tatiana deserved the recognition; she'd more than earned it.

Of course, that didn't mean that Marianne would hesitate to upstage her by withholding a few central facts and building a deep investigative piece around what was happening.

It had worked for her before, even though the *Timeless* debacle was not a multi-journalist occurrence, she'd kept the stories separate enough that she was able to sell very different angles to very different outlets... and became a household name among journalists almost overnight. Hell, she'd even sold a restaurant review about the place where a family member of one of the criminals involved in the piece had served her the best Italian meal she'd ever eaten, and that counted old Grandma Caruso's Christmas dinners.

So she didn't respond and simply checked if Max and Vasily had left anything in the fridge. When she approached, Max held out his hand. "I kept you a sandwich."

"One sandwich? I could eat a horse." She grabbed the proffered food and stuffed half of it into her mouth.

Max laughed. "You don't look like someone who makes a habit of eating horses."

"I hate to admit this but I probably eat more than I should. My metabolism has always allowed me to get away with it, but lately, I've been having to get out and jog. Please don't tell anyone."

"I don't think anyone will care. You look fantastic."

"I look like something that a cat would bury in a litterbox. Come on. My hair is an absolute mess, and I had to wash off all my makeup because it made me look like a raccoon."

"You look even better without makeup."

The way he looked at her made her wish they were somewhere else, somewhere they could walk out together and she could spend the night finding out just how hard those muscles actually were. She would have felt completely safe: this was certainly a very dangerous man, a killer more than just in potential, but she knew that the fury and violence would be directed outward, not towards her. Anyone who tried to mess with Marianne, however...

She finished the sandwich and opened the fridge. Glory of glories, Sun-Lee had stocked the fridge with real Coke, and not the crappy diet varieties which tasted like plastic vomit. She popped a 600cc bottle and listened as Max spoke to the North Korean.

"We need to get out of here quickly. We need to get back to base."

"That's easy enough," Sun-Lee replied. "But there are two problems. The first is that the creature you saw earlier, the arachnid monster, lives here, and will likely return soon. But that's not the biggest problem. The biggest problem is that Selene Grosjean is after us."

"Why would she look here?"

"Because we're here, and she will come after us."

"She doesn't know where we went."

"She knows we came in this direction, and those woods back there aren't big enough to keep her busy very long. So she'll come this way, and she has bigger guns than you do." He glanced at the spear in Max's hands. "And none of her men are carrying sharpened sticks to defend themselves."

"We can deal with her and any of her men. Hell, we could do it with our bare hands. The problem with people like Grosjean is that they never come after you in combat situations. They work in the shadows and with the politicians." Max spat as if the word had left a bad taste in his mouth. "That's how she takes away your capacity to defend yourself. But here, where there are no rules, we're going to fuck her up good, and leave the corpse for the carrion eaters."

"I take it you don't like her."

"No. Before I kill her, though, I'm going to torture her until she tells me what she knows about my brother."

"Well," Sun-Lee said. "While I can only applaud your intentions toward her, we should really get moving if we prefer to get out of here alive. Could you lend me that spear?" Thus armed, he began to tear into two of the computers on the desk. He pulled out the drives and stomped on them repeatedly.

"What's in there?" Marianne asked, heart sinking as the thought of valuable—and more importantly, newsworthy—data was damaged beyond recovery.

"Everything we know about how they designed that spider monster you saw out there, including where I suspect the man who did it is hiding."

"Come on. Let's get moving," Max said. "Which way should we go?"

"Down."

"Why? What's down there?"

"Old stuff and a tunnel almost no one uses anymore."

"Oh great, more tunnels."

"Come on."

***

Sun-Lee hadn't been kidding about the old stuff. As soon as they descended one level from the office, any resemblance to a modern office building disappeared and the carpeting and grey paint was replaced by an equally thick layer of dust. Lighting was by yellow incandescent bulbs fifteen feet above their heads.

Long wooden tables, strong, eternal, stretched out into the distance. Empty metal shelves lined the walls, and the remains of chairs littered the room.

"What was this place?" Tatiana asked Sun-Lee.

But it was Max who replied. "This is a staging facility and weapons assembly plant."

"Seven floors of it," Sun-Lee added.

"You mean this is where they built nuclear bombs?"

"I don't know if they ever had any here," the Korean replied. "We went over the whole thing with a Geiger counter, and we only found a few traces of radioactivity in a few corners." He shrugged. "Not sure if it means anything, of course, it's been a long time. But my guess is that they never had much nuclear material here. Probably just depleted uranium shells."

"This was a munitions production facility for the Afghanistan War. There're rumors that they used it to build up untraceable ordnance using western-type shells because they were sending them to several tribal groups to use against their neighbors, and the Soviets wanted to be able to blame the Americans for arming both sides of the conflict. Of course, that's all moot now."

"The facility was actually built in the Second World War. Slave labor put this together. It's supposed to be haunted."

Tatiana paled, but Marianne just raised an eyebrow. "You're shitting me. People believe that?"

"Russians are quite superstitious people," Sun-Lee replied.

Max was about to reply when something skittered in the distance, and both soldiers had their guns out and advanced. Whatever it was didn't sound too big, which might be worse; the small stuff came in packs and this dim factory floor might be the best place for a pack of ambush predators.

Max and Vasily advanced in the direction of the sound. Something came out from under a table and stood directly under one of the lights. Marianne gasped. "What the hell is that?"

"Don't shoot!" Sun-Lee said. "That's Chiffon!"

Max gave him a disbelieving look. "What? That looks like a... cat-lizard. Definitely prehistoric."

"No, it isn't. It's a pet." Sun-Lee knelt down and the creature rushed across the floor and leapt into his arms. "And it's the most modern creature anywhere on the planet apart from the big arachnid thing. This is a combination of cat DNA with all kinds of other stuff. Reptile, elephant, even penguin. I haven't even begun to unravel how the bastard did it, but it's one of my obsessions."

"Great. Just what we need. A pet."

"Don't worry about Chiffon. He'll stay out of our way, and will probably know when something is sneaking up on us before we do."

Max laughed ruefully. "Well, he couldn't really do any worse, could he?"

He walked towards the exit and the stairs.

***

Luca shook his head to clear it. The ground ahead of him had suddenly turned tricky. Well, trickier. He'd already been having plenty of difficulty trying to move the body without having to deal with these new obstacles.

They had a name, he knew. He'd once been able to deal with them easily, instinctively. But there had been something different about him then. He didn't know what, but different.

He gingerly placed his feet on platforms that were too small for them, putting all his concentration into balancing. It was a long fall if he went over.

And as he concentrated on something else, the name came to him: stairs. These were stairs.

He was so delighted with the discovery that he almost rolled down. With his big, heavy body, he knew that he would be badly hurt by a roll that his old body would have survived with a few bruises.

Old body. What kind of thought was that? How could someone change his body?

Luca didn't know, but he moved the unfamiliar tail and managed to regain his balance. He didn't think he'd be able to do that consciously. The body did it without any command from his mind. He didn't even know how to move a tail.

Which was strange, because he definitely had a tail... why wouldn't he know how to use it?

He shook his head again. He did that all the time, because it just didn't seem to be working correctly. A voice from behind made him look back. He caught the scent of the woman. She was speaking, but it was hard to understand more than a few words she said. Something about looking for something... or for someone.

He just kept going down. Whenever any of the other creatures with him did something wrong, the woman was certain to speak sharply at them, so he supposed they must be going the right way. When she did, he would try to do what she asked; that was the central thought keeping him going. The woman could do good things for Luca. He supposed she would do good things for the other two monsters, the feathered things he occasionally saw near them, as well, but he didn't care much for them. The important part was what she could do for him.

Things went fuzzy for a few seconds. That seemed to be happening more and more often as time went on, and it was welcome. He would suddenly be a few paces ahead without remembering the intervening time, and certainly without having to make the effort to walk. It was a relief to find himself at the foot of the stairs without having had to descend.

The space was enormous and he could hear every echo, from the skittering of rodents to the hollow sound of wind. There was nothing wrong with his hearing—in fact, he could hear so well that there were things he couldn't even identify.

Still, he listened. His body seemed to demand that he do so. Also, he sniffed the air, another thing that seemed alien but, at the same time, felt right somehow. There was something on the wind... something that smelled like the woman with them, a human smell. Human sweat, human soap. Humanity.

He headed where his nose pointed. He was having a hard time navigating the terrain. He bumped into things and scattered them—chairs, something said-but the scent was getting stronger. It was behind this... door, he remembered with a flash of pride. Door. The scent was behind the door.

He pushed it with his nose. It budged but didn't open. There was a small shiny object, illuminated by the daylight that filtered from the gap in the walls behind him. He thought it was something to do with opening the door, and he tried to grasp it.

His hands weren't working how they should. They couldn't get a grip: the fingers were all wrong, the arms too short.

Anger filled his existence, a red, blind rage that exploded like the sun in the morning and subsumed his capacity for thought. He roared, slamming his body into the obstacle.

With a tearing sound, the door splintered and fell at his feet, and he was inside.

Yes. He'd been correct. This was the source of the smell of humans. Right here. He could smell four… maybe five distinct humans. Women and men. They had been here, their smell still lingered. It was a warm, living smell, not a cold dead one.

But the room itself was empty. The owners of the beguiling scents were nowhere to be seen.

Luca stood aside to let the others pass. The man, the woman, the two monsters. They milled around the space and he caught some words, but they were in a language he couldn't understand. The woman knelt next to some uninteresting rubble on the floor, stuff that didn't even have any smell and the man with her made his way across the room to open another door, one which illuminated a small box.

Smells wafted out of the box… refri… no, the name was too long to bother remembering, but the smells were of food and for once, both sides of his mind responded to the same stimulus. This was familiar, to the thinking part, the part he'd come to consider his mind, it was human food. His body didn't care. It just registered the food. Glorious, familiar food. There could be nothing like it, not even the smell of the woman compared with this.

He reached the door in two steps, but he still wasn't the first to arrive. One of the monsters with them beat him to the draw and Luca tried to push it aside, but his effort was met with snapping jaws and a line of fire across his chest from some kind of strike.

It angered him. Without bothering to give the man in the way time to run, he launched himself at the monster with a roar of rage. He felt the soft flesh give way under his teeth, tasted the warm blood flowing into his mouth.

And that was the last conscious act. Then, the final monster joined the fray and Luca lost track of events completely.

He came back to himself with a start. He stood in a pile of gore, his stomach full of meat and three carcasses at his feet, two monsters and the man. He'd eaten his fill, but he'd also need time to recover from the injuries suffered in the melee. Of course, those puny monsters had lost. He knew they were inferior beings. It was a pity the man had to die, but a body that small could never survive in a real fight. The man hadn't.

He turned to survey the room, the food having brought a little more clarity to his thoughts, a little more power to his memory. It was an office, chairs and furniture askew, and broken computers everywhere. It was lit by artificial light from overhead and, standing against one wall, stood the woman he was helping because she could help him.

"Are you sane again?" the woman asked. "Nod if you are."

Luca nodded. That, at least was an easy movement.

"Good. I need to know where they went. The people who were in here before. Where did they go?"

Luca sniffed the air again. The scent that had been so warm when they entered the room paled in comparison to the searing hot odor of death and raw meat, but it was still there, and there was a thread leading to… another door.

He dispensed with any attempt to open it using the knob, even though he was proud to remember both the name and what it was used for—the food had done wonders—and simply bashed through into a long hallway.

The woman followed a few meters behind.

CHAPTER 9

The stairs grew darker as they descended. Some areas had artificial light, but the further down they went, the more likely the lights were to be out, which meant that they had to depend on the natural light filtering through the hole in the wall. Marianne put her hand on the handrail and immediately regretted it. Cobwebs and dust covered her fingers and she shook them off with a shudder.

"Does anyone use this?" Max asked.

"I do, at least a couple of times a month. My personal assistant does as well. She is in here more often than I am," Sun-Lee replied.

"Not today, though?"

"No. She is on a trip abroad."

"How convenient." Max cursed as they entered another pitch-black area. His words echoed like a demonic summons in the stairwell. "So how do you get up the stairs with no light?"

"I just use the flashlight from my phone. Unfortunately, the battery's dead because we used it to send a satellite signal this morning so Tatiana could tell the world what's happening here." He smiled smugly. "I think it will make this place front-page news all over the world."

Max didn't seem to be listening. "Well, if the roof hadn't collapsed, we'd have no light at all, so I guess there's that."

The light Max was referring to was quite tenuous, and less and less of it made it through the floor space into the stairwells as they descended.

But there were only a dozen or so flights of stairs, descending six floors, and they soon reached the bottom.

The final stairwell opened onto the gap where the floors had fallen in. There were a couple more stories beneath them, a sort of sub-basement, but no sign of office or assembly space on those levels. There was simply an empty concrete area with a pair of wrecked helicopters in the middle of it.

"That's where they kept the monster," Sun-Lee explained.

"Who was in charge of it?"

"Selene, of course. She ran most of the more sinister programs."

"It figures," Max replied, but Marianne wondered. The North Korean had spoken a lot about keeping the data away from the woman, and also about he and his assistant coming into this place... all of which gave Marianne a strong sense that, no matter what might be happening in the central facility out by the highway, the monsters in here were much more related to Sun-Lee than anyone else. She would be surprised if Selene knew what was going on.

Max's mind was on more practical matters. "Where now?" he said.

"Along that ledge, and then down a corridor to get to the tunnel entrance."

Max led, with Marianne and Tatiana behind him, then Sun-Lee and Vasily bringing up the rear. The ledge was a small piece of wooden-floored corridor, a meter wide, that skirted the drop beside the sub-basement where the helicopters lay.

Tatiana grabbed her hand, and Marianne squeezed back. "You okay?"

"No. I hate heights. It would have been better to do this in the dark."

Marianne chuckled at that. She'd seen Tatiana leaning nonchalantly on the railing of a penthouse suite twenty-five floors above the streets of Rio de Janeiro. Of course, she'd had a drink—the latest of several—in one hand and an interesting male model to talk to, so she was probably unconcerned about the drop.

Hell, this one even looked survivable, if painful. Maybe a couple of stories. Still, you probably didn't want to be lying among the wreckage of the helicopters with multiple exposed fractures waiting for someone to either rescue you or feed you to the dinosaurs. If you didn't die of some infection, first. The whole floor looked and smelled like it was covered in bat guano.

"How do you feed a monster that size?" she said out loud.

"That's actually one of the interesting things we were studying. The beast is enormous but, when it's not out hunting, it expends a tiny amount of energy. It can go up to two months without food at the very least. It goes into a kind of catatonic state, but it woke up as soon as we chickened out and opened the door to send some food inside. We try not to let it go that long anymore, though, and a cow a month is ample for its basic needs."

"Hell, I eat a cow a month," Max said.

"This thing can probably eat a lot more than that. But a cow a month keeps it from going catatonic, so we're using that until we understand it better. We have to take care of our specimens, especially the ones we can't replace."

"'We, Mr. Sun-Lee?" Marianne asked. She couldn't help it, the journalist in her was just too strongly ingrained to ignore. "That makes it sound like something you were very much invested in."

"I was. The man who built that monster is a genius… possibly unparalleled in human history. Studying his work is like trying to decipher Da Vinci. Unfortunately, it got to be too much for me. Even my conscience has limits."

"Too bad we are nowhere near knowing what those might be," another voice, a woman's voice, broke in. "Because you sure as hell haven't reached them yet."

The voice was Selene's and they all looked around to see where she was. Finally, Marianne spotted her standing in the shadows on a ledge on one side of the basement hole. She was pointing an assault rifle at them.

"Don't move," she called out to them. "I won't miss."

"Neither will we," Max replied. His gun was in his hand, and it was pointed unwaveringly at her.

Marianne didn't understand why they were talking. Did they really think that they would be able to engage in idiotic banter and also kill someone if they were shot at? If she'd been in their situation, she would never have talked, but simply fired while she had the element of surprise on her side.

Of course, she wasn't the kind to ambush people, except the in journalistic way, so it was a moot point. She would never find herself in the situation except, possibly, as a victim.

The silence continued for a few more seconds, before Max broke it. "So now what?"

"Now, you'll put down your guns and we'll talk."

"You must be out of your mind."

"I'll shoot the woman first. Do you want that on your conscience?"

"No, but I'm still not stupid. How about this; I promise not to shoot you if you come down here."

"That won't work. I'd much rather take you alive, but your death isn't something I need to avoid."

"Even at the cost of your own?"

She shrugged. "It would bring me peace, at least."

Movement in front of them caught Marianne's attention. One of the dinosaurs—it could have been the twin of the one she'd been face to face with at YekLab—blocked their advance. It had appeared out of nowhere and stood at the far end of the thin ledge along the side of the drop.

"Look!" she said, pointing.

Max chanced a quick glance, but his gun never wavered from Selene.

"I think you'll agree that it would be best if you just surrendered now," the woman said. "I have you outgunned and out-monstered."

"This changes nothing. If that thing moves, I'll shoot you anyway."

"But then how will you control it? I'm the only one it will listen to. Hell, even I'm kind of iffy on that. It's already killed one of my men."

"I'll worry about that when it happens. In the meantime, we've got a stalemate."

Selene Grosjean glared at him.

"At the very least, give me Sun-Lee and the women. They're trying to send Russian secrets out to the world."

"From what I've seen, these secrets deserve to get aired."

Selene laughed, a genuine, if sardonic sound. "I can see your tombstone now. Max Alexeyev. Scumbag and traitor to his country."

Marianne saw Max's gun tremble. Something had hit close to home. "I never told you my last name," he growled.

"Ah. I must have you confused with your dead brother. He told me his last name. Then I had him blown up... he didn't even die in combat. He was just discarded when he was no longer useful. But at least he was useful for a while, unlike you."

Everything seemed to happen at once.

"Bitch!" Max screamed. He fired three shots at Selene, but the woman had already dived to one side and taken cover behind a tank of some kind, crushed when the ceiling collapsed.

The dinosaur in front of them roared and snapped at Max's arm, causing him to overbalance and topple into the pit. Luckily for him, he landed on a piece of helicopter which broke his fall and saved him from dropping at least ten more feet.

Suddenly a shadow fell over everything, but Marianne couldn't look up to see why. With Max in the hole, she was face to face with the dinosaur. She screamed.

The dinosaur screamed back, a roar of absolute terror.

Tatiana pulled on Marianne's arm and dragged her backwards along the thin ledge. Gunfire erupted, an automatic weapon. Marianne waited for the slugs to tear her apart, but she didn't even hear them impacting the walls... strange.

She looked up at Grosjean. The woman stood on the other side, shooting her rifle... upward.

That was when Marianne understood the shadow. The arachnid nightmare was coming home.

It looked angry.

She nearly fell off the ledge in her drive to try to get under the dubious cover of a pile of rubble. Anything was better than being stuck out in the open.

***

Max looked up. The monster climbing down at them was enormous. Eight shiny black eyes stared… but he couldn't tell what it was they were staring at. At him, at Selene, at something else, there was no way to guess. He had no clue how spider eyes worked.

The walls, already damaged by the initial collapse and the monster's climb from the depths, crumbled as it descended, but the creature never looked like it was about to fall; eight legs must have distributed the weight well enough.

Selene might be a bitch, but at least she was serving a purpose. By unloading an entire clip at the monster, she was definitely calling attention to herself… and therefore away from him. His flight instinct was fully awake and aware, making it difficult to stay still, but he wasn't getting any specific warnings from the sixth sense that often warned him when he was the object of observation. If it was his money, he'd bet that the thing's inscrutable attention was elsewhere.

A minute later, the feeling was confirmed: the creature finished scuttling down the wall, dislodging alarming chunks of concrete that dropped around him, and stood on the wreckage of the downed helicopters.

One leg barely missed crushing Max to pulp, and that was the one that confirmed his feeling that the thing hadn't seen him. He was underneath the beast's stomach, pulse racing while he searched for the weak spot, the missing scale—even though the arachnid had no scales— that was always there for the hero to exploit in the movies. There had to be something, some weakness. But his scan, even in the full sunlight that reached them through the shaft above, revealed nothing. If anything, the bottom of the monster looked even more heavily armored than the top, with thick ridges running across it.

He would need an RPG to even dent the thing.

Max rolled to the side and emerged from under the spider, careful to stay out of its sight, which meant rolling towards its back as silently as he could.

That gave him a much closer look at the tail than he'd ever wanted. Black, like the rest of the creature, it was segmented in ten-centimeter increments, topped with a stinger as long as the spear he still held in the hand not holding the handgun.

But there didn't seem to be any vulnerability there, either. Even the articulations looked impenetrable. And he didn't want to draw attention to himself.

The creature's weight had levered one of the helicopter panels up so that it reached the ledge above. He hurried up, balancing the need to reach the top before the thing decided to move with the even more pressing need to not be seen or sensed or whatever... he thought spiders were particularly attuned to vibrations in their surroundings—with hairs or something—and he didn't want to let it know he was there.

But the monster seemed to have other concerns. In a sudden frenzy, its pincers assaulted the pile of rubble before it, sending rocks the size of motorcycles into the air.

He saw no sign of Marianne or Vasily anywhere, but his heart fell as he realized that they must have hidden behind the very pile that the thing was attacking; there was no other reason for such vigor.

With a huge swipe, the rubble was cleared, big rocks flying through the air with crushing force.

In the space they'd occupied, a single figure stood: Tatiana, the Brazilian journalist, wearing a look he'd seen before, the look of someone petrified with fear, rooted to the spot. He wanted to shout at her to run, to duck, anything, but to react. But shouting would just get him killed, too.

Her motionlessness lasted only a split second as the monster considered its next move now that it had uncovered her and then she seemed to wake with a start, took half a step back and screamed, a sound of pure terror. She took another step back, and started to turn, probably to run.

That was as far as she got. With an audible hum, the tail, dormant until then, suddenly flashed up and over the entire creature and impaled her sternum, tearing her chest in half. Blood flew everywhere, spraying the walls behind her.

Tatiana's head, mouth still screaming, now silently, and shoulders fell to the ground, completely separate from the rest of her torso.

The monster's pincer then grabbed a leg and, almost contemptuously, tore off a morsel of what had once been a beautiful, vibrant woman and ate it.

It left the rest of the dead flesh where it had fallen and turned slightly to face Selene.

Selene wasn't a poor journalist who'd never stared death in the face. Like Max, she sensed the danger and dove aside an instant before a claw decapitated her. She rolled behind a partition and out of sight.

The creature, apparently unfazed, simply clobbered the wall behind which Selene had disappeared, tearing it apart like paper. It wasn't paper; a brick rebounded off another wall and landed by Max's feet.

While the monster was busy ripping the building apart—he wondered how they'd managed to keep it contained if it could remove brick walls at will—he scanned the lower level for any sign of Vasily or Marianne. He also glanced back in the direction where Selene's pet had been waiting, at the far end of the ledge. It would be silly to lose track of it. Dead was dead, and if he had to die, better in the pincers of the Godzilla spider than in the jaws of a second-rate monster like the dinosaur. Spetsnaz warriors were meant to die epically.

There was no sign of the deinonychus, so he inched across the ledge, carefully looking away from Tatiana's mangled remains. He tried to go slowly to avoid calling attention to himself.

He needn't have bothered. The colossal spider-scorpion was hard at work trying to dig Selene out, and every once in a while, the bark of a handgun could be heard. Max grinned: she must have dropped her rifle... and if the rifle rounds hadn't done much, her pop gun wasn't going to help her. Selene Grosjean would become a monster munchie.

Couldn't have happened to a nicer bitch-whore from hell, he thought. And, better still, by playing hard to get, she was buying Max some very valuable time.

A screech behind him turned his legs to jelly. He whipped around in time to see a charging form shoot past, actually whipping him with feathers as it went. Selene's tame dino, running the wrong way. Any intelligent entity would have known that the correct direction was away from gigantic spiders. Fortunately, he was already off the ledge. Even more fortunately, the dinosaur ignored him completely and, in an almost ridiculously comical display of—what? Loyalty? Instinct? Stupidity?—it launched itself at the monster, easily ten times its size, landed on one of its arms and started biting the nearest pincer.

The spider went completely still again. It was huge and well-armored, but it seemed to take a few seconds to process any change in the situation. That was all well and good, but buying a couple of seconds was only useful if one could actually attack the thing or escape effectively. That didn't seem to be the case for the dinosaur, however.

"Max," he heard Vasily whisper. "Over here."

Vasily's head poked out from what-before one of the walls was torn away-had been a lavatory. Due to the angle of the walls, it was hidden from view because the monster's head was simply too big to fit around into the thin passage leading to it. And the walls were nice load-bearing concrete, not brick. It was a well-chosen hideaway.

Max dove in and found the reporter there, too. It felt like a weight came off his shoulders, but he certainly wasn't expecting her to hug him like a long-lost cousin. Vasily spoke. "I'm sorry, I couldn't save the other woman. She just wouldn't move, and I was too far away to reach her before…"

"It's not your fault," Max said. "This isn't a normal situation, and she wasn't trained for this kind of thing. Where's the Korean?"

"I don't know. Last I saw him was when the spider attacked the pile of rocks we were trying to hide behind. It scattered us all. I landed on Marianne, and I think Sun-Lee was pushed the other way. Only Tatiana stayed where she was because none of the stones hit her… she was the unlucky one."

Max looked out of the doorway. The rocks had flown in every direction, but there was still a good pile on one side. Odds were that the erstwhile director was under it. Max shrugged. The man might not be as bad as Selene, but he was a cold, heartless bastard. No one would lose much sleep for that man except, possibly, the employees of whichever escort service he used in Yekaterinburg. He was rumored to be very rich as well as powerful.

A war seemed to be raging between the two monsters in the shaft. Somehow, the dinosaur was still alive. It was either smarter than it looked or a lot luckier than it deserved to be.

Most importantly, it was a distraction.

"We need to run, right now," Max said.

"Are you crazy?"

"Maybe. But I'd rather try to get out of here than hide in the fucking thing's nest. How long do you think it would take to root us out?" He turned to Marianne. "Can you run?"

She smiled. "It seems like that's all I've been doing lately. A little more won't hurt me."

"Good. I'll go first, then you. Vasily last. Okay?"

"Okay," she replied. Vasily nodded.

"Go!"

They sprinted across the ledge. To Max's complete surprise, they arrived on the other side without dying horribly and sprinted down a staircase at the end. Vasily stopped about halfway down and lay on the stairs watching what was happening behind them. After a few seconds, he joined them.

"It's the craziest thing," Vasily said. "The little one is very fast, but even more, it's smart. It's staying to one side, where the tail can't get him and forcing the big monster to rotate around and around. He even hides behind things and comes out where the other one isn't expecting it. I've never seen anything like it. It's the kind of thing I would do in combat."

"Well, with any luck they'll kill each other."

"I no longer believe in luck. Well, except bad luck."

"That makes two of us."

They continued down the hall. It was quite wide once they got off the stairwell, and he wondered whether trucks used to haul missiles through this one as well.

Then the hall turned to the left—a gentle curve that would have been navigable by tractor trailers—and opened up into a well-lit tunnel that could have been the twin of the one that brought them to the valley, right down to the lack of use and encrusted cracks in the ceiling. The only difference, and one that was as welcome as it was unexpected, was a row of golf carts parked along the wall.

"This should make things easier," Max said.

"Not fancying a walk?" Vasily replied. He jumped into the nearest cart and floored the accelerator. Nothing happened. "It figures. Dead as a Jew in a Cossack pogrom."

"A what?" Max said. "Sometimes you talk like a country bumpkin from a hundred years ago."

Vasily laughed. "You should have seen me a hundred years ago: Everyone thought I was the latest fashion. Maybe I should have kept up with the times."

"And with the fact that we no longer kill people for having the wrong religion."

"Back in my day, we'd kill them for having *any* religion. The state had to come first."

"Vasily, you're an asshole. Can you get these things to run?"

The soldier, while he spoke, had already begun to dismantle the cart, popping open the plastic cover over the battery. "I think so. This power pack is only a couple of years old, and these industrial ones should last a lot longer than that. Now where…" He looked around the tunnel. "There! A charging station. I knew nobody could be stupid enough to leave this many carts lying around unless there was a way to charge them nearby."

"This is Russia," Max reminded him.

"Not even here, Max."

He chuckled and went back to check on the girl. She had walked ahead a little and was sitting on the back bumper of a cart beside a maintenance port that penetrated about five meters into the wall.

"You okay?" he said.

"No. I'm not fucking okay," Marianne replied. "I lost two friends in this disaster. Tatiana was a good woman; she was going to be one hell of an important journalist one day. I lucked into my big story, but she was always going to make it. Everyone knew it."

"I'm sorry."

"Yeah, I know. You've done everything you can." She stood and he saw a single tear running down her cheek.

He reached out and brushed it away.

That earned him a lopsided smile. "You know, if the situation were different, I'd take you home. You're exactly my type," she said.

"What, tall and handsome?" he said, trying to lighten the mood.

"No." The smile disappeared. "You're completely wrong for me. Dangerous, uncivilized, violent."

He was taken aback, and she must have noticed because she suddenly stood on tiptoes and brushed his lips with hers.

Max returned the kiss. At first her lips were hard, but then she opened her mouth and accepted him. She even pulled him into the little access port and let him press her into the wall, kissing him like there was no tomorrow.

Then she pushed him away. "Keep holding that thought," she said.

"I would much rather express it now," he replied.

She didn't answer, just laughed a dark little laugh. "Get us out of this alive, and we can get it on. I can't shake the feeling that every monster back there is still out to get us. Especially that crazy woman."

He pulled away, and her arm lingered on his. He nearly closed up on her again. Something about the way she held herself told him that her determination to get out alive was warring with her desire to give all her emotions an outlet that very instant. He pulled away with a number of regrets. And went back out into the main tunnel.

"How are we doing, Vasily?"

"Are you in a hurry?"

"Yeah. And though I have no idea what might be coming through that tunnel behind us, I am just going to assume it will be nothing less than the entire People's Liberation Army. So yes, I want to get the hell out of here."

"Then you're in luck. This one was actually reasonably charged. I just need fifteen more minutes to top up the batteries."

Fifteen minutes… damn. That would have given them time to do more than kiss. Not to do it right, but it was better than this yearning. But he couldn't go back now. Vasily would immediately know what was going on, and he'd hide somewhere and watch.

"How's our little lady holding up?"

"Scared. Angry. Just like anyone would be in her position."

"Tell her from me that I'm impressed with how she's holding up. It isn't often that I wish I spoke English, but that one almost makes it worth it."

Max smiled. "I'll tell her." Vasily was a good guy. You had to scratch below the surface for it to become evident, but his heart was in the right place. Of course, that wouldn't stop him from trying to steal the girl if Max dropped his guard, but that was only natural among soldiers. Yekaterinburg was an actual city... but the ratio near a base was sometimes fifty soldiers to every buck-toothed, cross-eyed peasant woman of forty. It was quite normal for things to get competitive.

Vasily shouldn't expect English lessons from Max any time soon.

*** *

The evenly-spaced lights and the hum of the wheels on the concrete were hypnotic. Already bone-tired, Marianne began to doze, and caught herself with a start. She couldn't allow herself to sleep until she was safe, and that meant somewhere outside of Russia, preferably New York.

She concentrated on keeping her eyes open. To do so, she thought about Max, and all the reasons he was utterly wrong for her. This was a man who killed people for a living. No one had forced him to choose that career path, he had done it because he *wanted* to be surrounded by guns and explosives and other men who also wanted to do violence in the name of nationalism. Because, once you came down to it, that was what it was. She understood that many were seduced by the dream of serving their country... but she'd never been able to see it that way, despite more than one long argument with true believers.

That made her chuckle and took her to a bar in Los Angeles where she'd met a guy named Carlos Gutierrez, who was some kind of... she wanted to say sergeant, but she wasn't really sure. He definitely wasn't an officer, as that was a class whose sexual deviations he described in particularly graphic language.

The guy had spent an hour-over way too many drinks-explaining why what he did was a privilege and an honor, and protesting that he couldn't understand how some people didn't see it.

When Marianne had replied that she was one of those 'some people', the guy had just grinned and said, "Well, there's a long-standing military tradition to forgive such ignorance if the score is gorgeous."

"Did you just call me a score?"

"No. You're a broad for now. You only graduate to score if I get your panties off."

That one had been all wrong for her, and she'd fallen for every subsequent line up to and including when he poured her a glass of wine and said: "Congratulations. *Now*, you're a score."

But that was actually sane compared to some of the guys in her life. At least she hadn't fallen in love, and at least he was a guy with which they had a cultural background in common.

Her true regrets always came back to the same guy.

Konstantinos.

She laughed to herself. Now *that* was one fucked up dude. A petty criminal who'd gotten in over his head and then became a freaking monk of all things. And she'd slept with him.

Of course, the man was brilliant. He'd written a book that turned the publishing world on its ear, and then, after helping save her from the criminals who didn't want the truth about his old activities to surface, he'd returned to the monastery, eschewing promises of money and fame.

He'd been smarter than Marianne, that was for certain. When he had the opportunity to remove himself from the cloistered life and enjoy himself with her at his side, he refused. He knew that he was too fragile to live in a world that afforded him such freedoms, knew that he would collapse under the weight of being responsible for himself. So he left it, and her, behind.

The funniest part of it was that if one of her friends had told Marianne that she was involved in something like that, Marianne would have sat her down for a long and heartfelt talking-to… once she stopped laughing. A criminal and a monk. A man who took orders and lived, of all places, on Mount Athos, the one piece of land on the planet where women were literally forbidden to tread. Not kept off by custom or prejudice but actually proscribed by law?

It sounded like a bad joke, an exaggerated case study for a practicing psychologist, pulled from the plot of an over-the-top, if entertaining, erotic-romance-crime mashup. Hell, she would have called the resulting novel *Timeless*, since that was the name of the book the guy had written and the way life seemed on Mount Athos.

She would have told her friend that, at the bottom of it all, she had chosen this guy precisely because he was trouble. She was self-sabotaging, and all she had to do was to stop, look at herself objectively and find a guy worthy of her.

That was what Marianne had been trying to do ever since the monk disappeared back into his medieval world without a phone and without an internet connection.

She'd gone out with stockbrokers and surgeons, with actors and poets. A few of them were jerks, some were worse than that. But there were also plenty of good guys in the mix, men who treated her well and were genuinely interesting to talk to. Some were quite adept in bed, too.

But none lit the same spark. None made her yearn to see them again, and to see them every day. That had been missing from every single one of them.

Until now.

Of course, she wasn't in love with Max. She just found him attractive. But she knew all the signs. As soon as she could take a breath, stop running from stuff that wanted to kill her, she would ache to be with Max, to have him take her hand and lead her to the altar, or whatever it was Russians did nowadays.

He's a killer, she told herself. *A special forces soldier working for the fucking Russians. Come on. Their specialty is killing people in the night, people who never even saw them coming. Probably noncombatants. Women and children.*

Which was all true, but when she was staring up at the ceiling above her bed in the middle of the night after returning safely to the US, that wasn't what she'd remember. She'd remember the man who'd risked everything to save her from becoming just a dead tourist, a corpse with a bullet in its head beside a Russian road. The man who'd helped her pull through dangers she'd never imagined... all because he'd decided it was the right thing to do.

Yeah, the moral argument was going to lose, and lose big.

***

Max drove, pedal to the floor. The cart was probably the slowest vehicle he'd ever been involved with, but it was still better than walking. He was tired of walking. In fact, he was so tired of the very thought of it that he would give his men a nice rest from any long hikes when he got back.

The good thing was that, with Selene dead, he would be in the clear: all he had to do to explain losing two soldiers was to say that she'd commandeered them to help and he, as a loyal Russian, had rushed to her aid.

Of course, that would only work with his superiors. The families of his men were a different matter altogether. He dreaded, more than he'd ever dreaded anything, having to tell someone that their father or husband was gone, never to return.

He wondered what Marianne was thinking. She'd been strangely silent the entire way. She wasn't crying, just staring straight ahead with her eyes half closed.

Then he heard it. Behind them, a sound like someone tearing a large metal structure apart.

No. Not someone... some*thing*. He knew immediately that the giant spider had found the exit, and was tearing away the stairs to expose the tunnel. A mere metal latticework from the Soviet era wasn't going to hold it for long.

He exchanged glances with Vasily who was sitting on the parcel shelf behind him and tried to coax more speed from the cart.

It was no use. They were going as fast as they could.

CHAPTER 10

Selene groaned and felt her head. That bump on her forehead was not going to do much for her complexion. She was already worried about getting old, and this clusterfuck had probably added years of wear and tear to her features.

Not that she cared for beauty per se. She'd always had it and always taken it for granted, but it wasn't her objective. It was just another tool, like staying fit, spending an hour at the firing range or keeping up with the latest political news in the world. Beauty gave her an edge. Men who insisted on thinking with their dicks—and in her experience, that didn't leave many of them out—would be at a disadvantage, distracted by things other than the matters at hand.

It was very satisfying to her that so many men simply missed out on the fact that the person who would, a few minutes, hours or weeks later, be putting a bullet in their head was the one they'd just undressed with their eyes.

But she had other tools, and when she got back, all of them would be strained to the breaking point as she fought a multi-front war trying to kill the renegade Spetsnaz troops and the North Korean while staying alive herself. There were no guarantees.

She got to her hands and knees. A dusty chunk of concrete the size and shape of a hardbound book fell from her back and onto the floor with a clatter.

Selene froze. Making noise was a good way to become dead.

But she realized that any noise would be lost in the background. Something—not her—was making a huge din. She hadn't noticed it before because of the ringing in her head.

She made a mental note to get herself checked for a concussion. She'd taken a bigger hit than she realized.

Rising carefully to her feet, Selene surveyed the area around her. She'd been lying a good three meters farther from the ledge than she remembered standing. In fact, the last thing she could recall was that the monster had done something that made her think it was coming for her, so she'd jumped behind a wall.

There was no sign of the wall now, just a bunch of small rocks and brick fragments.

The furious sound came from the hole where the helicopters had fallen, and she needed to know what was going on, despite a certainty that finding out would put her in even more danger.

Selene walked unsteadily, trying to avoid twisting an ankle on the rubble. She smirked. That would be a pretty dumb way to bring her own death onto her head. A sprained ankle that made her too slow to run from even the small dinosaurs. She'd be really pissed if she went all the way up the stairs on a bum leg to get killed by some Jurassic runt.

The helicopters were right where she'd left them. It seemed like they might be a little more dented than before, but she honestly couldn't tell. They were pretty fucked up to begin with.

Surprisingly, the pit wasn't the source of the noise.

She took another step and her foot landed in something soft. She looked down, and regretted it immediately: she was standing in a large gobbet of meat. What kind of meat, she had no idea, but after watching that Brazilian woman get filleted, she could make a pretty good guess.

Whatever. She'd seen dead bodies before; she just put it out of her head and kept walking. The important thing now was to identify the source of the noise. Whatever was making it had the capacity to wreak some serious havoc, and she wanted to be sure she knew where it was, what it was doing, and how long it would take until it killed her.

With the kind of day she'd been having so far, she found it unlikely that anything making that much noise was doing it for any other reason than to finally kill her off.

There! She saw a thick black pole in a place it shouldn't be. No. Not a pole, a leg. One of the big monster's legs. It stuck out from a hole across the pit from her.

Not a hole... a burrow. The thing had dug itself a nest, like those holes surrounded by spider's webs one saw in the chinks in brick walls.

Whatever the reason, it didn't appear content with what it had achieved. Every five seconds or so, the screeching would reach her, the leg would wriggle, and a chunk of metal would be pushed out of the burrow.

Among the mangled, unidentifiable bits, three steps from a steel staircase popped out.

The monster was digging into a stairwell. But why?

It probably had its reasons, and she wasn't necessarily dying to find out. She turned away.

A whimper caught her attention and she returned to where she'd fallen to dig out her handgun. Fortunately, it was buried only under a layer of dust and she was able to retrieve it easily. It looked all right, so she dusted it off and walked towards the sound.

Someone had survived the monster's rage.

She'd fix that.

She clambered over a collapsed wall and stopped.

The sound wasn't coming from one of her enemies. It came from one of her own, her last deinonychus.

How it had survived was beyond her. The killing blow—because, alive or not, it was certainly dying—had spilled most of its intestines onto the dusty floor onto the red mud that sprung from combining gallons and gallons of blood with the tons of dust that seemed to have been created when the building collapsed.

As she came into its sight, the monster tried to move its head.

"No," Selene said. "Stay still."

She sat beside it and it mewled plaintively, an insane sound to come from a creature that size. It was the sound of a dying baby bird, drowned in a storm after its mother flew to safety, not of something bigger than a horse.

The arm—it was huge despite looking puny compared to the rest of the dinosaur—inched towards her and she took one talon in her hands.

The mad, brown-and-pupil eye never left her face. The whimpering didn't stop. It was as if the creature was trying to talk to her, the human brain inside making its final attempt to communicate despite not having a voice box to talk with.

That lasted only a couple of minutes. Then the eye filmed over and the whimpering stopped.

Selene wiped a single tear from her cheek, angry with herself. Weakness would get her killed. She'd seen countless people die, men, women and children. Many had died at her hand, others by her orders. She knew that you could never let your guard down, or it would be you on the wrong side of the garotte to the neck.

That this creature, a pathetic thing that was once a man, and also never was a man, had died for her made no difference. It was just another dead thing.

But her rage, the rage she always carried, had disappeared. Her anger was beating to be let out. She let it come.

Because she now knew what the monster was digging for. It wasn't making a burrow... it was chasing the little creatures that had escaped it. Or maybe looking for a way out.

Either way, she understood. It was angry, it was confused.

And it wasn't the kind of creature that would just lie down and take it. It was going to make its feelings felt.

Selene smiled at the black leg which was all she could see of the abomination. Yes, they understood each other.

***

Park Sun-Lee watched Selene as she watched the monster. He was still stunned at how utterly stupid everyone seemed to have become all of a sudden. Instead of getting themselves out of harm's way by going deep into the old Soviet factory, where tons of concrete would buy them time until the monster disappeared, they'd just stood there, allowing themselves to be slaughtered.

Even Tatiana, who he thought was smarter than that.

Hell, even one of the uplifted deinonychus, who should definitely have been smarter than that.

And now, Selene gave every indication that she was going to follow the monster. That was just about as dumb as anything he'd seen so far.

Dumber still, Park realized that he was going to chase Selene. She was ripe for ambush... convinced that everything in the complex was dead, she would be looking for danger in front of her.

That wasn't where the danger would be.

Waiting was the hardest part. He wanted to run up behind her and push her into the sub-basement, but that just wasn't feasible. Selene wasn't the kind of woman that you could just walk up behind and attack with your bare hands. Well, maybe one of the Spetsnaz guys could take her, but it was beyond his own ability.

So he needed to remain silent and wait until Selene left the area. Then he would sprint up the stairs and retrieve the gun he'd stupidly left in the safe in his office. Once that was done, he would be equipped to deal with Selene both as she deserved and as prudence dictated: he would shoot her in the back.

Philippe's spider monster had disappeared a few minutes ago, but Selene just stood, rooted in place like she meant to remain there forever. Was she waiting for something? He didn't even want to breathe in case she heard him. The troops called her the witch-woman, something that he, as a scientist who was secure in the knowledge that she really couldn't do anything to harm him, always discounted.

It was one thing to snicker at the enlisted men from the familiar confines of the corridors of power, quite another to try to laugh it off in the ruins of a Soviet weapons plant surrounded by the flesh torn from recently dead victims.

Perhaps he wouldn't have had chills if she'd sat down to have a good cry or shown some other human emotion. But that wasn't Selene. The woman was standing, still as a statue, looking in the direction the monster had disappeared, waiting for the coast to be clear enough to continue. She was like the Terminator.

Park smiled. That would make shooting her all the more satisfying. When he got out of this mess, he'd let the truth leak. Hundreds of Russians, both in the military field and in espionage rings around the country, would raise a glass in his honor... a nice change from the way people normally spoke about him.

Finally, Selene walked. She stepped across the ledge around the opening which led to the sub-basements. He watched her walk. Any man with a pulse would have watched her walk, but only those who knew nothing about her would have acted on the impulse to do more than watch. She was death on the hoof.

When she finally disappeared into the pile of debris the monster had pulled up, Park counted to sixty, forcing himself to go slowly, and then sprinted up the stairs, opened the safe and pulled out the Type 70 pistol he'd brought with him from North Korea. The idiots in Pyongyang had trusted him, thought he was part of the power structure and could therefore be allowed to leave the country. Luckily, on his first outing, they'd sent him to Damascus... a place from which it was extremely easy to lose his minders and disappear.

Everyone had thought he'd defected to one of the Western powers, and spies by the dozens, hackers and anyone who worked on gathering personal information for the régime was co-opted to try to find him.

In the meantime, Park had been installed in a small hotel in Latakia, a place that, he'd later learned, would have been a cheap motel anywhere else, but which, to his North Korean eyes, seemed the pinnacle of Western decadence. No one cared who he was or where he came from, and it would have been hard to find common ground anyway, as most Syrians only spoke a very tiny amount of English, and Park spoke no Arabic. His interpreter—who worked for the Ministry of Security, of course—was one of the men who were probably locked in a dungeon in Pyongyang, being slowly tortured to death for the heinous crime of allowing an important scientist to defect. The hotel clerk thought he was Chinese.

The problem, of course, was how to get out of Syria. Latakia was not expensive, but his supply of lira, though generous—no one back home really understood how money worked abroad—would not last forever.

Park was not without contacts in the outer world, but using them was risky. Who wouldn't be on Pyongyang's radar?

Vladimir Petrovich. That's who. Park had sent an email to his old colleague. The man had replied that Park should stay where he was and that Vladimir would try to help. Just a week later a man had sat across the table unexpectedly while Park was having lunch at his favorite terrace restaurant overlooking the Mediterranean.

"Are you here to take me back?" Park asked, resigned. He'd been expecting the net to close over him ever since he'd run for it.

"No. Vladimir sent me. I work for Mother Russia, not for your petty dictator."

Park's hackles rose and he almost defended his homeland. But then he realized he was being tested. "Good," he replied. "Do you have a way out?"

"Parked in the port."

"Where are we going?"

"Away."

Park smiled. He hated this kind of thing, but it was the sign of a professional to never let anyone know more than they needed to.

Pyongyang's misjudgment had been Moscow's gain. Once they were satisfied that Vladimir hadn't exaggerated Park's credentials, they gave him a lab and a team. Once he proved in the lab that he would be a huge asset, they gave him money and luxury and women. Whatever he desired was his to command.

But he was destined for bigger things. His team was well trained, so they could continue his work, once they understood the ambitious scope. But Park wouldn't be there to lead it.

The gun felt nicely heavy in his hand. A little reminder from home that he'd refused to give up even when his new Russian masters had assigned him a security detail. He knew that, sometimes, you had to protect yourself.

The Russians had just shrugged. They were convinced he wouldn't leave his position as long as he lived like a king.

They, too, had misread him, and they, too would learn it at their cost.

A North Korean could never be his own master while he was stuck in Russia. And though the luxuries abounded, he was always very aware that the money he was spending wasn't his... and that none of the women ever came back for a second bout. They were probably spies sent to keep an eye on him, being debriefed in Moscow as soon as he let them out of his bed.

Not that he held it against them. Quite a number of them were very good at what they did, and that was the only thing that mattered. He would soon be a plutocrat in his own right, and that would bring a higher class of whore... the kind who would stick around so that *she* was the one getting the luxuries.

He went down the stairs—thanking a childhood of North Korean physical training for the fact that he could, despite living the good life for the past few years and was in anything but excellent shape, overcome the physical strain by sheer willpower.

When he reached the opening where first Philippe's monster and then the woman had disappeared, he paused to listen.

He heard something, but not what he expected. Not where he expected it, either. This sound was behind him.

His heart sank. He knew in his bones that the game was up, that Selene had known where he was all along and had simply returned once he'd cleared out to ambush him. She was a crack marksman, the bullet would hit him dead center in the back of his head.

So he turned around slowly, not even raising his gun. When you were a dead man, a few more minutes of life were more precious than all the hope in the world.

It wasn't Grosjean.

Chiffon, the little monkey-like creature, sat on a rock, scratching itself as it observed him. Park breathed a sigh of relief and strode over to ruffle the thing's hair. He'd grown quite attached to it over the past few months and understood why Philippe had been so loathe to part with it when Park had taken it. In fact, other than to take a few blood samples and study how the different genetic parts interacted, Park had refused to hurt his pet. "Well, come along then," he said. "We need to get moving if we're going to shoot that bitch."

As the words came out, he considered once again just what he was thinking of doing. He had a chance to get the hell out of there now. He could talk his way out of any questions at the main complex back by the road. He could say that Selene had gone rogue. They'd believe him.

But that would mean having Selene on his tail forever. As soon as she talked her way back into her masters' good graces, she'd come after him. It wouldn't be a good life.

So there was really no choice. He needed to see her die, or he would be a hounded man.

Chiffon jumped off the rock and came with him.

The first obstacle was the hole the monster had dug to get into the lower level. Though the tunnel where the stairs had been was wide enough to take a truck, it was also uneven, and he had to climb down. It took him an hour: an hour in which Selene could be escaping.

Once down, he headed for the tunnel. It was the only place big enough to hold a monster that size. He just hoped they hadn't taken all the good golf carts. When he came on official business, he normally drove up in a small pickup truck, but they kept the carts—left over from when the facility had belonged to the GRU—charged in case an assistant needed one.

Damn. The orange one he usually chose was gone. The rest, he knew from experience, were pretty much all crap.

But he knew something the others didn't: he knew where the charging station was at the other end, which meant that, if he needed the cart to drive up the mountain path they would almost certainly have to take, he could charge it there. And that meant he wouldn't have to spend too long charging the thing. He could give it a ten-minute quick charge and get moving.

"Come on, Chiffon," he said. "Let's go."

The monkey-thing jumped onto the nearest cart as he extended the cable to the charger. If he was too late, no worries.

Maybe Grosjean thought he was already dead.

***

Selene cursed the cart. She could have made better time if she got off and ran... but only if the tunnel ended soon. Otherwise, she would lose time when she tired. That meant that she had to stay with the program and keep her butt on the cart. She couldn't waste any more time.

The monster was going after someone, and Selene was betting that it was going after Max, the North Korean and the reporter.

Unfortunately, the drive also gave her time to consider what she should do next. Sun-Lee was either dead or would be once she caught up, which meant that her superiors' desire to have someone take the fall for this debacle would, to a degree, be sated. The problem was that even a scapegoat might not be enough to get her off the hook.

This was, quite honestly, a clusterfuck of spectacular proportions. The intelligence agency she worked for was small, elite and so vicious that it made Stalin's version of the KGB look like a bunch of teddy bears. They were not noted for tolerating failure.

She'd played the game long enough to know that the odds of getting out of this one alive were about fifty-fifty. Unusually, however, they would increase with the body count.

Thanks to the reporters and Sun-Lee, the world now knew about the escaped dinosaurs at YekLab, but that was not a real issue. The dead were employees of the same lab that had been conducting the research. They could pretty much be shrugged off as a private company that had, for profit reasons, gone well beyond the bounds of legal action. The morons on social media would lap it up. They believed the myth that evil billionaires were responsible for all their self-inflicted ills.

The world press would flock there, but that was easily dealt with. They'd be shown a dead deinonychus and told that the creature was the one that had caused all the damage and that, unfortunately, the people responsible for creating it had died. Then they would be shooed back to their countries.

Her one major concern was whether Sun-Lee had managed to transmit any images out of the valley they were now leaving. If he had, she was screwed no matter what she did... The man had a satellite phone. Someone had trusted him.

Trusting people always ended with dead bodies scattered across the landscape. It was a lesson best taken to heart.

So she needed to keep him alive a couple of minutes to ask him if the story was out.

If he was dead, the first thing she needed to do was to check the internet as soon as she got out of the tunnel.

If there was any news about the events of that morning, she needed to run.

But where to go if the situation deteriorated beyond her ability to fix it?

That was a question whose final solution would have to wait. The first thing she needed to do was to get out of Russia. From Yekaterinburg, that meant getting to Kazakhstan.

Unfortunately, Astana was a little too friendly with Moscow for her to be able to remain in the country once she got there. She'd need to head for the Caspian Sea and try to make it to Azerbaijan and then to the Black Sea via Georgia. That part of the journey would require Crypto, and lots of it—which, of course, she had. The problem would be to find smugglers who accepted Lightcoin. She had no idea how easy that would be.

Only when she made it to Bulgaria could she risk using her false IDs and traveling on her Swiss accounts. Even if her masters could trace her, it would take a while. After that, there were really only three options, places that could swallow her up without a trace: Latin America, Southeast Asia and Africa.

She would stick out a little too much in Africa, but Latin America... that could work. The vastness of Patagonia was easy to enter—the Argentine authorities let everyone and anyone into the country—and very difficult to search. French tourists were a dime a dozen, and no one liked talking to cops.

Yeah, that would work.

It was good to have a backup plan, but plan A was still in operation. If she could salvage something from this train wreck, she would try that first.

She tried to coax more speed out of the cart, but it stuttered, so she eased off. Having to walk would just slow her down.

A second later, she slammed on the brakes. She'd just finished taking a gentle curve in the tunnel and saw, up ahead, the silhouette of the giant monster blocking the light. It was moving slowly.

Getting closer was not an option, and she hoped it didn't have any weird sensory equipment that would allow it to feel air vibrations from a mile away, like spiders who could sense the vibrations of their webs. If so, she was dead.

What the hell was it doing?

It soon became clear. It was trying to get out. If it was anything like the one back at the main facility, the door at the end was a camouflage element with two openings, one about the size of a regular garage door and one big enough to admit trucks. Max's group would not have bothered with the big door. They didn't need to open it in order to drive a golf cart out.

The monster was another story, however.

After poking its snout through the smaller opening, the creature must have reached the same conclusion. It began to tear at the doorway with the same noise and energy it had used to remove the stairwell.

Selene moved her cart slowly back to the curve in the tunnel. She would know when it was time to advance because the noise would stop.

In the meantime, it was healthier to stay out of sight.

***

Park thanked the spirits of his ancestors for the noise in the tunnel. Had there been no noise, Selene would have heard him approach.

As it was, he almost stumbled over her. The curve had hidden the woman from view until the last moment, and he slammed hard on the brakes fifty meters from her position.

Thankfully, she didn't see or hear him. She was staring straight ahead, as if waiting for a signal to proceed.

He engaged reverse and pulled back out of sight, and then descended from the cart.

His gun was in the front pocket of his pants and he removed the clip just to make certain it was loaded. He'd been responsible for a number of deaths, things he'd ordered directly or by default. There had been times when people working with deadly pathogens hadn't received the information they would have needed to protect themselves. He'd been the one to authorize that, and in fact had been lauded for it; the dead men and women had been of suspect loyalty, and the people he worked for had asked that they have an accident, which Park had duly supplied. He'd also sent people to deal with large dinosaurs... and many had failed to return.

But he'd never killed someone in direct combat. He'd never fired a gun at a living person. Even in his North Korean days, where they'd forced him to train with the firearm, he'd been an indifferent marksman at best and terrible compared to most who worked for the government. His war was fought in a lab, or on a computer. Guns were for cavemen.

And yet, here he was, given the opportunity to strike a blow for freedom. Admittedly it would be his own freedom, but it was still better than nothing. All he had to do was to get close enough to shoot Selene in the back without missing.

If he missed, he was dead. Selene was not a chubby scientist whose only claim to ever having been an athlete was surviving the Pyongyang régime. She was a gymnast and a killer and, moreover, she was one who'd kept her training up as opposed to letting herself get fluffy. She would probably weave over to where he was standing and pull his head off his shoulders, not even bothering to waste a bullet.

He stayed where he was. He couldn't risk it, and would have to wait until he somehow got closer. Either that or accept that he was going to have to live the rest of his life looking back over his shoulder. Selene was not the type to forgive and forget.

That thought brought him to the monster. When Park had first been in Panama, the madman Philippe had told him about this kind of creature, even said that he had some of the genetic material on hand to create some of the deadlier things he'd dreamed up.

He also said he hadn't done it yet because some creatures were nearly impossible to contain. That, at least, had been true.

Park wondered why he'd decided to build this ultimate monster.

He looked down at the creature next to him. Philippe had sworn there was no human DNA in it at all, that the intelligence in its eyes was all chimpanzee, and the loyalty was all dog... but it was hard to believe as it sat there silently, waiting like a comrade-in-arms.

Even after being shown Philippe's diagram and having the big monster in his keeping for months, Park still didn't know what it was made of. Some of the characteristics seemed obvious, and they'd been able to identify the arachnid strands in the DNA they'd taken from it.

What about the rest? There was mammal stuff in there, and part of his team was convinced that they could see human sequences. But they were interwoven with other stuff, and no one could figure out how. Hell, no one could figure out what was in there that made this thing gigantic instead of just a regular-sized scorpion.

Only Philippe knew, and he wasn't telling. The man had an intuitive grasp of how the building blocks of life went together, a grasp that all of Park's computers had thus far proven unable to duplicate.

All of that, however, paled when compared to the question that had been bugging him since he started following Selene.

Why was the monster following the mercenaries? There was no reason in any of the DNA strands—or in nature itself—to explain it.

Food? Why bother? It was expending much more energy to capture them than it would gain by eating them. And even if the equation did work out, why not simply consume the dead deinonychus in the shaft? Why not go after other dinosaurs in the valley? Those would keep it alive basically forever.

It made no sense unless he looked at it from a human point of view, and that meant not only assuming it had human DNA in it, but also that said genetic material at least partially affected the way it thought.

Most animals didn't kill for fun, especially if it meant going to such an effort. If it was hunting the troops and Miss Caruso down for sport, it was a very unusual behavior... for an animal.

But for a human? The reason you went after intruders was to keep them from coming back and threatening you. Animals didn't do that, people did.

He wasn't going to be able to answer it there. In fact, if someone had asked him what the thing would do if faced with this situation, he would have been completely wrong.

Then he laughed to himself. If it was chasing the people to keep them from coming back for it, then it certainly had a lot of human intelligence. After all, wasn't that what Park himself was doing?

Too bad Selene was a much smaller target than the spider creature. Even at fifty meters, he could hit that thing.

CHAPTER 11

Max growled in frustration as the golf cart spun its wheels.

"It hasn't rained in three weeks, why the hell is it so muddy?" he asked, adding a few choice words in Russian.

"Probably a burst pipe under the trail," Vasily replied.

"Under the whole trail? Look up there. It's mud all the way up."

Vasily shrugged. "This is Russia."

Marianne had already gotten out of the cart and was looking at the path ahead. "It doesn't look too tough. We can walk."

"The problem is what to do when we get to the top."

"Why do we need to go up there?" she said. "We can go in any direction."

"That's where the road is. At the top of that ridge over there."

"Oh. Well, I'm just glad you know where we are."

"We've hiked in these hills for years. Great place to train troops. To think we never knew what was over that mountainside…"

"Do we need to go all the way up? I mean, the road must come down sometime, right?"

"It's much shorter than going around. There's a ski resort at the top, and the road goes through the parking lot. We can reach it without climbing all the way because one of the lifts is just up ahead. But it's still a fifteen-minute hike from here. Uphill both ways."

"Huh?" Marianne asked.

"Just an old soldier's joke." He turned to Vasily. "Leave the cart. We'll hoof it."

"Shouldn't we hide it somewhere?"

"I don't think the thing following us will be able to use the cart to guess where we went. It might actually be better if we could find a stream. If we could walk in the water for a mile, that might throw it off the scent."

"It's not a dog, Max," the soldier replied.

The sun was starting its long descent. He estimated that it must be around four o'clock, which gave them six more hours of daylight. It felt like weeks since they'd encountered Marianne and Selene playing out their little drama at the side of the road. To think that, just twenty-four hours earlier, he'd been the leader of a group of men in line to get medals for a quick, successful and unorthodox mission brilliantly executed.

What was he now? He didn't know. He might simply be a guy AWOL from his base, or he might already have been declared a traitor to the Motherland. He wouldn't know until he saw the colonel's expression when he got back. That guy would never get anywhere: he couldn't lie for shit.

To describe his mood as they started up the path as black would have been a serious understatement but, as the meters became kilometers, he began to unwind. He couldn't help it; this was his natural reaction to hiking in the woods. No matter what awaited him, no matter what chased them—and he hoped it wasn't chasing them but trying to find a way out—and no matter how poorly he'd slept the night before, he would arrive at the end of this hike relaxed and alert. That was how hikes worked on his psyche.

He started noticing the trees, not just as a tapestry of greens, greys and browns that slipped past as they walked, but as trees. Each had its own scent, a specific sound the leaves made as the wind caressed them. He watched the birds and noticed the way the sunlight slanted through the canopy.

Max was a city boy, but once you became Spetsnaz, they left very little of Moscow in your makeup. You spent so much time walking through the scenery that you became attuned to its ways, and would often find yourself standing at a stoplight long after it had turned green, just because the rhythm of a town was so different.

He could never live in a city again, he knew. Life as a soldier had ruined it for him. The walls were too close, the people packed together like sardines, half of them wearing surgical masks, the other half glaring at the mask-wearers. He remembered his days in clubs, smoke-filled boxes with people pressing against him on all sides. How far away that seemed to him now.

The trail was short, but they were already tired, bruised and scraped. Had it not been a deadly-serious situation, he would have been griping about the unreal training scenarios the brass kept thinking up. An uphill hike after a grueling clusterfuck of an engagement would have been exactly the kind of thing officers liked to foist upon the men.

And then he laughed. This was the reason they thought up those exercises, of course. Because life out in the field was messy, and because plans tended to go very wrong the instant they came off the drawing board. An American soldier had once explained the concept of Murphy's law to him and, while he understood what the other man meant, he was shocked that Americans needed to give it a specific name. Russians knew that when everything that could go wrong, did go wrong, it wasn't anything special—it was just life.

He kept those thoughts to himself, though. If anyone who'd lived through the bad old days of communist rule heard him, he'd be stuck for hours listening to the stories of having to wait in line for food and how things were so much better now and he didn't know just how good youngsters these days had it. He could do without that.

"Do you really think we'll need the spear?" Marianne asked. She was smiling, which was something Max couldn't believe. He'd seen action to the west, and had been involved in relocating civilians. They generally had two attitudes towards the people who were trying to save them. When things were easy, and they had to walk through safe areas, they were sullen and complaining, as if they blamed the soldiers helping them for the conflict itself. Then, when the shooting started, they screamed and cried and begged for the soldiers to save them.

Of course, as soon as the danger passed, they went back to being the same ungrateful pricks they'd been before.

Here was a civilian who, through no fault of her own, was having a much worse time than any he could remember, and she was talking to him like they were on a romantic walk through the woods.

Max was beginning to suspect there was something seriously wrong with her. He ached to get to know her better and find out what it was.

"I will let go of this spear under exactly one condition," Max replied. "I want to be back in a base surrounded by armed Russian special forces soldiers. Inside that base, I will go inside a tank and put a shell in the barrel. Only then will I let go of it... but I will leave the spear where I can reach it."

Marianne laughed. "You make everything about death sound so funny. Are you going to tell me you weren't scared back there?"

He sighed. This conversation was one he'd had a million times before. Every time a green recruit came into his unit, they eventually got him alone somewhere and asked him, in hush-hush tones, to admit that he'd actually been scared shitless. The only defense you had in those situations was truth, but no one would ever believe you until they received their own baptism of fire.

"The truth of the matter is that when it hits the fan, the training takes over. You don't really stop to think, you just react. The time to be frightened is mainly before the action, although I know some guys who, after running the worst gauntlet you can think of without even breaking a sweat would get the shakes so bad afterwards that you would think he'd wilt with the first shot... if you hadn't just watched him charge a machine gun post. We just do our job, and the ones who will be afraid are caught and weeded out early. We don't want those people with us.

Our job is to kill the people trying to kill us. Cowards just make that job harder."

"I think that's the most knuckle-dragging macho answer I ever heard," Marianne said.

He wasn't quite sure if she was serious or teasing; either way, he had to defend his honor. "I didn't hear you complaining back there."

Marianne took a while to answer. "You're right. I wasn't. And I'm not complaining now."

"It sounded like it."

"I know. I'm sorry. It's just that I live in New York, and no man in the city would ever casually admit that his job is to kill people. They'd say their job is to protect people, or to promote freedom... or something. If there's violence involved, it needs to be wrapped in a protective layer. Sanitized."

Now Max laughed. "The oath I swore was to serve Russia. It didn't say anything about freedom or protecting people. Except Russians... but most of the time, there aren't any Russians around to protect. So, I ask you again: does it bother you that my job is to go outside of my country and take down people who work against it?"

"Intellectually? Maybe. But I find that it doesn't bother me at all in real life. I'm starting to think that the whole toxic masculinity thing is just a way for insecure people to attack the alphas. Maybe we should go back to how it used to be. You should get a club, hit me over the head and drag me back to your cave."

"Now I know you're teasing me."

Marianne laughed. "You need to stop being so perceptive, or it's going to ruin your macho image. You can be a knuckle-dragger or an intellectual, not both."

He'd known women—even here in Russia, they had women who tried to show how modern they were—who would have said something like that in all seriousness. He knew enough to just walk away and let those particular harpies deal with their internal demons without his help. But he had the sense that Marianne was making fun of people who made fun of people like him even as she was also teasing him. Her words were the standard spiel, but her eyes showed affection.

"That's an easy one. I choose to be a caveman, now and forever. All the intellectuals I've met are miserable bastards."

"Yeah, me too," Marianne said. "But they wouldn't give it up for anything in the world. They use their intellect to feel superior to people like you."

"Until we beat them to a pulp behind a bar."

"You could go to jail for that."

"In Russia? Don't make me laugh. Besides, I only use my fists."

Marianne laughed, but uncertainly, as if she was trying to figure out if he was joking. He was, but it was fun to catch her at her own game. "You can still go to jail for that."

"That's awful. How are you supposed to gently teach imbeciles the facts of life if you're not even allowed to use your fists? How can they learn? Americans are denying a valuable social service."

Max strode ahead, leaving Marianne with her mouth open.

He smiled.

Suddenly, from a tree to his left, a grey creature fluttered at full speed into the air and above the trees. His smile deepened: a Ural owl. They were supposed to be nocturnal, but he'd spotted plenty in daytime.

Vasily nodded in its direction. "Those are good luck."

"We could use some for a change," Max replied.

"Look over there," Vasily said.

A break in the trees revealed a white-painted house actually made of concrete rather than wood. It was as familiar to the soldiers as the roadside restaurant, as it was a place where they could actually goof off with the approval of the brass, at least in winter. Skiing was an integral part of the skillset expected of a Russian commando. The house concealed the mechanism for the chairlift.

"Can you get it running?"

"Probably. But we'll have to break some locks."

"Go ahead. If anyone asks, I'll tell them I ordered you to."

"With everything that's happened, you think they'll ask about *that*?"

"You said it yourself, my friend."

"What?"

"This is Russia."

***

Marianne stared at the cables running up the mountain and the large, Alpine-looking hotel beyond them, shuttered for the summer. The sheer normalcy of the scene threatened to overwhelm her tenuous grasp on reality.

It looked like any number of places she'd been. Unused ski resort, waiting for the first November snows to get its early-season tourists. It wasn't the kind of place where you ran away from monsters and crazy KGB bitches, it was the kind of place you snuggled up with a lover whose wife thought he was working at some dreadful corporate gathering. Hot chocolate, fires and Jacuzzis would feature prominently in that scene.

Vasily disappeared into the house nearest them, doing something loud and violent to the door in the process.

"Now what?" she asked.

"We're taking the chair lift up to the resort. From there, I'm hoping we can hitch a ride back to civilization."

"You have civilization here? Why didn't anyone tell me?" She paused. "Don't mind me. It's just that being chased by crazy secret agents and dinosaurs has this effect on me."

"Does it happen often?"

"Not exactly this, but if you replace the dinosaurs with smugglers and criminals, it's happened before."

"Really? You've been involved with criminals?"

"I don't know if you'd call it involved. I stumbled on a smuggling operation, so they kidnapped one of my friends and chased me all over Greece and Albania. I finally got them off my back with the help of the Calabrese mafia in Lecce."

"Lecce?"

"It's in Italy."

He studied her for a few moments. "You're telling the truth, aren't you?"

"I wish I wasn't, but yeah."

"No wonder you're so calm and collected."

"I think you must be thinking of someone else. I'm scared shitless, just like I was the last time they put a gun to my head. At least this time it's just dinosaurs and a woman. Last time, I thought they'd rape me before discarding my body in the sea."

"You shouldn't put anything past Selene."

"Well, she's gone now, so I don't need to worry about it."

A mechanical groan emerged from the house Vasily had disappeared into, followed by a humming sound.

"There we go," Max said.

They went around the house to where the chairs emerged from the darkness within. "They keep them hooked up all year?" Marianne said.

"I think they're welded to the cable," Max replied. "This isn't one of your high-tech resorts in America."

Vasily jumped onto a chair. He called something back to them in Russian. Max laughed.

"What was that about?"

"He says he promises not to look backwards so we'll have privacy."

"You, sir, will behave yourself or I'll take a different chair."

Max grabbed the next chair, angled it for her and, once she was on, jumped aboard. "Too late now."

Marianne snuggled in close and said. "You should have asked what I meant by behaving yourself."

He kissed her. Hard. Like he meant it. Like he wished they weren't on a chairlift in the middle of nowhere.

She kissed him back, and then pulled away as Vasily shouted something. "What is he saying now?"

"He says to keep our clothes on, because the lift won't take the swaying. Also, he... gave me some pointers about what I should do to you which flatly contradict his original suggestion. If you don't mind, I'll keep those to myself."

"Please do."

They rode in silence for a couple of moments, about thirty feet from the ground, occasionally passing over a tree which Marianne could have reached out and touched from where she was sitting. The view was simply spectacular: if they hadn't been seated on a chairlift, she would have been reminded of drone footage of empty wilderness. Trees, occasionally broken by grassy patches, and hills as far as the eye could see. It brought to mind camping trips out west.

"I can't believe that it's so peaceful, can you? How can something so empty be so dangerous?"

"The emptier a place, the more dangerous it is. Empty places are where the world hides the people who wouldn't be tolerated anywhere else. They feed on the emptiness; they use the isolation to train their followers. Out here, tendencies become steel-hard beliefs."

"You'd think they'd lose all their recruits. I'd be mellow all the time if someone stuck me out here," she said, snuggling into his uniform and taking in his smell. Yes, there was an undercurrent of sweaty guy who hadn't showered after a couple of days of strenuous physical activity, but there was also a smell that was uniquely his, masculine yet with a slight hint of vanilla for some strange reason.

"They use the peace to indoctrinate. Anything pure can be twisted."

"What a world you live in, in which even peace is war and violence."

"I didn't create it."

"I know. But can you stop talking about it long enough to let me enjoy the view for a while?"

He held her tight, and she enjoyed the play of the breeze on her face as it tried to blow her hair out of place.

Her first clue that something was wrong was that Max stiffened and pulled away. Her next was the crack of a gun, a sound she'd grown to recognize over the past day.

"Is someone shooting at us?"

"No... it's Vasily."

"Why? What's he shooting at?"

"That!"

Max appeared to point to a tree. She was about to tell him that she couldn't see what he was talking about when a wing popped into her sight over the leaves. The scale couldn't be right...

But it was. The wing was leathery and see-through, and it belonged to a flying thing like the one that had attacked them on the stairs in the main facility. Vasily's shots didn't deter it in the least. It flew straight toward them.

"Damn," Max said, "we must look like a meal on a string to that thing." Then he chuckled. "And now you're going to find out why I kept the spear."

Ignoring Vasily despite the continued shooting, the creature made a bead for Max and Marianne.

She tried to remember what Ronnie had called these monsters. Ptero... she knew it hadn't been pterodactyl, because she'd heard of those, and this was something different.

It didn't come to her, no matter how she tried, and she felt like, somehow, her failure was an affront to Ronnie's memory. Had she really thought they were out of it? No wonder Max had been adamant that he wouldn't relax until they were safe on the base. He was more experienced than she was and his instincts were telling him that they were far from safe.

She couldn't believe how quickly he'd been proved right.

Max let go of her—she wanted to scream at him not to do it, to hug her tight, come hell or high water—and stood on the bench of the chair, his legs straddling her on each side. Then, pointing the spear in the dinosaur's direction, he braced for impact.

A moment later, the monster arrived. It blocked out the sun and sent a blast of air over them. Even though she'd promised herself she wouldn't, Marianne screamed.

Max, on the other hand, seemed completely prepared. As the creature closed on them, he thrust the spear out and it tore through the membranous wing.

The wound didn't stop the thing's momentum, though, and it crashed into the chair, Max and Marianne. The wire holding them up swung crazily, like a mad pendulum.

Max kept one hand on the spear, and with the other, he grabbed the monster's beak, trying to keep it from pecking them to death. The claws, Marianne saw, were busy trying to keep a grip on the cable.

"Shoot it!" Marianne screamed.

"I can't. If I let go, I'll fall. See if you can get the gun out of my pocket," he grunted back.

She tried, but it was impossible from where she was sitting. She bent around his leg to try to get into position, but just as she was about to get her hand in his pocket, both Max and the ptero-whatever shifted and she missed. "Stay still."

"I'm doing the best I can," Max replied testily. "It's quite a bit stronger than I am."

Then he did the craziest thing Marianne had ever seen. He pulled his arm away from the creature's beak and punched it in the neck.

It screeched and pulled back, just as the chair's sickening pendular motion pulled the chair away.

"Max!" Marianne screamed and reached out for him.

It was like clutching at the wind. The momentum of Max's weight, combined with that of the monster, tore him out of her grip.

She watched them tumble into the trees twenty feet down, heard the crash of breaking branches and then the vegetation hid man and monster from view.

"No!"

She gripped the rail and sobbed, forgetting where she was in her anguish. Only when she felt something pulling at her fingers and an iron grip tearing her from the seat did she come back to herself.

Vasily was holding her up, pointing at the chair she'd just been on, as if apologizing for manhandling her. It was already on its way back down.

"Thank you," she said.

"You. Home," he replied, struggling with the unfamiliar words.

"Yes. I need to go home."

"Me take."

Marianne nodded, wondering what she'd done to deserve any of the sacrifices people seemed to insist on making for her. Would everyone end up dead just to get her out?

But what could she do but keep going? Lying down to accept her fate was not part of her nature.

***

Max grunted as the ground knocked the wind out of him. It felt like they'd hit every single branch on the way down and that most of them had punctured, prodded, scraped and gouged him without doing much to actually slow him down.

The only reason he wasn't killed was that he landed on the flying monster, whose torn wings looked like half the tree was stuck there. If Max himself had taken a bone-jarring hit, the dinosaur had taken a bone-pulverizing one. It lay very still.

Ignoring the pain, he forced himself to his hands and knees and studied his assailant. The head and neck were a greyish-pink color, mottled with black spots. Had he not seen it flying powerfully through the sky without difficulty, he would have thought it was a diseased member of whatever horrific species it represented. The beak, longer than his outstretched arm, was almost the same color, slightly more grey than pink, with smaller black patches.

That color was only broken up by a band of that looked like grey fur running along the upper torso and the top of the wings which, on closer inspection, turned out to be down-like feathers. Hooked claws protruded from the middle of the wings, and a short, stubby tail emerged from the bottom of its torso. Blood covered everything.

"Well, at least you stopped me from breaking my neck," he said. Then, painfully, Max attempted to stand. Miraculously, nothing appeared to be damaged enough to keep him from standing. Only sharp pain in his left wrist told him he wasn't going to be using the spear to defend himself any longer. Possibly broken, more likely sprained, it was just lucky he was right-handed. And it hurt to breathe. Probably cracked ribs.

Man, was he going to be in pain tomorrow.

But that wasn't his major problem. The major problem was that today still wasn't over, and he still had to live through it.

For a second, he debated whether it would be better to hike up what remained of the hill or go down and take the chair. He finally decided to go up. It was slightly closer, and would be much quicker overall. Time was of the essence.

And besides, there might be more flying dinosaurs looking for a quick aerial snack around.

Three steps towards the summit, a searing pain shot through him like lightning. He looked back to see a claw trying to tear his butt off. One of the monster's feet had impaled itself in the flesh of his gluteus, sending fiery agony through him every time it moved.

He screamed as he pulled away. Then his training took over and he rolled aside to put a bit of distance between him and his assailant and came up in a crouch facing the creature.

Incredibly, dragging half a forest in its wings, the monster stumbled to its feet. A big, beady eye stared at him for an instant.

The monster struck, its neck snapping towards him at a tremendous rate.

Only Max's reflexes saved him. He turned aside as the closed beak attempted to impale him and then fell back as the same bloodied foot talon raked his legs.

The gun sprang to his hand as if by magic and he looked for a place to shoot the creature. Normally he'd take a chest or a head shot—from that distance, it would be impossible to miss—but he was worried about that. He'd heard that dinosaurs had a brain the size of a nut surrounded by a wall of brain. Worse, he had no idea where the animal's vital organs might be. It would be pretty stupid to waste a precious bullet on a non-lethal shot.

The hesitation almost killed him as the dinosaur's beak flashed out again. Max thought he'd backed out of range, but it leaned forward and almost managed to impale him. His quick reaction limited the damage to yet another deep and bloody scrape.

And the monster misjudged the strike, or maybe the branches stuck in its wings changed its center of gravity. Whatever the case, it overbalanced and fell to the floor, neck extended.

Max was on top of it in a flash. He landed on its neck, both hands taking a stranglehold on the long throat.

Unfortunately, it was a muscular appendage, as thick as his leg, and his injured left hand wasn't strong enough to exert any pressure on it. In fact, though his whole weight was on the thing's neck, he was being pushed off as it tried to lift its head.

"Oh, screw this," Max said. He pressed the muzzle of his gun against the back of the dinosaur's head and pressed the trigger.

A tremendous heave tossed him away, and he slammed into a tree and likely collected another large crop of bruises for tomorrow, as well as sending a blinding blast of agony from his ribs. He gritted his teeth through the pain and didn't take his eyes off the dinosaur.

The movement that threw him must have been a death spasm. The dinosaur wasn't moving. He backed away slowly, on all fours, until there was no way it could reach him again. Only then did Max get back to his feet and begin walking, trying not to think of what Vasily would say when he showed up with a punctured ass.

The first thing to do was to get out from between the trees. It would be much faster to go up the ski slope, even if that meant he was also much more visible.

The climb was agony and, despite his determination to reach the top as quickly as he could, he had to stop every few minutes to rest his buttock. He kept looking down, but he wasn't able to see much—the trees directly to his right blocked his view of the base of the hill and the hotel.

By the time he was about a hundred meters away from the top, he was seriously doubting his ability to reach the summit. He could deal with pain, but the sense that his movements would debilitate him, that each step was tearing a larger and larger hole in a huge muscle made him want to stop.

So he did what they'd taught him to do in this kind of life and death situation: he lowered his head and took one step at a time. And then another. And another. The pain could wait until he was safe; there was nothing wrong with him that a decent surgeon couldn't fix. He'd never seen anyone permanently disabled by a muscle tear, why would he be the first?

He looked up. Fifty meters. The sweat pouring down his forehead had little to do with the heat—the afternoon was still pleasant, and a mountain wind ran across the slope. It wasn't even caused by the pain, at least not fully. It was mainly due to the fear of hurting himself badly.

Max wasn't the kind of guy who'd fold in the face of armed enemies, or wilt under an artillery barrage—he'd survived both and come back for more—but he wasn't at his best when injured. He expected his body to be at his disposal for whatever feat of endurance or strength he decided to perform. On command, no questions asked.

He didn't take sick days, and never admitted to having something hurt. And his men followed his lead.

His fear was that he wouldn't be mentally strong enough to reach the top, and when he bent his head again and began to step forward, part of it was training, but even more was shame. He needed to prove to himself that he wasn't as weak as he felt right now.

Step. Step. Stumble. Step.

He was there. Incredibly, he'd reached the summit.

But where were Marianne and Vasily? He could see the parking lot and the road from where he was standing, and they weren't there.

He turned back in the direction he'd just climbed from.

It looked like the whole Ural countryside around Yekaterinburg stretched out below him, the low hills and the green forests. The grass and the lakes, shimmering in the afternoon sun.

Marianne was right. It didn't look like the kind of landscape that would be full of monsters. It looked like the kind of place where you went for a camping trip to get back in touch with your center or your tai or whatever those new age people called it.

Even the hotel and the house that held the chairlift motor looked out of place in that peaceful country. They were the only visible signs of civilization.

He turned to search for his companions when something nagged at him and he turned back to look. What was it?

The hotel was ugly, but not a problem. Likewise the engine room. Then what? His sixth sense told him something was wrong. What?

"Oh shit."

There were two golf carts parked at the base of the muddy trail. Someone had followed them.

And whoever had followed them had to be behind the monster that was already following them... and that meant the monster was out, too.

Hopefully, the spider would have lost itself in the countryside to become the Russian Army's problem, but if that cart was Selene...

He didn't think he would be able to deal with Selene right then. He was too badly hurt.

He needed to find Vasily. Like right now. He began to walk, painfully.

"Well, at least it's all downhill from here."

CHAPTER 12

Park watched Selene leave the tunnel.

The entrance was now torn to pieces and very much not camouflaged. The door lay in a pile of rubble outside the tunnel. If no one fixed it, it wouldn't be long before the urban explorers came calling. They wouldn't be able to resist a huge underground tunnel smacking of secrets and Soviet times.

It was almost an industry. He remembered the photos of the Balaklava submarine base he'd seen online, not to mention the tank graveyard right outside Yekaterinburg itself, which caused such a scandal when people decided it would be a fun place to hang out completely drunk. He hadn't arrived in the city when the authorities cleaned up that mess, but it was legendary among the population.

And now the tunnel would join their ranks. Assuming no further journalists were allowed into the valley of dinosaurs, but also assuming that no one in officialdom would take the time to explore the unsafe-looking collapsed hole under the tarmac, it would be fascinating to watch the news begin to leak.

At first, the discovery would be nothing but yet another old Soviet tunnel leading into some kind of bunker. Almost yawn-worthy, and not something to send explorers flocking to see where it went.

But eventually, *someone* would go have a look. And they would find a factory floor with traces of radioactivity—urban explorers in Russia were always looking for that—from the Afghan war days... and the wrecks of a couple of modern helicopters at the bottom, plus the rotting carcass of some large animal... which the urban explorers would likely just ignore. They'd assume it was a yak or a bear or something.

Even the smartest people could be blind to what was right in front of them, of course. But those discoveries would raise a few eyebrows and, again, eventually someone would look up and ask where it came out. After all, a hole that size would have been seen by passing hikers... so why hadn't anyone heard of the place?

Eventually, someone would climb the stairs and emerge into the valley of lizards just in time to be eaten by a pack of velociraptors or one of the bigger meat eaters.

He almost laughed to himself. The whole thing would be legendary, and there would soon be programs on the *Discovery Channel* that mentioned the Yekaterinburg conspiracy with the same breathless style of docu-drama narration they used for treasure hunters and ancient aliens.

He wondered if any of them would try to track him down and interview him anonymously, a silhouette in a darkened room. He doubted it; though those programs sometimes got wind of something interesting, they never seemed to really be able to penetrate into the secret stuff people were actually hiding. In this particular case, only the sheer difficulty of concealing twenty-ton dinosaurs would give the conspiracy hunters a hint of the truth. Even then they'd probably go off on a silly tangent like concluding that the closed-off valley, undiscovered for tens of millions of years, had preserved the dinosaurs and allowed them to survive.

And the bunnies would watch the drivel in droves, inspiring yet more annoying pseudoscientific babble on channels that were supposed to be documentary-focused. People were morons.

Selene, however, wasn't. She was extremely smart, and it would have been suicide to follow her in his cart. Fortunately, there was only one place to go from there, so instead of following the track, he abandoned the cart and cut across the hill and through the forest to watch her, trying not to make any noise. Being mentally tough enough to walk for any length of time was one thing. Being good at forests was quite another. A misstep onto a twig could make him dead.

He turned to Chiffon. "Be very quiet," he said, feeling a little bit foolish as he did. This was an animal that had been born and raised—and more importantly had *survived*—in the Darien Gap. It would be silent. Park was the problem.

He reached the top without incident and waited.

Selene parked the cart next to the one the soldiers and Marianne must have taken and started up the path. Park let her get out of sight before following. There was still only one place for her to go.

When he reached the top of the hill, Selene was standing thirty meters from the chairlift, looking around. To Park's horror, the lift was working, which meant that all she needed to do was to grab a chair and she would be out of his reach. He couldn't risk taking a seat behind her: if she saw him, he was a dead man.

That left only one option. He pulled out his gun and ran in her direction, betting on the noise of the chairlift to hide his approach. He needed to get close enough to actually hit her.

So, despite the gun being in his hand and pointed in the right direction, he didn't fire. He got inside the fifty-meter range that most competent shots would have felt comfortable with and kept going. Chiffon loped beside him, apparently amused at this new game.

At forty meters, Selene must have felt something amiss, because she began to turn. At thirty-five, she saw him and hesitated for a second. At thirty, she went for her gun.

He fired.

She fell.

Still, he didn't stop running. He crossed the distance between them, panting like he'd completed the Olympic marathon instead of running less than the length of a football field. Kneeling beside her, the first order of business was to take the gun from her nerveless fingers and place it in his pocket.

The bullet had hit her in the right part of her chest, below her left breast. She was bleeding quite badly, but it didn't look like a wound that should have killed her directly. He felt for a pulse and found it immediately—strong and fast.

He couldn't leave until he knew she was dead, so he put the point of his gun against her head.

Park found that he couldn't pull the trigger. This wasn't self-defense, it was the cold-blooded murder of a defenseless woman. Well, defenseless unless she woke up and killed him with her bare hands.

All that remained was to wait for her to die. He was in no hurry, and the wound looked serious enough to kill her unless someone operated on it. Then he would be free, utterly free, to make a run for it.

Not knowing what else to do, he grabbed her under the arms and pulled the unconscious woman towards the open door of the white house that held the motor for the chairlift.

As he dragged her, he wondered what had become of the giant spider. He looked up the hill to see whether it was in sight, but all he spotted was some unusual movement in the trees near the top of the hill. Could that be it? He didn't know, but it was no longer his problem. After months of study, he was off to do what he should have done in the first place: talk to the man who'd built the monsters. Park was on the last leg of his long Russian sojourn. Soon, he would be following a very different trail, one that began in Western Africa.

The darkness and noise of the motor building enveloped them. He left the door open to allow at least a little light to fall on them and placed Selene on a concrete floor where he could watch over her.

And there she lay, in a ray of golden afternoon light, her hair looking honey-colored in the illumination. If he hadn't known her, he would have found the sight breathtaking. The pallor of her skin made her look like an angel and, unconscious, she appeared much younger. When you worked with her, you forgot that she was still a young woman, in her early thirties at most; the hardness of her expression made it feel like you were talking to an ageless evil.

He almost walked away, leaving her to live or die as the fates ordained.

But he couldn't live with the uncertainty, even if the price was to watch the light go out of an angel's face.

***

Somewhere below the conscious level, a part of her brain was screaming that something, somewhere was terribly, terribly wrong. But she just didn't have the energy to deal with tedious realities at the moment.

Selene recalled the one time she'd failed on a mission. It hadn't been her fault, but she'd been convinced that the powers-that-be in Moscow would pull her off of active duty and recall her. That was the fate that awaited failures and burned agents.

But they hadn't burned her, her superiors had understood, and she was still around to crown her field career with an assassination two years later.

Her failure had taken place in London. On a fine spring morning, Selene had been assigned to walk to a specific park bench in Princess Gardens, that tiny park surrounded by the buildings of Imperial College. She arrived much too early because the last time she'd walked there, Selene had gotten lost among the maze of tiny streets and mews to the west of Harrods.

This time, though, she'd gone straight up Exhibition Road, not taking any chances, with the result that she arrived while the courier who occupied the link on the chain immediately before her was still present.

Dressed in a grey suit, looking like a civil servant, the courier had light, thinning hair and sallow features. He was pretending to read a newspaper but, as she watched, the man casually bent forward and placed something under the bench.

Selene walked past, of course. She wasn't supposed to cross paths with the courier at all, much less spot him during the dead drop. But something about the way he did it set off every one of her alarms. He should have been more careful, checking if anyone was watching before executing the drop. If he had, he would have seen her—a stranger to him—walking past less than ten meters away, and simply waited until she was out of sight.

But he hadn't, and that scared the crap out of her. Instead of doing what she'd originally planned, which was to turn left at the north end of the park and return for the package ten minutes later, she turned right when she reached the northern end and walked towards a convenience store located across the street from the park's northeast corner. She bought herself a bottle of water and a pack of cigarettes, some beastly British brand, and pretended to enjoy a quick smoke while leaning on the railing at the top of the ramp that led up to the store, slotting between two clumps of students.

It gave her an excellent view of the park.

Five minutes later—and only five minutes before Selene was scheduled to appear in Princess Gardens—the courier stood and headed away, walking south.

A man walking a dog turned to look, following him and, without making a production of it, pulled a phone from his pocket and made a call.

It was all perfectly natural, and had he not had to force his dog—a big yellow Labrador—to move in the direction the courier had headed, she wouldn't have noticed anything amiss.

But as the man jerked at the leash, his sudden hurry was completely at odds with his cover. He needed to get out of the park now... and there was only one real reason she could see for that: the courier walking away.

Selene tried to keep her eyes off of the man. She didn't want to get spotted herself.

What now? If they had the courier under surveillance, they'd also be watching the bench. They couldn't have missed the drop; if she'd seen it, a professional watcher would have been certain to notice.

So she went to Harrods, abandoning whatever valuable piece of intelligence the courier had dropped to its fate. She bought an expensive hat and fought to keep her ever-present rage under control.

Then she went home and waited for the call.

"I didn't run into James," she said. It was the code phrase for a botched pickup. "I think he was with some friends."

Silence on the other end of the line greeted this admission as some poor analyst had a panic attack. A moment later, another voice came on the line, slightly deeper, older.

"Did you happen to run into anyone else?" the new voice said in patrician tones. This man, whoever he was, would have passed for British nobility by his accent alone.

"No, I had a lonely time of it, I'm afraid. Just some people I thought I recognized, but who didn't know me," she responded.

"Ah. That's too bad, but it can't be helped. Maybe I can take your mind off of things. Would you like to get together for a drink? Say around seven in the usual spot?"

"Are you sure your wife wouldn't mind? You're normally home by seven." Selene was ad-libbing, trying to warn her handlers that it was possible she'd been spotted and followed. She didn't think so—she'd looked around obsessively on her way home, and taken a roundabout route—but the possibility existed. The British government could have flown a drone with decent cameras high above her head and she wouldn't have seen it.

"I'll deal with her," he replied.

The car that picked her up at fifteen minutes before midnight was a black Volvo; the driver said nothing, but handed her a card with a single name scribbled on it: Ignatius. Then he drove her past stately Georgian houses in the direction of Clerkenwell before turning off into a tiny dead-end lane or mews. The car stopped and the driver solicitously opened her door.

As she descended into the darkness—only the headlights bouncing off the brick wall in front of them gave any light—she was certain that it must be the end of the line, that she had been brought there to dispose of her, and that, from out of the darkness, a bullet would enter her head and she would be gone.

None of that happened. The driver just indicated, still silent, the door to their right, a numberless black-painted steel panel set in the bricks of what appeared to be a warehouse. Then he backed down the narrow street and disappeared, leaving her temporarily blinded by the headlights.

This was her chance. The driver didn't stop to see if she went inside; she could run in any direction she wanted, disappear into one of the less-well-policed places on the map and hope the Russian government lost track of her.

Of course, that could be exactly what they expected her to do. This could very easily be a test, and if she failed, a knife in the back before she even made it onto the main road would be her fate.

Better to play along.

She knocked on the steel door through which she could now hear the faint strain of music. It opened instantly to reveal a tiny foyer, maybe three meters long and two wide, mostly filled with a large blonde man who beckoned her inside and closed the door behind her.

"Who're you lookin' for?" he asked in a thick northern accent.

"Ignatius," she replied.

The man nodded knowingly and winked. "All the way in back. Just beside the kitchen entrance." Then he hesitated for a second. "And I'm sorry, miss, but I need to search you. For weapons, you know."

Selene grimaced to herself, but nodded. Normally, she would have maimed this guy before allowing him to put his hands on her… but this wasn't her game, they weren't her rules, and getting groped might conceivably save her life. Or it might just get her killed by her employers. She fought down the rage, the desire to see if her hand-to-hand training would work against a much bigger opponent, and submitted.

To her surprise, the man frisked her quickly and efficiently, not spending an instant more than necessary on any part of her body. When he was done, he stepped back and opened the door behind him.

She nodded in respect, and he returned the gesture. She had to assume a doorman wouldn't have known who she was… and that told her a lot about him: he was a professional. Probably a murderer and a sociopath, but not a sleazebag who preyed on those who couldn't defend themselves. Unless, of course, he was being paid for it.

The door opened onto a scene that could have been lifted straight out of a mafiya club in St. Petersburg. A glass bar was crowded with men in dark suits. The baristas behind it were wearing the skimpiest of outfits, showing more cleavage than they concealed.

But at least they were wearing clothes. The two dancers on the circular stages that served as islands between the tables were wearing little more than a few belly chains and earrings between them, and their motions were designed to make their nudity extremely evident, even through the clouds of cigarette smoke.

Selene ignored them. She knew why they were there—to show that the place could operate without fear of official censorship, so that the people inside felt safe—and also know both where they were recruited—in the slums of Russian industrial towns—and where they ended up—dead of something violent or contagious, usually within a few short months. Most of the men ignored them as well. These were experienced operators who knew the truth: the meat on display was just meat. Only newbies and muscle that would remain forever at the bottom of the totem paid any attention to it.

Selene was neither, so she walked confidently towards the indicated table.

She passed a Babel of languages. German here, French there. Even Arabic, coming from the table of one Saudi who was openly staring at the nearest dancer and drinking Blue Label from one of a pair of open bottles. She smirked. There was a man who confused cost with quality.

English and Russian were ubiquitous, forming the backbone of the language soup.

Interestingly, in a place where the women were obviously decorative—girlfriends showing as much flesh as they could, waitresses in tight mini-shorts and, of course, the dancers—not many glances flashed onto her. People knew that a woman dressed in business attire in that place was likely to be in the business of death, not the business of love.

They could get both elsewhere, so they didn't stare, just glanced at her long enough to commit her features to memory.

Ignatius turned out to be a pudgy, balding man with watery blue eyes. She sat across from him and stifled an urge to plunge a knife into his chest. The table in front of her was set, and it would have been the work of a moment. She hated him immediately.

"We should have met somewhere else," she said. "Now, every small-time jackass in the city knows my face."

"This place was convenient," he replied, "for a number of reasons." He counted on his fingers. "First, the driver says you weren't followed. Second, no one saw me come in here. Third, no one here will ever talk about anything that has to do with me. They know better. Fourth, there are many people in here, and no one knows who you came in to meet with. And five, I was hungry. The only one that matters is five."

"And when the British come to take you away?"

"Oh, they won't. I'm not the kind of man the secret police takes away."

"You're just a functionary."

The man calling himself Ignatius laughed. "Perhaps it's best if you continue to believe that. Now tell me what happened."

She went through the failed meeting. The man's expression never changed, but his features began to swim in the smoky ambience.

"I will report that you did well, and haven't been burned. You will leave now. There's a car waiting outside. But first, I have one last question: why are you here with me when you've just been shot in the chest?"

Selene opened her eyes with a start and coughed. The entire left side of her body was numb and she felt cold. She was surrounded by noise, some kind of machinery. The place was dim, only a flash of sunlight entering from the door.

Park Sun-Lee stood over her, a gun in his hand.

"You won't need that," she said.

"Would you believe yourself?" he replied.

"Never."

Park nodded. He didn't lower the gun.

***

He looked down over her, feeling his body tense. He'd hoped she would slip off peacefully, but that didn't seem possible now.

"Are you going to shoot me?"

"That depends. Are you going to attack me?"

But Selene was no longer looking at the gun. Her eyes had shifted over to where Chiffon hid behind Park's leg. "What the hell is that? Where did you find a monkey?"

"It's not a monkey," Park replied, shifting to one side so Selene could get a better look at the creature. "It's called Chiffon, and it was designed by the same man who built the big black monster."

"What for?"

"He seemed to want a pet. I think there is something more behind it, but I'll need to talk to him to find out what it might be. I think the man is hiding a great sadness."

"You seem to know a lot about a guy you only spoke to for less than an hour. Or did you lie about that as well?"

Blood was beginning to pool on the floor around her, and Park looked away. It wouldn't be long now. Blood loss would take her, even if the bullet hadn't hit anything important. He didn't want to shoot her again. "No. I reported the meeting exactly as it happened. But you'd be surprised at just how much you can learn from a person by studying his work and reading his file. Yes. There's great sadness there."

Selene coughed. "He would have made a good Russian."

"I don't…"

He was cut off mid-phrase as Selene lunged at him, both hands groping for the gun. Her sudden movement was just enough to grasp the barrel.

Park tried to pull it away, but she was still strong.

He should fire the gun. At the very least he would blow a hole in her hand, and he might be able to hit her torso and end it.

But something other than his unwillingness to shoot made him hesitate. Selene wasn't pressing the advantage of having caught him off guard. She seemed content to do nothing but hold the barrel and pull it gently downward.

The movement seemed strange. Did she want to ensure that he wasn't pointing the gun at her anymore? That any shots would hit the ground?

No. She simply didn't have the strength to keep her hands up and the weight of her body was forcing her down.

A moment passed and Selene released her grip with one hand, using that one to steady herself as her knee hit the ground.

Could it be a trick? Was she trying to get him to bring his guard all the way down? He didn't think so. She'd lost too much blood. The lunge had taken everything she had, and now she was defeated. He pulled the gun away and her fingers presented no resistance.

Now on all fours, breathing shallowly, she looked up at him. "Can you help me sit? Please?"

The pain of having to beg could be seen in her eyes. She wasn't lying... the time for dissembling was gone.

Park put the gun in his pocket, put his hands under her arms and lifted. She was a lot heavier than her lithe form made her look. He dragged her a few feet and placed her against a wall so she wouldn't be sitting in the pool of her own blood.

"Thank you," Selene said.

"I'm sorry," he replied.

She snorted, a weak gesture. "No you're not. You might be remorseful now, because you're watching me die, but you're not sorry." Selene spoke slowly, measuring each breath, as if she had all the time in the world. "You know I would have killed you."

"Yes."

"And you're not sentimental. You're a complete bastard. That's why we never had any trouble working together. You're just like me."

"I don't think anyone is just like you," he replied. "You... you seemed to enjoy it." Was that the kind of thing you said to a dying woman, cut down in the flower of her life? He didn't know and, at any rate, he'd already said it.

She thought about that. She thought about it for a long time, and when Park thought she must have breathed her last, Selene shook her head. "No. I didn't enjoy it. I did what I had to do, to get back at the world for taking the life I deserved. I was angry almost every moment of every day. Angrier than you can imagine."

"I worked with you. I can imagine."

"No. You can't. That they would do that to me, just because of who my father was..."

"Do what?"

She looked up at him. He got the impression that she could barely see him, that her eyes weren't quite focused. "You wouldn't understand."

"And now, are you angry?"

Again, the long pause. "No." She sounded surprised. "I always thought it would end with a bullet to the head, instantly." The pauses were getting longer, her words more widely spaced. "Or, failing that, after a long session with the torturer, where the pain would make death seem like a welcome friend."

She made the effort to hold his eyes, then smiled wanly. "I certainly never thought it would be you with me at the end. I didn't expect it to be painless, numb... peaceful. No. Not peaceful."

She stopped speaking and Park was about to reach over and feel her pulse when he saw her eyes move.

"Thank you for staying with me. I always expected to die alone. So thank you."

He didn't reply, and she didn't speak further. After ten minutes, he leaned forward and closed her eyes so they wouldn't stare at him while he checked her pulse. He'd never heard of anyone thanking their killer... but then, he'd never witnessed the death of anyone quite as damaged as Selene Grosjean.

No pulse. She was dead... and he was free.

Park stood and turned to go. Then he paused. He'd never left a dead body behind. When there had been deaths at the lab, someone had been on hand to take care of it. Just leaving her there, dead, offended his sense of order.

He shook it off. There was a lot he had to do.

"Chiffon, would you like to go see Philippe?" he said. The little monkey-thing looked up at him, not understanding. "Well, come along, anyway. I wonder how I'm going to explain you at the border," he thought.

He'd stop at an ATM somewhere, and grab some cash to do the explaining for him. The nice thing about Russians—and hopefully Kazhaks—is that they understood universal languages extremely well... and there were few languages more universal than rubles in that part of the world. Dollars and Euros, perhaps... but getting hold of those would mean stopping at a hotel.

No matter. A border guard on an isolated road was unlikely to quibble at being bribed with the wrong kind of currency.

He walked back to where he'd left the golf cart and realized he was suddenly in no hurry at all. A great sense of peace came over him and he accessed the hidden charger on the exit side of the tunnel.

Half an hour later, he pushed aside the branches hiding a dirt track and drove in the opposite direction to where the soldiers and Selene had gone. The path was maybe a couple of kilometers long, and led to a logging road that went another five before it hit the highway.

Park pulled out his phone. He still couldn't believe the soldiers had taken him at face value when he told them the battery was dead. Of course, if they'd checked, they would have found that the phone was, indeed, dead... but that was only because Park had removed the battery after sending out Tatiana's story. He didn't want Selene tracking him through the phone. The people he worked for had promised it was encrypted and untraceable, but believing that those same people wouldn't be able to find it was a good way to end up dead.

Unfortunately, he would have to use it a little more. The first was a quick app operation to get a Yandex cab, which told him he would have to wait ten minutes for the car. It must have been from one of the nearby villages, as Yekaterinburg was an hour away.

Then he scanned incoming messages and smiled: his advertising had borne its first fruits. Finally, using an encryption app the Electric Buddha had sent him through a different channel, he composed a message to the nameless middleman.

Tell the clients that deliveries will begin in August to African clients and September to those in Asia. Production of certain specimens has already begun in a convenient location, and they will be ready for delivery.

The Americas will be served by year's end.

The taxi drove up, a dilapidated Lada that would likely have been ordered off the road by the police anywhere else in Europe. The driver smiled and asked him where he'd like to go. He was missing two front teeth on his bottom jaw. He didn't even blink when Chiffon jumped aboard. This was a man who knew not to ask questions.

"Take me to the nearest ATM," Park said. As the car drove off, he removed the phone's sim card and tossed the pieces out the window. He wouldn't be using it again, and everything he needed was in the memory card.

The ATM was in Kivograd and, armed with an enormous wad of cash, Park walked to a taxi stand containing a bunch of cars that made the Lada look like an airport limousine. He climbed into the first one in line, gave him a glare that challenged him to say anything about his pet and said: "Drive out of town."

The man complied.

"Now where?" the driver asked, unease visible in his features. He was not quite certain he liked the direction things were going.

"Kazakhstan," Park replied, handing him a chunk of the wad, five times what a normal round-trip fare would have been in that area.

The man grinned. "You're the boss," he said, and gunned the engine.

Park Sun-Lee sat back and smiled.

CHAPTER 13

Marianne slipped on a loose rock as she looked behind her. The spider monster was still coming their way, although far behind, just starting to move down the mountain.

After descending from the chairlift, once she had gotten hold of herself, Vasily had led her through the parking lot and to a road that, other than the presence of the ski resort, looked exactly like every road she'd seen outside of Yekaterinburg: an endless strip of two-lane blacktop losing itself in the infinity of trees.

There were no cars on the road. Five minutes stretched to ten and ten to fifteen, but there was no sign of traffic. It figured: who would come to a ski resort in the middle of summer?

Vasily didn't seem overly perturbed. He showed no signs of impatience, no indication that anything was wrong. He could easily have been a soldier returning from nothing more unusual than a long and dirty hike.

Until a crash behind them announced that their eternal companion, the spider-monster, was on their trail. Again.

They'd fled headlong down the hill, and were now trying to decide where to go.

"Do you think it saw us?" Marianne asked.

Vasily just looked at her blankly, and she didn't know whether he'd understood and simply didn't believe she could ask or, more likely, he just didn't catch the English.

"Come. This way," he said, and tugged on her arm.

She wanted to ask him why the monster was following them. Did it want to eat them? Did it think they were a threat? Was it simply revenge for having invaded its lair? Marianne didn't know. More and more, she was certain that she would die without knowing, killed by an evil that was completely opaque to her, something that didn't think like humans. Something alien.

Maybe it even was an alien. Nothing on Earth looked like that, that was for certain.

Vasily's fingers dug into her arm as he tried to force her to speed up.

"I can't move any faster," she gasped. "Go ahead, save yourself. Enough people have died on my account."

Vasily shook his head and slowed down.

That, he understood, she thought angrily. *Apparently, nothing is going to stop these idiots from killing themselves on my behalf. I suppose this is what it must have felt like to be one of those princesses from tales of chivalry.* She shook her head. *Fucking frustrating.*

But she went with him because not going with him would have meant going on alone, and she was too scared to do that.

Out of the corner of her eye, something called to her. The yellow… it meant something.

"Over there," she said, pointing.

To their right, at the bottom of the hill, sat a yard full of construction machinery. Bulldozers, road scraping machines, or whatever those were called, steamrollers, a big shovel-thing. Hell, there was even a crane with a wrecking ball among the vehicles.

Vasily nodded, and they left the barely discernible footpath to cut through the shrubs on the slope. A minute later, the monster behind them changed direction and followed after them.

"It's still coming," she said.

Vasily looked behind him and shrugged. His entire body showed that he wasn't surprised… quite the contrary; it seemed to her that he would have been shocked at anything other than persistent pursuit.

He must have been one hell of a conversationalist, she thought. Fatalism as your defining trait had fallen out of favor in her generation. Most people she knew would have been complaining all the way. She chuckled to herself with the thought that some of them would probably be organizing to protest the giant spider.

She nearly fell and decided to look where she was going. They still had a big lead, there was no need to look back over her shoulder. There would be plenty of time for that later.

A ten-foot tall fence loomed ahead of them. Vasily touched it gingerly, and found it wasn't electrified. "Up!" he said, pointing towards the top.

Marianne began to climb, putting her feet in the links, certain that the thing would collapse under their weight at any moment.

But it was sturdily built and barely swayed, not even when Vasily joined her and began to climb.

They reached the top and, again, Vasily checked carefully. Failing to find electrified cables or razor wire, he threw a leg over the fence and balanced there for a second, one foot on each side, bottom a couple of inches above the wire. Then he reached down and grabbed Marianne's wrist to help her get over the top.

"Thank you," she said.

He smiled back at her and dropped to the ground. She climbed laboriously, keeping her eyes on the grass below her to avoid looking at the monster.

Only when her feet were solidly planted did she look up.

"Oh shit," she breathed.

The spider-monster was halfway down the hill, and not slowing in the least. It would be on them in seconds.

Vasily pulled her towards the nearest machine-a road scraper with wheels as tall as Marianne. He pulled the flimsy plastic door open, nearly tearing it off its hinges, and sat in the driver's seat.

He fiddled with some wires, becoming more and more desperate as the monster approached. Marianne wanted to tell him to hurry, but he was obviously doing everything he could.

The spider reached the fence. She hoped that would slow it down somewhat—it certainly wasn't going to be able to climb. But she soon realized that the monster would simply be able to step over the obstacle, as if it was jumping a puddle.

It didn't seem to be in the mood for puddle-jumping, though. The creature brought a massive pincer down on the fence and flattened a section. Then it seemed to try to pull it physically from its moorings— but the fence was much too solid for that. It came up in one piece, even though three of the concrete posts holding it down popped away.

This enraged the spider. It grabbed the fence with both pincers and appeared to fight with it, pulling this way and that, sending sod and clumps of dirt into the sky. Finally, more by accident than by design, the fence folded in such a way as to leave space for the spider to crawl under.

"Time's up," Marianne said.

Vasily was still fiddling with the wires, cursing in Russian.

"I mean it. We need to go, now," she said. "Look." She grabbed the man's head and turned it so he could see the approaching monster.

Vasily paled, but she had no time to feel satisfaction that he was, in fact, human because he suddenly pushed her out the door of the machine—not the same door they'd entered through, but the one on the opposite side. She landed on her butt on the ground and looked up to see Vasily trying to free himself from one of the levers on the floor of the vehicle.

She could hear cloth tearing as he tore at his uniform pants, but there was no way he would survive. The monster was too close.

And once her wall of protective men was gone, she would die, all alone, ten thousand miles from her home. There wouldn't even be enough of her left to identify.

The monster's tail went up and struck. Marianne closed her eyes.

With a sound of ripping cloth, a body landed on her. An instant later the crash of impact, tail on machine filled the air.

Vasily. Alive!

He stood and pulled her to her feet. Together, they ran between the machines. There must have been forty or fifty of them in the lot, some tiny, some huge, most yellow.

Behind them, the monster appeared to be venting its frustration about Vasily's escape on the machine they'd vacated. Good. That would give them time to...

To what? To climb another fence and die out in the open?

That would never work. She tugged on Vasily's arm. "Over here," Marianne said. She pointed under a bulldozer. The thing looked indestructible, and there was a space on the floor between the two caterpillar tracks big enough for them to squeeze into.

Vasily understood immediately and dove into the dark gap. She followed at a more sedate pace until she realized that she was unconsciously trying to spare a set of clothes that was ruined beyond any hope of repair.

She crawled like a kid then, concentrating on not bumping her head on the machine's underside.

A few chinks in the tracks allowed light in. More importantly, they allowed Marianne to look out at the monster.

"It's still demolishing the other vehicle," she said.

"Shh," Vasily replied. At least that was universal, and he was right. They didn't know how well the monster could hear... hell, their breathing might be enough to give them away.

A big yellow chunk of machine flew through the air and landed point-first in the grass, quivering, right in Marianne's line of sight. Why could the monster tear metal that way? It shouldn't have been possible. The chunk it had thrown was cut raggedly, as if the pincers had done it. The thing might be armored, but those were steel plates.

Of course, it was a created creature, not a natural one. Perhaps the designers had put some different material into its claws specifically to allow it to tear into metal.

Why would anyone do that?

For the same reason people built atomic bombs, she concluded. To kill a lot of people in the most horrible way possible.

A terrible silence filled the lot, and she wanted to hope that the creature had decided they were a lost cause. Perhaps, in its distraction, it had simply missed the two insects trying to lose themselves among the yellow machines. Perhaps it had gotten hungry for something bigger and drifted off after the smell of sheep on the wind.

She didn't let hope flower, however. This creature had been after them for hours. It had dug its way through steel and concrete for the express purpose of killing them. It wasn't going to lose the scent now, not when it was so close to finally achieving its goal.

Vibrations came up through the ground, confirming her fear, and then a leg came into view, followed by the carapace. She was stunned to see that the monster had been hurt. This close, Marianne could see seeping cracks and deep gouges in the armor. The claws might be strong enough to cut metal, but the burrowing through steel had taken its toll.

She doubted that would save her, though. The bulldozer above them thundered with a colossal impact.

They were found.

***

Max knelt on the ground, unable to believe his eyes. The monster had passed him without stopping, headed exactly in the direction that Marianne and Vasily would have gone if they hadn't seen anyone in the parking lot.

He didn't need to be psychic to guess that it was still following them. It was always following the main body of their group, even as it chopped that group to pieces. Tatiana was dead. Sun-Lee, though hardly a friend, was buried somewhere in the old basement factory. Max hadn't fallen to the spider, but he'd fallen—quite literally—from the trail.

So unless the creature was seriously pissed at Vasily or Marianne, it was following the scent of the largest group it could locate.

Max didn't care why. All he knew was that one of his friends, as well as the most alluring woman he'd ever met, were in mortal danger, and he needed to help.

The monster disappeared from view over the side of the hill, and he followed after as fast as his injuries allowed. He laughed at himself ruefully: did he really think he was going to be able to do anything? Short of stumbling over a cache of abandoned RPGs or an armored division just waiting for him to tell it what to do, he didn't have much chance of pulling off the impossible.

But still, Max ran after the monster; his conscience would never allow anything else. He reached the crest of the hill and groaned. The descent was steeper than he would have liked, and the thing was already halfway down. He spotted two small dots in the distance, just on the other side of a tall fence and realized that they must be Vasily and Marianne.

That fence wouldn't be much help, he reflected. They climbed into a machine and he realized that Vasily must be trying to start up a road grader. That might be a good idea. With the blade retracted, the machine might just be able to outrun the monster on their tail.

But the road grader remained resolutely in place. No movement, no sound of a diesel engine coughing to life, not even a cloud of blue smoke.

The spider, meanwhile, had stopped fighting with the fence and was advancing on the machine they'd selected.

Max kept running, always on the verge of rolling the rest of the way, ignoring any number of alarming pain warnings from his body. His hand was killing him, but his butt, at least, seemed to have gone numb save for certain fiery lances of agony.

He still had no clue what he was going to do.

The spider-monster attacked the cab of the machine, sending glass flying everywhere. He huffed in relief when he saw two figures scurrying away.

Max stopped at the uprooted fence. This was realistically as far as he could go without being seen immediately. The machines blocked him from sight of the monster's forward-mounted eyes, but if he got any closer, he was, quite simply, toast.

He looked around. Absent a tank battalion, Vasily's idea of trying to make a run for it seemed solid, but the machines in that compound weren't built for speed. There were a few forklifts, and another pair of road graders that seemed like they might be able to move at a decent rate. The rest were tracked vehicles, great for navigating mud, but slow as hell.

If only…

There! Half-concealed by a huge crane with a wrecking ball hanging from the tower was a dump truck. Not a sports car, but that should be able to keep up a steady hundred kilometers an hour—more than enough to outrun any monster.

He ducked under a section of mangled fence and, keeping watch on the monster, edged around the perimeter of the compound towards the truck. He needn't have been so careful: the spider appeared to have anointed the road grader its new worst enemy, and was tearing it back to its component molecules. He sprinted—or more likely hobbled a little less slowly—towards the truck, staying behind as much cover as possible.

A sudden silence announced that the time for stealth was past. He looked back to see the monster advancing on a bulldozer, and he would have bet any amount of money that his companions were under it.

But he was nearly at the truck. He just had to pass the final vehicle, the crane.

Max ground to a halt.

The truck had only three wheels, the axle where the front right should have been was supported on a pile of cinder blocks.

Behind him, he heard a thump. Then another.

The monster was attacking the bulldozer. Vasily and Marianne would be dead in minutes, if they weren't already.

Max leaned his hand on the fender of the enormous yellow crane and screamed in frustration.

***

The monster on top of the bulldozer appeared intent on going through the metal above them to reach the tender morsel inside. The first two blows had landed hard enough to sink the tracks into the ground as dust and gunk fell from the floor of the machine onto them.

Marianne screamed in pure terror, certain that they would be crushed. She put her arms around Vasily and pressed him close. He said soothing things in Russian, not bothering to try to speak English. But even in this extremity, with the certainty of an unpleasant death looming, Vasily remained calm. It was a pity she would never be able to ask him how he managed to keep his emotions under control. Or maybe he was just the classic soldier stereotype who thought emotions were for the weak.

Maybe it was best not to know. People's pasts often hid horrors of the worst kind.

The beast struck again, but this time, though more crap fell on her head, the treads didn't sink further. For some reason that was extremely important to her. She couldn't bring herself to believe that the creature would ever be able to tear away all the metal above them, so if they weren't crushed, they might live. Hope, as they say, dies last.

She pulled away from Vasily and crawled towards the track, where a sliver of light indicated that she could see out through a chink among the wheels.

Vasily whispered something in Russian. She couldn't understand the words, but it wasn't hard to guess the content.

"It already knows we're down here," she replied. "No harm in having a look."

He said nothing more and she pressed her eye against the gap. The opening was near the top of the track—the bottom was buried in the earth—where one of the road wheels met the steel tread. She had to bend her neck to see through it.

What she saw was breathtaking. The creature was right there, less than ten feet away. She saw thick legs and then, by contorting her neck even further, she looked higher up and was able to see the circular torso in all its glory. She wished she hadn't. The bottom four eyes were visible from this angle. Those eyes were mad, black, watery. They appeared to be looking everywhere at once, as though they could see straight through the iron right into her soul.

If someone had told her that the creature was feeding on her terror, she would have believed it without a second thought.

It was certainly tracking her through everything. You could almost feel the hatred in those enormous orbs.

The creature reared back and brought a pincer down on the metal above her. She wondered how the bulldozer was holding up under the ferocious onslaught.

Her question was soon answered. A grinding screech sounded and, moments later, a large chunk of yellow metal thudded to the ground beside the monster hard enough that the earth shook.

The piece was big, too big, and her sense of security evaporated. At the rate it was working, the shield above them would be gone in minutes, if not sooner.

The claw came down again, the metal screamed, another piece, a jagged sheet this time, landed beside the first. That piece wasn't even painted yellow: the monster must be tearing at the machine's insides. Those were soft, unarmored.

The next strike actually lifted the bulldozer slightly when the creature pulled the metal from it. Then it came down, striking her head hard enough to make Marianne see stars.

But her eye remained pressed against the makeshift peephole. She might be about to die, but at least she would see what happened and face it with her eyes open. Unfortunately, she had the feeling that the easiest way to face her death would be through the floor of the bulldozer. It would soon be showing daylight.

The monster reared back once more and Marianne braced for the strike. It definitely looked like it was preparing to demolish their makeshift hideaway once and for all.

She saw it begin to move, both pincers coming straight towards her when, with a sickening thud, the creature lurched to one side. Marianne saw a huge dent on the side of the exoskeleton, with a network of cracks radiating out from it. Dark fluid began to gush from the wound.

Had someone hit it with a missile?

No, there was no explosion.

She tried to see what the hell happened. Maybe the bastard had been hit by a meteorite? It wouldn't stop it, but it definitely deserved it.

Movement to one side caught her eye and she looked away from the battered monster to focus on it. A large grey sphere, apparently floating in midair hovered out of sight.

"Oh good," Marianne said. "Now we've got flying saucers."

Then she laughed until she cried.

***

"Yes!" Max exulted.

The ball had actually struck true. He would have bet any amount of money that it wouldn't have worked, that he'd have hit anything other than his intended target. When he fired the crane up and began to move the wrecking ball, it seemed utterly unwieldy, impossible to control. This crane was much taller—and the ball much bigger—than what you saw in old movies, and his first clumsy attempts had nearly wrapped it around the crane and, for a terrifying moment, he was certain that it was about to crush the cabin where he sat.

But it had swung harmlessly by and he'd managed to swing it on a wide arc in the intended direction.

Of course, the creature he was aiming at was so big it was hard to miss.

After the first strike, he moved the ball away slowly, but the monster appeared stunned, unable to understand what had happened to it, where the unseen assailant had materialized from.

So Max swung the ball again, on a longer arc this time. He aimed at the monster's torso but missed, so instead of delivering a killing blow, all he did was shear off two of the spider's legs as the ball flew past.

It still felt incredible to actually be able to damage it.

He expected the spider to roar, but it kept an insect-like silence. That was the creepiest part of it. The loss of two legs—even when the complete complement was eight-had to hurt like hell.

The creature had now identified its tormentor and struck at the ball with its stinger. The entire valley seemed to ring with the metallic clang of impact. More seriously, though, the ball accelerated and Max thought the momentum would topple his crane.

But the crane was balanced by outriggers that dug into the ground and absorbed the movement. Now he was at an angle, but still mostly vertical. He swung again.

He missed. This was harder than it looked, and the monster was now mobile. As the ball went past a mere three or four meters from its eyes, the creature's attention was suddenly drawn to the crane itself. Max could see the monster angling its torso to look up at the moving pillar. Then, it scanned downward... downward until all eight eyes found Max.

He swallowed as the creature lurched in his direction. It no longer moved quickly and every step appeared to be the prelude to a disaster, but it came inexorably, leaking whatever black liquid passed for blood in giant insects.

Max swallowed. The ball was reaching the outer part of its arc and he needed to correct the angle. There wasn't much time remaining until the thing reached him and if he had to abandon the crane... well, they were pretty much fucked.

He had time for a couple more passes, though, as the monster navigated the maze of vehicles separating them.

Max began to swing the ball to try to hit on the first pass when he realized the monster had begun to climb over a bulldozer and then stepped onto a grader, bending it like a banana.

It would be on top of him much quicker than he expected.

The ball missed by a mile and he frantically tried to line it up for a final blow before the monster pulled him out of the glass cabin and tore him to pieces. The projectile was moving very quickly and went way out.

The spider was nearly on him. A pincer hit the crane and jolted the entire structure. He moved the lever and realized that the impact had straightened the ball out. Now there were two colossi heading straight towards the cabin: the monster and the wrecking ball.

He watched, transfixed, as the monster reared back.

A second before the tail lashed out, his attention was drawn to the ball. It was coming at enormous speed right towards him, at eye level.

His training took over. A giant insect might mesmerize him, but a huge chunk of metal on a gravity-fueled collision course with his favorite head was something he knew how to deal with.

Max dove out of the cabin and onto the ground, rolled and ran as fast as his lacerated leg could go.

A deafening crash sounded behind him and liquid splattered onto his back before something much more solid hit him in the back of the head and he fell to the ground... which also hit him in the head.

***

Max rubbed his head and gasped in pain. His wrist, he remembered was badly hurt. His head as well, but he needed to feel it with his other hand.

He'd nearly been knocked out, and was still a little woozy, but he got to his feet. He needed to run.

Wait.

Was he running away from something? Was he running after something?

He sat down. He must have been hit harder than he realized. He needed a couple of minutes to get his thoughts together.

He was sitting on grass. The closest thing to him, five meters away, was a twisted and mangled crane. It must have hit the ground pretty hard, because it had dug in quite a ways.

Crane... wrecking ball. That crane had had a wrecking ball on it. He was pleased to have remembered that.

And then he remembered the rest and sprang to his feet. Ignoring the sudden dizziness, he looked around. The monster had to be there somewhere. He might have managed to hit it with the wrecking ball, but it was one tough son of a bitch. He followed the collapsed crane to its base.

There.

There was no need to run. The monster would never again be a threat to him... or to anyone.

From where he was standing, it looked like the mad scientist who'd created the spider-monster had decided to take things one step further and merge monster with machine. The crane and the spider, under the irresistible force of the out-of-control wrecking ball, had blended together, proving that at least parts of the spider's armor were softer than metal.

Though the crane had broken off about six meters from its base, the bottom segment had embedded itself into the spider's body—or rather, the blow of the ball had driven the spider into the crane. The top of that broken column protruded from the monster, covered in black gore.

The ball itself had lodged into the back of the creature, tearing the segmented tail off and adding to the force with which the spider smashed into the structure ahead of it. Everything was covered in liquid goo.

"Well," he said, raising an imaginary glass in its direction, "fuck you to hell."

Then he went to look for Marianne.

***

"That thing's been gone for a long time," Marianne said. "You think we should go out?"

Vasily just looked at her, obviously not understanding a word.

She pointed. "Out? Run?"

He shook his head and then, as if to prove him right, they heard the biggest crash yet. Only one thing could have made that noise, and the hope died inside her. The monster was still out there and whatever had injured it was now receiving its punishment.

"Oh God," she said. "I wish it would just be over already."

Marianne heard footfalls approaching. The creature was treading carefully, probably because of its missing legs. She moved away from the peephole and towards the center of the battered bulldozer. She didn't want to watch any more. She just wanted to curl up in a ball and wait for death with her eyes closed. As long as there wasn't any suffering, she was fine with whatever.

"Marianne?" a voice said.

She opened her eyes to look at Vasily, but he hadn't spoken and looked just as surprised as she did.

"Marianne?"

"Max?" She knew it couldn't be. She'd seen him fall. But it certainly sounded like him.

"You're alive? Can you get out of there?"

She was already moving, pushing herself towards the back of the bulldozer. In a couple of places, the floor was battered almost to the ground, but she squeezed through, thanking her stars that she hadn't had anywhere near enough to eat over the past couple of days. That probably made the difference between being able to make it out and not...

Marianne finally got her feet out, then her legs. Her butt was a tight squeeze, but after that, it was smooth sailing. A moment later, she sprang to her feet.

Max stood in front of her, holding his wrist, covered in sludge and smelling like a sewer.

She didn't care. Two steps later, she had her arms around him and kissed him. Then, when she was sure he was real, she pulled away. "What happened to you?"

"You mean after I fell off the chairlift?"

"Yes."

"I killed the flying thing. Then I killed the spider thing. In hand-to hand combat."

She felt her eyes widening and said: "Really?" which she hated herself for saying as soon as the word left her mouth.

Max laughed, and then grimaced.

"You're hurt," she said.

"Not really. Sprained wrist, maybe broken. Also I have a punctured... leg... from one of the bird-thing's talons. That's why my pants are covered in blood. Oh, and I think I cracked some ribs." He held her gaze. "In other words, I'm perfectly fine. This could have been so much worse."

A voice from under the bulldozer spoke and Max laughed.

"What?" Marianne said.

"He says: yeah, it could be worse, you could be stuck under a big yellow hunk of metal."

Vasily's feet protruded from out of their former shelter, but that was as far as he'd gotten. He was much bigger than Marianne.

"He's right."

"I see a shovel clipped to one of the machines. This will only take a minute," Max replied. Then he spoke in Russian and hobbled off to get the spade.

It took them considerably longer than a minute. Max's wrist was too weak to do much, and Marianne was no use at all. By the time they'd gotten Vasily out, night was beginning to fall.

A pickup truck appeared at the fence. A man got out and stared at the demolished barrier for a long time, holding his head comically.

Max called out to him, and he sprinted over. A long conversation in Russian ensued, and Marianne began to feel faint. She was obviously managing to keep her feet from adrenalin alone, and that was wearing off quickly.

"Max," she whispered.

He turned to her and suddenly looked concerned. "Are you all right?"

"Can you ask him if he has some food?"

A protein bar and a flask of vodka appeared almost immediately and she felt worlds better. But the Russians continued arguing. She tugged on Max's sleeve. "I want to go home," she said.

Max said something to Vasily and, between them, they walked the protesting man back to his truck. Vasily took the wheel and the man sat in the passenger seat, making one phone call after another. Max and Marianne sat in the back. Marianne fell asleep on Max's shoulder almost as soon as the truck started moving.

CHAPTER 14

As Max and Marianne emerged from the infirmary, a group of soldiers waiting at the door asked them to accompany them, in English. She looked to Max for guidance, and the blond man just nodded, so they went without protest. The situation didn't feel particularly threatening. The men were relaxed, just carrying out orders, escorting a couple of people who weren't deemed dangerous—and one who was a friend—into a room.

Of course, there was very little Max or Marianne could do even if they had decided to cause trouble. They were inside a concrete office building in the Spetsnaz base surrounded by pretty much every Russian commando in the region. Not even Max would go very far, although his peers would likely go easy on him and simply immobilize him non-lethally.

Besides, the doctor had explained to Max that any kind of strenuous activity would tear the stitches on his ass, hurt his ribs and very likely do some unspeakable damage to his fractured scaphoid which, once the Colonel got done with him, would need to be immobilized... and possibly operated on if the cast didn't heal it.

The doctor had explained all of this in English, likely in the vain hope that she would be able to make him see reason and take care of himself. It was almost as if the doctor had zero experience with men who thought that only dangerous things were worth doing—unlikely, as he was a Spetsnaz officer, as far as she could tell from his uniform. Maybe he was just an optimist at heart.

The uninjured Vasily had been separated from the group and, presumably, already debriefed. In any event, he wasn't waiting for them when they reached the large room the troops deposited them in.

It was a classroom, she thought. Or, considering where they were, it might be a briefing room. Metal chairs and desks were distributed on the concrete floor, and there was a whiteboard at the front. Twenty-five normal-sized students could probably fit comfortably... so maybe twenty guys Max and Vasily's size.

Max turned to her with a serious expression. "Call me old-fashioned, but I was hoping to see your ass before showing you mine. Or at least both at the same time." Then his poker face broke and he burst out laughing.

Marianne smirked. "You keep acting this way and you may not get to see it at all."

"I thought you wanted me to choose. I choose caveman, and this is how you treat me?"

She turned serious and gestured around the room, indicating the base, the whole of Russia and their situation. "Are we going to be okay?"

"That depends on what you mean by okay. We probably won't be shot. I heard from one of the soldiers that Selene was found dead of a bullet wound near where we took the chairlift. They'll probably suspect us."

"But we didn't do it."

"Yes. So the ballistics people will clear us. But that leaves the more complicated part, the politics."

"I just want to go home."

"You will, I promise. It might take a while, however."

"I don't feel like waiting a while."

"This is Russia. It might take a while anyway."

"No. Can I borrow your phone? I saw you charging it in the clinic."

"Of course."

"I need to make an international call."

"Do it. I... Let's just say I wouldn't deny you anything, ever."

She got up on her toes and kissed him. She wished they could finally be alone somewhere.

Max pulled away again. He was always doing that.

"Are you going to call someone important?"

"Yes."

"A politician? A senator? The American President?"

"Nope. I'm going to call someone who will give me immediate results if he knows what's good for him."

"Who?"

"My editor."

A soldier opened the door and motioned for Max to follow him. Max looked back at her, shrugged, and left.

***

Terrence Vaidal glanced at the clock. It was five-thirty in the morning. No one should be calling about work at five-thirty, but the phone buzzing was the one that only work people had.

It would be about work. Everyone in the industry knew that he would take a call about a story at any moment, day or night. He needed to stop doing it.

The number was not one of his contacts, and it was longer than it should have been, a string of meaningless numbers. He debated whether to just let it roll over onto voicemail, but finally pressed the green icon with a sigh. "Hello," he said.

"Terrence, it's me." The voice was unmistakable. It had haunted his working days for years, and haunted his dreams for a couple of unforgettable weeks. Now, it haunted his conscience.

Relief flooded him. "Marianne, are you all right? We saw what happened. The monsters... We feared the worst."

"Yes, I'm safe," she said. "But I need your help."

"What is it? Money? Diplomatic pressure? Please tell me you don't need a doctor."

"Right now, I need you to tell me, in thirty seconds or less, what you guys know."

Vaidal brought her up to speed about Tatiana's story. Marianne was silent for a couple of beats, and then spoke in a flat voice. "Tatiana's dead, Terrence. And Ronnie."

"Ronnie... oh God. What happened?"

"That's part of the story."

"Fuck the story. Tell me where you are. I'll send people to get you. Are you sure you're all right?"

"I'm fine. Surrounded by Russian commandos who won't let anyone hurt me. Relax. The story first. Promise me you'll run it now. Today, first thing—it's early morning there, right? It's just after midnight here, and I'm really tired, but I think it's morning, right?"

"Yeah," Vaidal replied, trying to keep the sarcasm out of his voice.

"Good. Also, you're going to have to write most of it, because I'm nowhere near a computer or an internet connection. I'll give you the telegraph version. Do you have a notebook?"

"It's five-thirty, I'm in bed."

"I'll take that as a yes." She paused for one second while he scrambled to grab the notebook that lived—as she knew because she'd seen it—beside his bed. "After the stuff with the dinosaur at the lab, Ronnie and I rented a car and..."

***

The colonel waited in his office-a spartan cubbyhole that showed little sign of use save for the fact that it contained a few books on a shelf.

Max had only been there a couple of times, most recently to be informed of his brother's death. He took a long look at the officer and saw the man was unhappy, but not overly so. Annoyed more than upset.

The guy would never be a decent poker player. Anyone could tell what he was thinking.

"Sit down Max," the colonel said.

"Yes, sir. Thank you, sir." He sat, wincing as his butt came into contact with the chair.

"You look like shit."

"Thank you, sir. I don't feel much better."

"However you feel, you aren't anywhere near as unhappy as I am. Here I am, minding my own business when, suddenly, I get the call that there's been a major incident with national and international security implications right on my doorstep. There are dead soldiers, dead journalists, dead people from security organizations so secret I'm not even supposed to admit might exist, dead helicopters from an important defense contractor, dead dinosaurs—and living ones, too—and a dead monster no one thinks should be able to exist.

"I'm thinking that's all fine. I don't do the spy stuff, I just have to respond when the shit hits the fan, so if the intelligence boys dropped the ball and didn't ask for Spetsnaz support, I am perfectly all right. The political stench can't touch me. So, while I'm trying to explain to the boys in Moscow that, since no one told me about anything, it isn't my fault, it turns out that two of the dead soldiers are, in fact, mine, and two more walk out of it all with a few scratches."

"I'd say we got more than a few scratches."

"Speak for yourself. Vasily looks like he just came back from the beach. If you're a bit of a wimp, it's not my fault." The colonel took a breath and Max tried to keep his smile from breaking out. The fact that he was being chewed out like a recruit meant that he wasn't going to the firing squad... not as long as his superior officer could help it. And anyone trying to storm a Spetsnaz base against the commander's will was not going to have a good day. The colonel went on. "Initially, my first instinct was to tell Moscow that your unit had gone rogue and murdered half the human and monstrous inhabitants of the woods outside Yekaterinburg but then I realized that they would never believe me. It would have taken at least five of you to do that much damage."

"Marianne helped. You don't know her. She's the most dangerous person in the country. The Americans are probably already threatening the Kremlin with a nuclear strike if we don't let her go now."

"I have her file," the colonel said, indicating a print on his desk. "She's not that important."

"That's what you think."

"That's what I know. Now tell me what happened; Moscow is especially interested in the fates of Selene Grosjean and Park Sun-Lee. General Orlov was very agitated about them for some reason."

"I think they're both dead, but I didn't see it for myself." Max was stalling. He was trying to remember what he'd agreed with Vasily that they would tell the colonel. Finally, he shrugged and went with what he remembered. "It started when we were going to lunch out at the gas station. We ran into Grosjean on the way and she asked us to accompany her to the complex because there was a reporter who'd been stopped by one of her men, and that there was something else going on. That reporter turned out to be Marianne." By offering as little detail as possible at this stage, Max hoped he wasn't contradicting anything Vasily had told their superior officer. Fortunately, the colonel's deficient poker face had not registered any alarm so far.

"And you didn't think of calling it in?"

"We thought it would be a quick thing and when we realized there was trouble at the facility, we couldn't get a signal. For some reason our phones didn't work there."

"They have a jamming field... I think they don't trust their employees."

"I'm not surprised. I'm convinced it was one of the employees that caused all the problems. Both the escape of all the dinosaurs and the explosion in the main containment area had to have been inside jobs."

"Why don't you tell me everything in order?"

"Okay. As I said, we realized that there was something wrong inside. The guards were all gone and the place looked deserted, so we advanced and entered a large enclosure..." Max went on to tell the story of the following two days with only slight modifications. The only thing he changed was that Grosjean wasn't a prisoner but part of the expedition at all times. But he kept the rest of the narrative almost completely untouched, especially since most of it had occurred without the presence of the people in whom Moscow was interested.

The story took an hour to tell, and Max was feeling exhausted and in pain when he finally told the colonel what happened in the machine lot.

"And the girl?" the colonel asked.

"What about the girl? She was just along for the ride. Grosjean wanted to shoot her, but we decided to wait."

"Is she really just a journalist, or was Grosjean right and she's a spy?"

"Definitely a journalist."

"Grosjean didn't seem to think so."

"Grosjean is a crazy woman who kills people for the hell of it."

"Now she's dead."

Max didn't bother to pretend to be surprised. "How do you know?"

"They found her body."

"Good."

"You make it sound personal."

"I never liked her."

"No one did, but we can't go around shooting everyone we don't like."

Max bristled. "I didn't shoot her. In fact, I did everything in my power to keep her alive. We got separated twice, and she seemed to be at war with Sun-Lee, but I had nothing to do with her death."

"It looks bad. You and Vasily were the only ones who got out."

"I didn't shoot her." He studied the colonel for a few moments. "But you already know that, don't you?"

His superior grimaced. "The bullet inside her was fired from a North Korean gun. The story you told us about Grosjean and Sun-Lee being at war appears to fit the evidence and the bodies we found, and it matches with what Vasily said, so I can only conclude that you did your job to the best of your ability, and that your involvement in this mess was purely accidental. You are free to go."

"Really?"

The colonel's face hardened. "That isn't what Orlov recommended, but Orlov has a hell of a lot of explaining to do in Moscow, and he probably won't survive the political fallout. I predict that, in a month, Orlov will be a man with a nice pension, a dacha in the country and precisely zero power or influence. With Grosjean dead and Sun-Lee in apparent disgrace, I doubt anyone will want to raise a stink about a couple of soldiers who aren't talking to anyone. We at least came out of this well so far, and I plan to keep it that way. One way to do that is to act like you did everything right which, as far as I can see, is correct. Every shred of evidence we have fits your story exactly, and I know you well enough to know that you wouldn't have done anything stupid.

"So you are still on active duty, except you have some medical leave coming. And anyone who argues... well, unless they are in my direct chain of command, they will have to come and get you, and I don't think that would be a good idea."

"What about Marianne?" Max said.

"The reporter? She stays where she is for now. Moscow wants to talk to her."

"Can't you do anything? I mean..." Max never got to finish, because the colonel's phone rang.

The man picked it up and spoke into the receiver. "Yes, sir," was all he said. He said it a number of times.

Then the colonel hung the phone up and gave Max a sour look. "That was General Kaminov. He just got off the phone with someone important, and he says we need to release the woman. Right now."

Max chuckled.

"I hate to say I told you so. Actually, I don't hate to say I told you so. I told you so. Do you want me to drive her?"

The colonel rolled his eyes. "You can't even drive with that hand."

"Yes I can."

"Whatever. Just get her off my base."

***

"Can you drive this?" Max asked.

Marianne studied the controls. It looked like a big SUV, nothing too tough. "I'm a bit rusty on stick shift, but I learned to drive on one of them, and I managed that rental... so I guess I should be all right."

"I don't think you'll be able to break it, even if you try," Max said. "They're designed so that the kids right off the farm can operate them without damage. You should see some of what passes for driving around here."

Marianne laughed. "You should see the George Washington Tunnel."

"Maybe someday. Now tell me the truth. Who did you call?"

"I already told you. My editor."

"I believe you," Max said, even though his face registered anything but.

She fiddled with the gears until she found first and stalled the car immediately. She got it moving on the second try. "Well, after working that clutch, I won't need to go to the gym," she said.

"My colonel is convinced you're a spy. He wanted to keep you on the base to ask you some questions. Your editor must be a very important man."

"I'm not a spy," Marianne said, recognizing the unspoken question in the comment.

"I know. That's what I told him. Just take this road. We'll reach Yekaterinburg in fifteen minutes or so."

"All right." They drove in silence for a couple of minutes until a soft sound from the passenger seat made Marianne look over. Max, leaning against the door, was snoring softly.

She slowed and turned onto a dirt track that cut across the main road. She drove until she couldn't see the asphalt behind them, then stopped the car on the grass along the track and turned off the headlights. Complete darkness fell outside, while the interior was illuminated only by the dash instruments.

Marianne watched Max sleep next to her. His two-day beard looked prickly, but he looked fantastically handsome in a fresh uniform and after taking a shower. She, on the other hand, had been forced to put the dirty clothes she'd been wearing back on... but at least the shower had been wonderful and the troops had even closed off an entire shower room for her use, posting a guard on the other side of the closed door to ensure her privacy.

Seriously, she probably would have taken the shower even if the whole base had been watching her. It ranked almost as high as food—which she'd also received—on her list of priorities. A point in favor of the Russians is that they'd let them get cleaned up and go to the infirmary before putting Max to the question. She didn't think an American CO would have acted the same way. It would probably have gone against some process or other.

She watched him sleep for a few minutes, just enjoying the sensation of having him beside her while not running from anything and not being hungry and afraid. On one hand, being there with him felt perfectly safe, but in some corner of her mind, she half-expected to be attacked by an escaped dinosaur or a rogue soldier working for that crazy bitch Selene.

Nothing happened and she began to get sleepy. She put the gear lever in reverse.

But she didn't start the car. Instead, she put the lever back in neutral and took off her belt. She leaned over into the passenger seat and brushed her lips against Max's.

He woke with a start. "Is everything all right?"

She smiled. "Remember that thought you've been holding?"

He looked confused for a second but then returned her smile and pulled her closer.

Marianne kissed him hungrily.

***

Dawn was breaking over the city as they entered Yekaterinburg. Max was wide awake now, and he directed her towards the hotel.

"Isn't it still dangerous to go there?" she asked.

"With Selene dead, we'll be fine. Besides, someone way up in the government has your back... they want you out of the country as soon as possible."

"Will they let me back in?"

"I don't know. Do you want to come back?"

She thought about it. "To be a soldier's girl? I don't know if I could live with the uncertainty. Knowing what you do..." She sighed. "But yeah. I guess I'd want to give it a shot. Maybe."

He nodded and they pulled up in front of the hotel and parked in one of the reserved spaces. The bellboy who emerged to tell them they couldn't park there took one look at the insignias on Max's uniform and decided he had more important things to do than enforce parking restrictions.

The front desk informed them that her room was being held just the way she'd left it, on orders from the government. Marianne asked about Veronica's room and was given the same answer.

"Let's go there, first."

The room held very little. A laptop, some clothes. Like most hotel rooms, it was devoid of human warmth. And worse, the clothes looked like they'd been purchased at a bad charity sale.

Marianne stood very still, surveying the contents. After some moments, he began to feel uncomfortable invading her grief, but remained silent.

"What do I do?" Marianne said.

"Did she have any family? A husband?"

"I don't think so. No. I'm not really sure if she even liked men. Or women for that matter. She seemed mostly turned in on herself."

"Isn't there anyone to tell?"

"I suppose Terrence would know that."

"Then let it go. Mourn her for yourself, not for others."

The silence stretched out for a long time. Finally, Marianne gave him a wan smile. "Again, you're failing at being a caveman."

"That's because I don't have the luxury of mourning my men, my friends, that way. When you have to tell a wife and two aging parents that their beloved isn't coming home... you appreciate being able to mourn for yourself."

She hugged him, then looked over the stuff in the room again. "What do I do with all of this?"

"Forget about it. I'll have someone ship it back to your editor. If I have to, I'll pay for it myself, but I'm pretty sure I won't have to. I think Russia wants to forget any of this ever happened, and that means they won't balk at a shipping bill."

"I wish I could forget," she said, before stepping out of the room.

It hurt for a second, that quick dismissal of the fact that there was some good in even the evilest of situations. But maybe Americans saw things differently. Russians always expected the world to try to crush them, so when something like Marianne appeared in the middle of a catastrophe, it was natural for Max to count himself lucky. He wouldn't have traded it for anything except maybe to have Yuri and Ivan back.

He closed the door softly behind them.

Marianne was looking up at him. "This is why I didn't wait to get back here before we... well, you know."

"Yes, I know," he replied. The memory of watching the sun come up and illuminate her naked skin would stay with him forever.

"I wouldn't have been able to... not with her things there. I can't even think of anything else now. Only Ronnie."

"I understand."

"Will you take me to the airport?"

"Do you have a booking?"

"I'll buy a ticket on the first flight out of here. I don't care. Just help me pack and get me there."

He nodded. He didn't ask when he would see her again. It wasn't the time.

Besides, she wasn't difficult to find. Famous journalists never were.

***

Terrence Vaidal was waiting at the airport. The man himself, not one of his flunkies. And he was on the inside of the security perimeter, flanked by a couple of uniformed immigration people and someone in a suit-an airport official, judging by his badge.

"How did you even know I was coming?" she asked him.

"Everyone knows. Your story went out yesterday morning. It made a bit of a splash, and there are actually demonstrators looking to grab you and take you to a protest outside the Russian embassy. I thought it would be easier if we could dispense with that."

"But how could you know what flight?"

"That was the easiest part. And I'm not the only one who found out."

One of the uniformed officials held out her hand. "Ma'am, could you please let me have your passport and come with us?"

Terrence nodded and smiled. "It's fine. They're here to help."

They ushered her out of the flow of people and into a back room where a computer scanned her passport and took her picture. "You're good," the officer told her. And then, in a quieter voice, she continued. "And I wanted you to know what an honor it is to be the one to welcome such a brave woman back to the States. We're proud to have you here."

They entered a long hall that led to an elevator which, in turn deposited them in an underground parking facility. "Terrence," she said. "What did you print?"

"Nothing you won't approve of. Only what you said over the phone, and I licensed some of Tatiana's images. You couldn't have done a better job yourself."

"Then why is everyone gushing? Why am I suddenly the darling of the protest crowd and the TSA?"

"Those weren't TSA."

"You know what I mean."

They entered a limousine that Terrence had waiting, a long, black one with tinted windows.

"It's that no one has been able to get a journalist into the area. Everyone's being stonewalled, and the Russians are denying everything. They even denied that you were in the country at all. If they could, they'd disavow any knowledge of your existence." He paused and looked out the window as the car exited the tunnel and merged with airport traffic. It was a bright day, and Marianne couldn't believe she was back and alive. Terrence went on. "And since no one could get the news straight, I allowed them to use your prose."

"I didn't write any prose."

"Yes, you did. It's on the front page of today's New York Times, under your byline. You are due a pretty fat check. How is it you didn't see that? Is your phone broken?"

"No. I just didn't turn it on. I want to be left alone."

"Then it's a good thing I got to you before the mob."

"Is it?"

"They weren't going to take no for an answer. These are hardcore human rights activists, and they wanted to use you for their purposes. Have you ever seen that type listen to reason or excuses?"

"All right. Thank you for that, then."

He sighed. "I know when I'm not wanted, although, dear woman, it wounds me to the quick. As soon as we get to Manhattan, I'll get out and take the subway to the office. You must be really tired."

"Thank you." They motored on for a few more blocks. Morning traffic was heavy that day. What was it? She thought it was a Thursday. No. Friday. No wonder. "Have you run the obituary for Ronnie?"

Terrence shifted in his seat. "No. I mean we thought about it, but she wasn't anyone people knew about. We thought it would look like navel-gazing when huge stuff was going on all around us."

"You mean it wouldn't have brought any more readers to the page."

He didn't respond.

"You're a bastard, Terrence."

"I have a business to run. Ronnie isn't news, no matter how tragic this is. We reported her death, of course, and a small résumé, but that's all we could justify."

"Oh, then I'll sell the obituary to the *Times*."

Terrence sighed. "Is it really that important to you?"

"Don't be a dick."

"All right, we'll take it. But it runs under your byline."

"Still thinking of the bottom line?"

"I said we'll run it. So write it and send it over." He had the look he always had when arguing with Marianne. A kind of dazed, glazed defeat.

She usually felt like smiling in his face in these situations... but today, she didn't feel like smiling at all. There was nothing to smile about.

Terrence must have noticed. As he descended from the limo, he turned back to her. "This time you're going to get the Pulitzer for sure."

"Fuck the Pulitzer," she replied as he closed the door.

***

Marianne sat at the computer, staring at the blank document in front of her. She didn't know what to write. All she had was the title: "Veronica Bee, an Appreciation of an Important Life", but now she couldn't think of how the hell she was going to be able to put all her rage into words.

It was more than just about Veronica. It was about the modern world, where Marianne, a famous name, would have merited the better part of a page, above the fold, if she hadn't made it back from Russia, while Ronnie only rated a tiny square and a quick mention because she was an American killed in the mess. Why did Marianne's fame make her more worthy of note than Ronnie's gentle, civilized obscurity?

She knew the answer. Famous names, especially when they got themselves killed in a dramatic way, sold newspapers.

This wasn't about selling newspapers. It was about acknowledging that Ronnie was chasing the same story as Marianne. And as Tatiana and the other journalists who'd died, all of which had merited rivers of ink in their respective countries. *Caipi*, Tatiana's news site, had a fully black homepage with only a photo of Tatiana to break the darkness. It made Marianne tear up just to look at it.

Unfortunately, it didn't help her write the obituary, and neither did the canned bio that HR had sent her. Who cared that Ronnie had spent her career as a research assistant at a museum or that she'd worked as a fact-checker for the *Washington Post* before joining *Update!*? No one, that's who. Not even Marianne.

The problem was that she didn't have anything else to fall back on. Like everyone else at the magazine, she'd had a cordial relationship with the weird girl from research... but not a deep one. She had never spoken to Ronnie outside work, and the longest conversation she'd ever had before the trip was the one that led to Ronnie accompanying her on the trip to Russia.

Guilt hit her like a hammer between the eyes. This wasn't working. She didn't have anything to say. She needed to figure out who Ronnie's friends had been, and that meant calling the office.

Marianne didn't want to call the office.

She wanted to call Russia.

But it wasn't time for that. Not yet.

CHAPTER 15

This was more like it. Helicopters and a large group of men, including zookeepers specialized in working with large animals, was the right way to hunt dinosaurs. Especially since the government had, over the past month, given up on trying to contain the story and decided that, if the dinosaurs were there, they would make excellent zoo exhibits.

The current official story was that a private company had created them for profit and that they had been unable to control the result. Conveniently, the people responsible for the disaster had been killed, so there was no real reason to investigate much further. All that remained was to round up the surviving specimens and get them to a safe place.

Precisely zero people believed it, but that was the story and everyone was sticking to it.

Or else.

Besides, that story had gotten Max cleared to participate in the operation to clean up the valley. The doctors had removed the cast and pronounced him fit just three days before, along with recommendations that he take it easy and...

He'd ignored them completely. If he sat this one out, Vasily would never let him hear the end of it.

So he was where he was meant to be: hanging out of the door of a helicopter and looking down at a herd of large dinosaurs. He knew that certain sectors had opposed the roundup, saying that this was a unique opportunity to study the creatures in the wild, but the last thing the government wanted was tourists poking around in a Cold War development zone and getting eaten by velociraptors.

"I think those are the ones we're supposed to be going for," he said, pointing out the window at a herd below them. "Try to put down on the other side of those trees so we don't spook them."

"Yes Captain," the pilot replied.

It took Max a moment to realize the man was talking to him. From being a possible traitor, Max had, instead, received a medal for his team's actions at YekLab and a promotion for the situation in the mountain complex and the valley.

It was a bribe, of course. Since no one really knew what had happened—the security video from the complex had been disabled—Max's story had become the official version, and he and Selene were being treated as heroes, while the North Korean and Orlov were being bandied about as the culpable parties. But since there was still some doubt, Max had been promoted hard to ensure he stuck to his story. He now had much more to lose.

Hell, they'd even made Vasily a sergeant, upping him three grades in the process. No one was going to contradict the official story.

Max had also been allowed to lead the first roundup, which was much better than being left behind at base wondering how things were going and whether Vasily would screw everything up.

This first strike had been designed to pick up five herbivores the size of hippos in cargo nets slung under the choppers, but to do that they had to tranquilize them and then defend the sleeping dinosaurs from carnivores… which meant tranking the carnivores, too… and that meant defending them from other carnivores. All in all, the operation was going to call for a lot of soldiers on the ground, armed with modified grenade launchers that shot extremely large tranquilizer darts.

It had all the hallmarks of an operation that could get out of control very quickly. If it did, the choppers were to be used as gunships. Fortunately, Spetsnaz Mi-8 helicopters were well armed, and the dinosaurs would find it unhealthy to do anything too chaotic.

But the idea was to keep the creatures alive, not mangle them with heavy machine guns.

The warm breeze and the smell of the grass reminded him of the last time he'd been out here, and that, in turn, brought back memories of Marianne, of his dead soldiers, of desperate days. He smiled. Those were nearly good memories now that time had done its thing. In ten years, he'd be looking back and wondering why disaster scenarios had been so much better when he was younger.

"All right," he told Vasily. "Use the trees for cover and see if we can get these things down before they spot us. Otherwise we'll have to use the drones." He turned away and then turned back. "And try to stay downwind of them."

Vasily rolled his eyes and went off to gather his men. For a few, it was their first time in the field, which might not be a bad thing. Dangerous enough that they needed to obey orders and take care, but at the same time, devoid of anyone shooting at them. A perfect way to blood the troops.

He let Vasily's squad get into position before standing beside a tree to watch the situation unfold. Each soldier took aim at one of the targets and, to his surprise, four of the men found their marks—the adapted launchers, he knew from personal experience, were inaccurate as hell.

Vasily ordered the man who missed to reload and try again, but Max stepped in. "No. I want to try the drone." He turned to the soldier. "I'm sorry about this, I know it won't be much consolation when you have to buy the rest of your team a beer because you missed, but it truly is necessary."

The soldier, dejected, just nodded and removed the trank dart from his weapon and stowed it in its assigned pocket. Max turned away and smiled. A conscientious kid like that would take this badly, but then he'd double up his range time and try harder. In a year, he would likely be the best shot in his unit with any sort of weapon, able to take down a tank at four hundred meters with his handgun... and he would be the most respected man in camp.

But Max still felt bad for the guy. The road to being a valuable soldier could be rough.

The drone was already in the air, so Max told the operator. "Wait for my signal. I want to see what you can do."

The four dinosaurs that had been tranked—grey, mottled creatures without feathers and with wide, ugly heads—were falling to their knees. The final beast seemed oblivious that anything was happening.

Max decided to help it out. He emerged from behind the tree cover and ran towards it, waving his arms. Either it would bolt or it would charge him—either way, he'd get what he wanted: a moving dinosaur to test their drone-mounted system with. He hoped it worked, because getting close enough to fire the grenade launchers at some of the carnivores out there didn't appeal to him.

The dinosaur looked at the approaching creature and ran in the opposite direction. Max glared after it. "Yeah, you better run, you prehistoric bastard." He chuckled at himself in the knowledge that a clash with a thing that size would mean death by trampling. Then he remembered where he was. "Igor," he called. "See if you can bring it down."

The drone whizzed out from behind the trees and swooped across the creature's line of sight. It didn't stop, but the operator corrected, hovered above the dinosaur and fired his dart straight down. A minute later, the fifth dinosaur was snoozing.

"Bring in the choppers," Max said.

The operation to get the slings and netting in place took much longer than the actual hunt. The animals were heavy and, while every detail of the actual transport had been minutely calculated, no one had thought of how to manipulate large creatures on the ground.

"Could you please bring a forklift next time?" Vasily groused once the first of the monsters was safely secured. He was sweating profusely;

even with ten men lifting, it hadn't been easy to slide the harness into position.

Max just relaxed and watched them work. None of the choppers could leave because they had to wait for the men who were still working, and Max couldn't help because, though he might be ignoring doctor's orders just by being there, he wasn't dumb enough to try to lift heavy weights with a weak wrist. That was just begging for trouble.

He reflected that this was a very pretty place. No wonder the refugees and political undesirables who'd been put here hadn't complained. He imagined that they must have had quite an idyllic existence before they were all killed by ravenous monsters. But that was life.

"I'm going to clear that pack of little raptors," he shouted to Vasily.

Pulling his gun out of its holster, he strode towards the little guys. They seemed more curious than aggressive and scattered at his approach, so he was about to turn back towards his men when something vibrated near his heart.

Damn the new phone, he thought as he fought to pull it away from a pocket too small for it. It was bigger than the one he'd had the last time he was there but, at least it was a satellite phone, which meant that he could talk even though there was still no service out in the valley. He recognized the number immediately.

"Hi sweetie," he said because he knew she hated to be called sweetie, and she got angry in the cutest way.

"Hi Neanderthal," Marianne replied. "Are you off in the mountains of Central Asia killing innocent goatherders?"

"Hey. Those goatherders are plotting to destroy humanity. I thought a connected journalist like you would know that already."

They laughed together. It felt good. He could almost visualize her huge, beautiful brown eyes.

"If you really have to know," he continued, "they have me playing park ranger at the moment. We're rounding up the dinosaurs to take them to a zoo."

"You went back there?" He heard the shudder in her voice.

"It's just a job. This is just a place."

"It's a dark place."

He laughed alone this time. "I was just thinking what an idyllic place it is. A place where we could retire together."

"Anywhere but there."

"Whatever you say. How about you?"

"They asked me to give a speech. I'm nervous as hell."

"Better you than me," he replied. "I told you this wasn't as easy as you pretended."

"I know. But it's important to me." She spoke to someone not on the line, and then returned. "I'm on in a couple of minutes, but that's not why I was calling you. I wanted to tell you that I'm getting on the next plane to Russia. I can't stand being so far away anymore."

"What about your work?"

"The news will have to take care of itself for a few weeks, that's all. I'm too tired to keep at it. And I just signed a very large deal to write a book... so money is not going to be a problem."

"That's awesome. I don't know how much time I'll be able to spend with you, but I promise you every night unless they deploy me to kill goatherders."

"I can live with that."

"Good luck with your speech. Let me know when you have the flights figured out so I can go get you at the airport."

"I will. See you." She hung up.

Max walked back to his men, thinking that he liked this one. No games of 'you hang up first, no, you hang up first,' no wildly premature declarations of love. Just a woman who did what she wanted when she wanted to do it.

Damn. This could get very, very complicated.

He grinned. Bring it on.

***

Marianne took a deep breath. What the hell was she doing? The man was clearly emotionally stunted. How could he return to a place where so many people, including a friend of his, had died?

She suspected she would never be able to understand, but she found that she didn't care. Her heart, which had been racing, had stopped fluttering. His calm outlook must have rubbed off on her. She still had to give a speech, but now she could face it with a smile.

Joao looked more nervous than she felt, which was ridiculous. She was bringing them money, funding a socially relevant program. Even if she completely fumbled the speech, everyone would go away happy. Unlike most of the news she was involved with, this one was a feel-good story all the way.

A man and woman approached her. He was sixty-ish and tanned, with hair that was nearly completely white and bright blue eyes. She was a little younger, with skin the color of coffee with a lot of milk in it. Just looking at her parents, you could tell where Tatiana had gotten her incomparable exotic beauty.

The man spoke in heavily accented English. "I wanted to thank you again for this."

Marianne smiled. "You've already been very generous in your thanks, Mr. Close."

"It is better in person. I'm glad to finally meet you."

The woman, who only spoke Portuguese was even more eloquent. She embraced Marianne and hugged her tight for ten seconds before releasing her, breathless but somehow uplifted.

"It's time," Joao said. Someone must have called him on the earpiece.

Marianne took a second to smooth down her suit, took a deep breath and began her walk. Long steps, confidence and a folder in one hand to keep that hand busy and not fidget. Every piece in its place as she strode through the glass-sided corridor that showed the modernist architecture in the government center of Brasilia outside the auditorium: green grass, white concrete and blue glass.

Joao held the curtain aside and she walked onto the stage. Thunderous applause greeted her. The crowd held everyone from Brazilian senators and cabinet members to media industry leaders, social project managers and journalists. A camera in back filmed the event.

"Thank you for having me," she began. "I'm used to talking about the news, not being the news and I would normally have done pretty much anything to avoid giving a speech. But today isn't about me."

A picture of Tatiana's face, blown up to twenty times its normal size, appeared on the wall behind her.

"Tatiana Andrade Close da Silva was a marvelous journalist. Eloquent, connected and knowledgeable, she was able to put facts together from data and communicate effectively with her readers.

"But more than that, Tatiana was a wonderful, generous human being. When I first came to Brazil to report on the world's most important Fashion Week in Rio," this, as it was meant to, elicited a round of applause, as everyone knew that Rio was in fierce competition with places like Milan and Paris for that title-but the parties were better in Rio, which made a huge difference in Marianne's mind, "she took me under her wing and showed me around. Some journalists worry about others stealing their stories and taking their readers. Despite the fact that her magazine, *Caipi*, is directly in competition with the one I worked for at the time, she never let that get in the way, and always helped me when she could. Not many would have.

"But there's more to her. She was also brave. I was present in the place where she sent out her final story. I know what she went through to get the truth out to her readers and that, to me, is the measure of a real journalist. A lot of things were going on around her when she filed her last words... but she ignored them. This was important to her.

"As journalists, we respect that. It's the mark of someone who truly loves this strange profession. And she did.

"That's why I'm so happy to have the opportunity to come here to announce the Tatiana Close Memorial Scholarship. This project has been created by *The New York Times* for two reasons. The first is to recognize Tatiana's contributions to truth, which is the highest objective a reporter can possibly have.

"The second, and equally important, is, each year, to give two Brazilian students in the final year of journalism school the chance to learn their trade in the editorial office of one of the world's greatest media companies. And, to ensure that we get more Tatianas; at least one of the journalists will be a woman, every single year."

This was met by applause, wholehearted by some, politically expedient by others. Marianne was not enamored by the affirmative action aspect of that particular clause—she believed that quality needed to be the only criteria in any field—but the *Times* had insisted, and they were paying for it. At least she'd managed to talk them around to leaving the second position open to be competed for by everyone equally.

But her job wasn't to give her opinion, her job was to talk about the program, and to honor a dead friend. So when the applause died down, she continued.

"This is something Tatiana would have loved. She always stressed how much she'd learned working at a major paper. Well, there aren't too many papers in the world more important than *The New York Times*. This initiative will create a solid foundation for Brazilian journalism that will create the independent thinkers and honest critics of the future."

She paused to let them applaud. This time, it wasn't tinged with politics in the least.

"But better still, it will introduce the New York media to the warmth and wonder of the Brazilian people. New York will never be the same."

She let them applaud. No one was going to stop the feel-goodies to point out that there were already thousands of Brazilians in New York. That wasn't what you did at this kind of event.

"Now, I'd like to leave you with some words from people very close to Tatiana: her parents."

She stepped into the background as the couple stepped up to the lectern and began to speak in Portuguese. The words rolled over Marianne. Her mind was in Russia.

She only woke temporarily to do a couple of interviews with the Brazilian press and then, once she'd shaken the last hand and received the last hug, she simply grabbed her wheeled carry-on and climbed into the car the Brazilian government had provided for her.

It was just after noon. She had begged off the cocktail event for the launch, saying she had to be in a meeting the following day and everyone had nodded, understanding. They all imagined that she would be at some kind of high-powered powwow with movers and shakers. It had been all she could do to keep herself from laughing. There would be moving and shaking, she hoped, but of a very different kind.

Then she leaned back on the leather seat and smiled.

This would be fun.

EPILOGUE

It was hot. It was humid. It was wonderful.

The huts were situated alongside the N2, the road that ran north and south on the Ghanaian side of the border with Togo. This section was the kind of infrastructure you expected to see in the developed world, with paved shoulders and well-maintained central lines.

Park had been on the road for two hundred kilometers already, and knew that there were better places and worse places along it, but nothing like what he'd expected from Africa. This was a road in a reasonably prosperous country which valued the mobility of its citizens, and it showed. It was quite well-maintained.

He was surprised and a bit unsettled. The whole point of establishing himself in Africa was to use the official indifference and general anarchy to slip away from the public eye for a while. Evidence of good government did little to make him feel secure.

Fortunately, the landscape outside the old taxi was more than enough to overcome any uneasiness. Low, equatorial vegetation with taller trees interspersed between the bushes, sprouted from the dense earth. There was no other place on Earth you could confuse this with.

And the roadside buildings made him smile. The country might be modernizing, the government might be building a developing society out of the ashes of colonialism... but the people still lived in Africa, and they seemed to like it. Everyone he saw was smiling.

"Stop here," he told the driver.

"Here? Are you sure? There's nothing here." The man's English was French-accented, and he had proved to be a charming and entertaining raconteur. Park would miss him, but he had pressing business in the cluster of huts ahead of him, be they ever so humble and low.

The modernization mentality had even arrived in this tiny and forgotten outpost. The thatched huts were not made of reed or adobe, but of unpainted cinder blocks. A couple of them even sported roofs made of corrugated plastic sheet. The inhabitants might not be rich, but at least their houses could pass for those of the poor almost anywhere.

He let the air play over his cheek. August was smack in the middle of Ghana's rainy season, and the warm winter wind blew heavy with the promise of evening rain.

The bar stood a short walk from the other huts and it was recognizable because there was a large rectangular gap in the wall which could be secured by a wooden panel when the watering hole was closed. When in operation, the panel was horizontal, sitting above the single wooden table and casting shade over the two chairs.

Only one seat was occupied, by a pale man wearing a white suit. His hat, a thing that looked like it belonged in an old film about Europeans in the tropics, sat on the table in front of him. A black cane leaning against the chair completed the scene.

The man's eyes followed his progress and then, with a sigh, he turned to the local on the other side of the dark rectangle. A drink was served from a bottle into a small glass and was waiting for Park when he arrived.

"So you found me," Philippe said, his face showing no joy at the North Korean's presence.

"I never lost you," Park replied.

The Frenchman had aged appreciably since their last meeting in Costa Rica. He thought that life on the run must not agree with him... but then Park remembered that the man had been on the run for the better part of a decade and had already carried an air of unhappiness with him when they'd met two years before. Something else had befallen this man.

"But I did bring you something." Park lifted the cover of the wicker basket he was carrying and a tiny head popped out.

Chiffon sniffed the air, hesitated with its head cocked to one side, and then leaped with a cry of pure joy at the man who'd created him.

In that instant, years seemed to lift from Philippe's face as an incredulous smile revealed overly-white teeth.

"Chiffon!" Philippe studied the creature, looking for anything that might be amiss before turning back to Park. "Apparently, I misjudged you. I was sure you were going to cut him to pieces."

"One does not destroy a masterpiece," Park responded.

Philippe nodded. "No. That is a fate reserved for its creator."

"I do not want to destroy you."

"I have difficulty believing that. The French arrived in Panama mere days after you left. Coincidence?"

"I did not have anything to do with that. I imagine the French can follow the same clues I did."

"Which means they're probably right behind you now."

"That is irrelevant. You will be long gone."

Philippe studied him for a long while. He sighed. "I sense your story is going to be a long one. Perhaps you would like to have a seat.

That drink was served in the spirit of basic hospitality but, in light of this gift, I believe I can extend a little more. Not friendship, of course, but at least I will let you speak."

"Thank you. I assume you know about the dinosaurs." He drank the liquid. It had the familiar taste of Akpeteshie, which he'd been drinking since arriving in Ghana.

Philippe smiled. "I have been following that since the news first came out. Not particularly elegant, but effective. That was you?"

"Yes."

"Then I assume the rumors of the Nothosaurs at the Argentinian Antarctic installation are true and you used that as the genetic base to retro-engineer the rest?"

"Yes. But it's not as easy as it looks. Nothosaurs are reptiles, not dinosaurs and…"

Philippe held up a hand. "There is no need to get defensive. I am not one of your Russian masters. I know exactly how hard something like that would be in the right hands. Or how easy."

"The Russians are no longer my masters."

"Ah. That is an interesting development. Who are you working for these days?"

As always, Philippe was extremely tranquil. He gave the impression of someone at peace with the world, someone who had received the worst that life could dish out. Someone who had no fear— and who had very little left to interest him.

"I work for myself."

"Ah. The illusion of independence. One of the world's lies."

"I plan to make it true," Park replied.

"An admirable goal, but not one which explains the reason for this visit." He stroked the head of the monkey-like creature. "Not that I'm complaining, mind you. You have, at the very least, brought some light to an old man's life."

"You aren't much older than I am."

"It's the experience that truly counts, not the years or the grey hairs." He drank deeply and asked for a refill. "So tell me, what brings you to darkest Ghana?"

"I have a proposition to make."

"Of course you do."

"I have a lab. We're gearing up to produce dinosaurs like the ones you saw."

"I see. And I suppose they will be harmless things aimed at the zoo and conservation markets, right?" The ghost of an amused smile flitted across the pale features.

"There's no need to be sarcastic. As I recall, your own creations weren't exactly used for peaceful ends by most of your clients."

"In that you are correct."

"We have a few lines of research that we think would interest you."

"I have everything I need right here. I'm working on theory at the moment. I won't need a lab for a few months."

Excitement flowed through Park at the Frenchman's words. That Philippe would be working on new theoretical directions was more than he'd dared imagine.

"I can give you materials, access to research that you have never seen before. Secret things I did myself. Some based on your work, other things my own. Even though you are the master, there is work out there that can enrich what you do."

"Where is this lab?"

"Right here in Africa. Straight to the north. In the desert. It's already producing. Our first shipment was sent off last week, to Nigeria."

"In the desert? That is a large desert."

"I'm sure you'll excuse me for not being more specific. If you decide to come aboard the project, you will be told everything."

"I'm more worried about that desert. There isn't much cover in the desert. Anyone can see you from above."

"We know that. The facility is beautifully hidden. Here is the satellite photo of the area, taken just a few hours ago."

Philippe studied it in silence for some moments. "How do I know this is real?"

Park shrugged. "All I can give you is my word."

The silence stretched. Park sweated in the sun as the Frenchman looked out into the distance. Finally, the North Korean couldn't take it anymore and he spoke.

"The French will never be able to get to you there."

"The French will find a way to get to me no matter where I go." Then he shrugged and finished his drink. "So I might as well go with you. At least it might be vaguely interesting."

Park exulted. They were the best in the world. He wondered what heights they could scale together.

THE END

CHECK OUT OTHER GREAT DINOSAUR THRILLERS

WRITTEN IN STONE
by David Rhodes

Charles Dawson is trapped 100 million years in the past. Trying to survive from day to day in a world of dinosaurs he devises a plan to change his fate. As he begins to write messages in the soft mud of a nearby stream, he can only hope they will be found by someone who can stop his time travel. Professor Ron Fontana and Professor Ray Taggit, scientists with opposing views, each discover the fossilized messages. While attempting to save Charles, Professor Fontana, his daughter Lauren and their friend Danny are forced to join Taggit and his group of mercenaries. Taggit does not intend to rescue Charles Dawson, but to force Dawson to travel back in time to gather samples for Taggit's fame and fortune. As the two groups jump through time they find they must work together to make it back alive as this fast-paced thriller climaxes at the very moment the age of dinosaurs is ending.

HARD TIME
by Alex Laybourne

Rookie officer Peter Malone and his heavily armed team are sent on a deadly mission to extract a dangerous criminal from a classified prison world. A Kruger Correctional facility where only the hardest, most vicious criminals are sent to fend for themselves, never to return.

But when the team come face to face with ancient beasts from a lost world, their mission is changed. The new objective: Survive.

CHECK OUT OTHER GREAT DINOSAUR THRILLERS

JURASSIC ISLAND
by Viktor Zarkov

Guided by satellite photos and modern technology a ragtag group of survivalists and scientists travel to an uncharted island in the remote South Indian Ocean. Things go to hell in a hurry once the team reaches the island and the massive megalodon that attacked their boats is only the beginning of their desperate fight for survival.

Nothing could have prepared billionaire explorer Joseph Thornton and washed up archaeologist Christopher "Colt" McKinnon for the terrifying prehistoric creatures that wait for them on JURASSIC ISLAND!

K-REX
by L.Z. Hunter

Deep within the Congo jungle, Circuitz Mining employs mercenaries as security for its Coltan mining site. Armed with assault rifles and decades of experience, nothing should go wrong. However, the dangers within the jungle stretch beyond venomous snakes and poisonous spiders. There is more to fear than guerrillas and vicious animals. Undetected, something lurks under the expansive treetop canopy . . .

Something ancient.

Something dangerous.

Kasai Rex!

CHECK OUT OTHER GREAT DINOSAUR THRILLERS

SPINOSAURUS
by Hugo Navikov

Brett Russell is a hunter of the rarest game. His targets are cryptids, animals denied by science. But they are well known by those living on the edges of civilization, where monsters attack and devour their animals and children and lay ruin to their shantytowns.

When a shadowy organization sends Brett to the Congo in search of the legendary dinosaur cryptid Kasai Rex, he will face much more than a terrifying monster from the past. Spinosaurus is a dinosaur thriller packed with intrigue, action and giant prehistoric predators.

LAND OF DEATH
by Eric S Brown & Alex Laybourne

A group of American soldiers, fleeing an organized attack on their base camp in the Middle East, encounter a storm unlike anything they've seen before. When the storm subsides, they wake up to find themselves no longer in the desert and perhaps not even on Earth. The jungle they've been deposited in is a place ruled by prehistoric creatures long extinct. Each day is a struggle to survive as their ammo begins to run low and virtually everything they encounter, in this land they've been hurled into, is a deadly threat.